# Series by Julie Johnstone

## Scottish Medieval Romance Books:

### Highlanders Through Time Series
*Sinful Scot, Book 1*
*Sexy Scot, Book 2*
*Seductive Scot, Book 3*
*Scandalous Scot, Book 4*

### Highlander Vows: Entangled Hearts Series
*When a Laird Loves a Lady, Book 1*
*Wicked Highland Wishes, Book 2*
*Christmas in the Scot's Arms, Book 3*
*When a Highlander Loses His Heart, Book 4*
*How a Scot Surrenders to a Lady, Book 5*
*When a Warrior Woos a Lass, Book 6*
*When a Scot Gives His Heart, Book 7*
*When a Highlander Weds a Hellion, Book 8*
*How to Heal a Highland Heart, Book 9*
*The Heart of a Highlander, Book 10*

### Renegade Scots Series
*Outlaw King, Book 1*
*Highland Defender, Book 2*
*Highland Avenger, Book 3*

## Regency Romance Books:

### Scottish Scoundrels: Ensnared Hearts Series
*Lady Guinevere and the Rogue with a Brogue, Book 1*
*Lady Lilias and the Devil in Plaid, Book 2*
*Lady Constantine and the Sins of Lord Kilgore *Coming Soon**

## A Whisper of Scandal Series
*Bargaining with a Rake, Book 1*
*Conspiring with a Rogue, Book 2*
*Dancing with a Devil, Book 3*
*After Forever, Book 4*
*The Dangerous Duke of Dinnisfree, Book 5*

## A Once Upon A Rogue Series
*My Fair Duchess, Book 1*
*My Seductive Innocent, Book 2*
*My Enchanting Hoyden, Book 3*
*My Daring Duchess, Book 4*

## Lords of Deception Series
*What a Rogue Wants, Book 1*

## Danby Regency Christmas Novellas
*The Redemption of a Dissolute Earl, Book 1*
*Season For Surrender, Book 2*
*It's in the Duke's Kiss, Book 3*

## Regency Anthologies
*A Summons from the Duke of Danby (Regency Christmas Summons, Book 2)*
*Thwarting the Duke (When the Duke Comes to Town, Book 2)*

## Regency Romance Box Sets
*A Very Regency Christmas*
*Three Wicked Rogues*

## Paranormal Books:

### The Siren Saga
*Echoes in the Silence, Book 1*

# Lady Lilias And The Devil In Plaid

Scottish Scoundrels: Ensnared Hearts, Book 2

by
Julie Johnstone

Lady Lilias and the Devil in Plaid
Copyright © 2020 by Julie Johnstone, DBA Darbyshire Publishing
Cover Design by Najla Qamber, Qamber Designs & Media
Editing by Double Vision Editorial
and
Louisa Cornell

All rights reserved. No part of this book may be reproduced in any form by any electronic or mechanical means—except in the case of brief quotations embodied in critical articles or reviews—without written permission.

The characters and events portrayed in this book are fictitious. Any similarity to real persons, living or dead, is purely coincidental and not intended by the author.

The best way to stay in touch is to subscribe to my newsletter. Go to https://juliejohnstoneauthor.com and subscribe in the box at the top of the page that says Newsletter. If you don't hear from me once a month, please check your spam filter and set up your email to allow my messages through to you so you don't miss the opportunity to win great prizes or hear about appearances.

If you're interested in when my books go on sale, or want to be one of the first to know about my new releases, please follow me on BookBub! You'll get quick book notifications every time there's a new pre-order, book on sale, or new release. You can follow me on BookBub here: www.bookbub.com/authors/julie-johnstone

# Dedication and Thanks

This entire series has an underlying plot of a close group of women who are always there for one another, so it seems fitting that this book should be dedicated to three ladies I know I can count on to be there. This one is for my gal pals Heidi Falconer, Harisha Patel, and Shelly Sheinler. Thanks for the hours of laughter, the encouragement, and the parenting therapy. My life is richer because of each one of you.

Writing a book is a journey, and my journey always starts with my mother. Without her encouragement from the day I was born to pursue my dreams, I may have not had the unwavering belief it takes to reach for something that can sometimes seem unattainable. She deserves a million thanks for everything she does for me constantly.

When I'm in the writing pit, someone has to be there to take up the slack, and that's my husband, Inge. He keeps the train on the track when I'm too busy to even realize it might be derailing. Thanks, honey!

I cannot write a book without thanking my kids. They are twin guiding lights that always remind me of the endless depths of love you can have for other people.

To my editor Danielle Poiesz, who has been with me quite a while now. Danielle asks the hard questions of my stories that force me to dig deep but make the stories so much richer for the effort. Thank you!

And to my editor Louisa Cornell, who has checked behind me on all things Regency. Your endless knowledge, from the type of tablecloth that would have been on a gaming table to the appropriate entrance at a club for a lady bird, always amazes me! Thank you!

Finally, to my assistant, Dee, who knows better than anyone, besides the people who live with me, just how far into my writing cave I crawl, and just how much I need someone to remind me life is going on around me when I'm in there. I thank you!

# Prologue

**The Cotswolds, England**
**1830**

*H*e was the most beautiful boy she'd ever seen.

In fact, the stranger standing by the bridge on the other side of the river was so shockingly handsome that a wave of heat and dizziness crashed into Lilias Honeyfield. It was either his artist-worthy face or the fact that he was wearing a kilt that was affecting her so. She'd never seen such well-formed calves—or any male's calves for that matter. Regardless, the result was the same: she lost her balance.

Her gaze darted to the water below, and she sucked in a sharp breath as she threw her arms out to regain her balance. A warning tingle swept over her skin at the possibility of falling into the cold water of the River Eye. Her belly tightened, teeth clenched, and toes curled against the damp, rough bark beneath her feet. She would not fall. She *refused* to fall.

Her friend Owen slowed to a concerned pace in front of her. "Lilias?"

"I'm fine," she assured him, finding the center point of his back and staring at it in the hopes that she would feel steady once more. But her pulse was beating faster, her confidence in herself shaken. It had been foolish to cross upon this log over such deep water while wearing so many layers of clothing, but that's what was required to get to the secret place she wanted to show Owen. She often came here to avoid her pesky younger sister, and she suspected he might need an escape from his father. The marquess was not a very warm person, and that was putting it kindly.

She bit her lip, glancing toward the water again. If she fell into the river, she'd sink like a stone, even though she could swim quite well. Owen might jump in to save her—they were friends, after all—but they were relatively new friends since he'd only moved to the Cotswolds a month earlier. Besides, he had not wanted to cross on this log. He'd said it was dangerous. He'd said they should not even be out here alone.

Owen needed to gain some courage, and she intended to help him do so. He was far too stuffy and proper. She'd been working on that since the day they met. She liked him well enough that she'd risk her safety to save him if he fell in, but would he do the same? Her mother said Lilias lived as if she were an invincible heroine in one of the Gothic romance novels she liked to read. It was probably true, though she didn't think she could be blamed. Life was deadly dull out here in the country at Charingworth Manor, and creating fantasies in which she starred made her days so much more interesting.

A quick glance toward the bridge confirmed that she'd not merely imagined the boy. He still stood there, and he was still staring at the water as if mesmerized by something in it. Whatever held his interest must have been quite fascinating for him not to notice them. And whyever was he wearing a kilt? She took another step forward, and her foot slipped slightly, forcing her concentration to Owen's back to keep her balance.

Owen didn't appear very strong, she realized. She eyed

his dark, superfine overcoat while slowly placing one foot in front of the other and moving forward, steadier now, toward the other side of the river. In fact, he looked as if he sat inside all the time worrying about all the things that might bring him harm. He was a worrier and most definitely not one to take chances. This day was a rare exception.

Upon further contemplating what would occur if she were to fall into the water, she had serious doubts that Owen could actually haul her out with the added weight of her shift, pantalettes, petticoat, and stays, not to mention the encumbrance of her gown. She quirked her mouth, considering. It was more likely she'd take him down with her. That was hardly the stuff Gothic romances were made of. Though, in truth, she didn't fancy him as much of a hero, anyway.

She allowed her gaze to skitter once more to the boy. His dark head was bent forward, the sun gleaming off his thick hair. Without looking up, he raised a hand to his neck, tugged on something for a minute, and then his white cravat was dangling from his fingers before it dropped to the ground by his shiny, black hessians and his overcoat.

*Scandalous.*

She liked him instantly. He was a mystery, and this was the sort of meeting that *could* be in a Gothic romance. She grinned and pressed her bare toes more firmly against the log, glad she'd removed her shoes and stockings, despite Owen's protest that it wasn't proper. Honestly, who cared out here in the woods? She didn't. The beautiful boy didn't. The heroines in her novels didn't let a little thing like propriety stop them, and Lilias wanted to be like one of them—strong, bold, and one half of a love for the ages.

"Who the devil are you?" Owen bellowed, making

Lilias jerk and teeter yet again.

She threw out her arms once more, and her heart lodged in her throat, even as her attention shot back across the water to the distractingly fine-looking boy. Her gaze crashed into his, and his eyes widened as hers did the same.

He wasn't simply beautiful; he was *darkly* beautiful. Like a true Gothic hero. Heat flooded her at the silly thought as she stared. Then she blinked, and her lips parted in utter shock.

*He's shed his shirt.*

It was her first glimpse of a male's chest, and it sent her right off the log into the frigid water of the River Eye.

Nash Steele reacted instinctively and dove in after the girl, though the boy she was with stood there gaping down at the river where she'd disappeared with a scream. The icy water took Nash's breath and snatched his senses for a moment, and flashes of the past froze him: His twin, Thomas, charging at him in rage when he'd found Nash kissing Helen. The uneven way Thomas had run because of his bad leg. The white puffs coming from Thomas as his weak lungs worked to meet the demands he so rarely made of his body. The early-winter ice cracking beneath Thomas's weight. Helen screaming as Thomas disappeared, followed by Helen screaming at Nash not to go after Thomas. Helen clinging to his arm, and Nash practically shoving her away so he could dive into the frozen lake to save the brother who had been born a breath and a scream after him. Nash searching but finding nothing but dark water and death.

A kick to his forehead jerked him from the torturous memories that had sent him out into the unknown woods surrounding his new family home in the first place. A curse was ripped from his lips, and he reached out in front of him, grabbing at the water with the desperate hope that he'd be able to locate the girl. His fingers grazed something solid, and he didn't hesitate. He curled his hand around the body part, registered that he likely held the girl's ankle, and a cry of relief bubbled from him. The joy was short-lived when her other foot connected with his nose. Pain burst upward and spread across his forehead. A crunching sound echoed in his ears.

*She broke my nose.*

He shoved the shock away as he caught her other foot before she kicked him again. With both ankles clasped, he jerked her toward him and down so he could circle an arm around her waist. She went rigid in his grasp and then wild. She swung out and tried to twist toward him, but he gripped her more tightly, knowing they'd never make it to the surface that way. His lungs were already starting to burn. She thrashed about, making it hard to keep hold of her, and she got him good several times. Still, he took the blows, not letting go. She was in a complete panic, and no wonder. Girls were required to wear too many layers of ridiculous clothing.

He kicked toward the surface, glad for once in his life that his parents had always demanded perfection from him in everything. He was a strong swimmer.

*As a future duke should be.*

His mother and father's words echoed in his head as he swam toward the light, holding on to the girl. He broke free of the water, hauling her up with him and gulping in greedy breaths of the cool air. A panicked scream blasted him from his right, and for one moment, terror gripped him. The girl was no longer thrashing.

*She's dead. She's dead as Thomas was dead. I've failed again.*

He turned her slowly toward him, and his eyes met hers, brilliant blue but filled with fear. Not dead. Just frightened. A tremor of relief went through him. "I've got you."

"I think I broke your nose," she replied, her voice barely above a whisper.

The girl was definitely stunned, and his nose definitely felt broken. It throbbed with pain, but before he could comment, the boy yelled, "Bring her to me!"

Nash frowned and looked around to find the boy, who was now at the shore. He was madly waving his skinny arms at them. "Is that your brother?" he asked, turning the girl around so her back was pressed against his chest. She shook her head as he snaked his hand around her waist. "Lean against me. I'll swim us to shore."

She did as instructed without so much as a word. By the time they got to the shore, the boy was there, frantically splashing into the water but stopping as it lapped against his boots. Nash released the girl as he stood and then helped her to her feet.

The boy shoved between them and turned an angry green gaze on Nash. "Don't touch her."

They were the exact three words Thomas had said to Nash when he'd found Nash and Helen kissing on the ice. Nash released the girl at once, and the boy shoved him out of the way to circle an arm around the girl's waist.

"Are you all right?"

"I—Yes, I think so," she replied, her voice shaking and the click of her teeth telling Nash that she was freezing.

"She needs to get out of the water and home into dry clothes," Nash suggested, looking toward the bridge and his own dry clothes, which he had discarded when he'd intended to take a swim.

"I know that," the boy said, sounding irritated.

Nash touched a finger to his aching nose as the boy started to lead the girl past him, but she stopped, her friendly gaze settling on him. "Thank you for saving me."

Before Nash could answer, the boy said, "I would have saved you if I could swim."

"You can't swim?" the girl bellowed in a way Nash had never heard a proper girl bellow before.

The sudden urge to laugh shocked him. He had not felt that desire since Thomas's death a year earlier. Nash clenched his teeth. He didn't deserve to laugh when Thomas never would again.

"Owen!" the girl exclaimed, snatching Nash from spiraling back into the past. "Whyever did you not tell me that?"

"I—" Owen opened and closed his mouth, his face reddening.

He'd been embarrassed. It was obvious to Nash but apparently not to the girl. She stood there, hands now on her hips and a quizzical look upon her face.

Owen's blush spread to the tips of his ears just as Thomas's used to. The instinct to act like a big brother as he'd done for Thomas roared to life.

"I don't think it's the sort of thing one goes around announcing," Nash offered, catching Owen's grateful look as Nash moved out of the water. Behind him came the splashing of someone following him.

"Wait!" the girl called. "Where are you going?"

Nash didn't pause. He'd only be here a few months before he was off to Oxford, and he neither wanted nor needed friends. And they certainly did not need to become close to the likes of him. He was a bad seed. He'd caused his brother's death. No one had said those exact words aloud, but his parents' silence had told him everything.

"Did you hear me?" she asked, closer now. "What's your name? Perhaps you'd like—"

"I heard you," he growled. "And it's Nash." He didn't say his title in case either of them had heard about his brother. Nash hated the pity and the curiosity that always surfaced when someone realized he was the Marquess of Chastain, the son of the Duke of Greybourne, older brother to Thomas, now one year dead.

*Tragic.* They'd shake their heads. *So tragic that Thomas fell through the ice. That he was born sickly. That you couldn't save him. How did the fall happen?*

The question was inevitable, as was the lying.

Fingers brushed his shoulder and then a hand grasped his arm. He stopped and whirled around. He didn't like to be touched. Not anymore. He shot her a withering glare, even as her large blue eyes latched on to his. He saw the moment she realized he didn't care for her hand on his arm. Her lips parted, and she released him. No color of embarrassment stained her cheeks, though. Instead, to his surprise, the girl gave him a determined look.

"I was going to say that perhaps you'd like to spend the day with us. I'm Lilias Honeyfield, and this is Owen—" The boy cleared his throat, and Lilias rolled her eyes. "I mean, this is the Earl of Blackwood and *the future Marquess of Craven.*" Nash could tell by her tone that she found the need to announce Owen's title ridiculous.

He liked her attitude toward titles very much, and he was shocked by how much appeal her offer held. They didn't know him, his secret, or what he'd done. They didn't know that he did not deserve to be happy. They didn't know that once, not so long ago, he'd selfishly decided he was tired of looking out for his sickly brother. Tired of trying to be perfect as his parents demanded and not cause them a moment's worry because they already had so much of that with Thomas. Tired of going unnoticed, except to be criticized.

He hadn't realized how lonely he was until that very moment, and it was all her fault.

"You need to go home," he snapped at the girl. "You'll freeze to death out here in those wet clothes, and I want no part of it. Not that I care," he added. Caring about someone brought responsibility, and if you failed, if you slipped just once... Well, they might just end up dead.

"Oh yes," she said with an all-too-knowing smirk. "I could tell by your jumping in the water to save me that you are exactly the sort of person who cares for no one but himself."

"I'm leaving," he replied, not liking the way the girl looked at him as if she knew him better than he knew himself.

Not waiting for her response, he swiveled on his heel and crunched his way across the carpet of gold, red, and brown leaves to the bridge where his overcoat, shirt, and cravat lay. He bent over, scooped them up, and twisted around, nearly stumbling backward to find the girl, Lilias, standing there, hands on hips, determined expression still firmly in place, and her head tilted back to spear him with the look of a hunter eyeing its prey. Behind her, Owen stood like an eager pup.

"You need a friend," she replied, matter-of-fact.

Owen cleared his throat, and Lilias's gaze darted over Nash's shoulder for a breath, an apologetic smile coming to her face. Then she settled those eyes—more the color of a stormy sky than a clear summer one—on him once more.

"You actually need two friends," she amended.

"No," he said, brushing by her. "I don't."

"You do," she objected, having the cheekiness to sound exasperated with him.

Owen gave Nash a sympathetic look as Nash started past him along the trail back to his house. Nash got no more than four steps when Owen said, "You might as well not fight it. Lilias will make you our friend one way or another. She's a fixer of broken things."

Nash stiffened at that revelation but did not slow his pace toward his home. "I'm not a thing," he tossed over his shoulder as he shoved low-hanging branches out of his way. "And you don't know me."

He lengthened his stride so the woods would swallow him up and make the boy and girl disappear. He chanced a look behind him and saw only trees. But then she bellowed, "I don't need to know you to see you're broken. We'll be round tomorrow, Nash—to call for you."

He laughed at that ridiculous statement as he strode toward home. They couldn't come to call on him tomorrow. For one thing, they did not know where he lived. For another, he was certain the girl's mother would not let her go galloping about calling on strangers who were almost men. He was seven and ten summers, after all. It wasn't proper.

That he'd even considered propriety made him laugh again. It felt strange and good, and that second feeling immediately brought the guilt and silenced the mirth.

He considered Lilias as he made for home, recollecting his hand inadvertently brushing against a swell of soft flesh on her chest. He pictured her face, large blue eyes streaked with gray, high cheekbones, full lips with a ready smile, and long hair that was light like a moonbeam, though he'd only seen a flash of it before she'd fallen into the water. Her wet gown had been molded to her, and when he thought on that and the outline of her curves, he realized the girl was not as young as he'd assigned her to be. So what the devil was she doing alone in the woods with a young earl crossing over a slippery log?

Proper girls didn't do that. Then again, a proper girl didn't kiss a boy as Helen had kissed him, and a good brother did not return the kiss of the tutor's daughter when he knew good and well his younger brother, the one he was supposed to protect, was enamored of the girl. But Nash had selfishly done just that. He'd wanted to act on his own desires for once instead of his obligations as a future duke and as Thomas's older brother. And the result had been Thomas's death.

It could not be undone. The withdrawal of his parents' affection could not be undone, either. It was strange that losing the little bit of love they had shown him had been such a blow. He could not blame them. His action had been the worst sort of selfishness, and he did not deserve to be happy. And friends equaled happiness, so he wanted none. It was a good thing Lilias Honeyfield did not know where he lived. He may not want her as a friend, but he didn't want to hurt her, either. He wasn't worried about the boy, Owen, coming to look for him. It had taken one look at his besotted face for Nash to know Owen would do whatever Lilias told him, as well as nothing she did *not* tell him, to do.

---

Four nights after meeting Lilias and Owen, the sound of pebbles being thrown against his window ripped Nash from his sleep. He stared openmouthed out his bedchamber window and down into the moonlit garden where Lilias

Honeyfield—or more properly, *Lady* Lilias—and Owen were standing. He'd gained that little bit of information about her when Nash had heard her speaking to the butler the first time she and Owen had appeared at his door. She'd informed Sterns that Lady Lilias and the Earl of Blackwood were there to call upon Nash, and Owen had added that Lilias was the daughter of Lady Barrowe and the late Earl of Barrowe, at which Lilias had shushed her friend. Of course, Nash declined to see them that day, as well as the three other times they had come.

But here she was—*again*—the persistent chit.

"Nash!" Lilias whispered furiously up at him, somehow managing to convey the tone of a bellow without actually yelling.

She was a slip of a thing with a halo of moonbeams for hair and what appeared to be a gathering of dogs surrounding her, and damn, if he could not look away. Lilias Honeyfield certainly was not a quitter. She'd somehow managed to figure out where he lived in less than a day, and he had no doubt that Owen had only come along at her demand. Her behavior was unheard of in polite Society, but she didn't seem to care.

He was about to close the window on the pair, but then he thought about how it was night, and dark, and she was a slight girl, and Owen was not exactly the sort of fellow who could protect a girl if ruffians should come upon the two of them. Of course, the dogs could, if they listened to commands, and if they weren't shot by the ruffians first. Though, it seemed doubtful that ruffians would be about in the Cotswolds. Still, he should not risk her safety. That would be unwise, and future dukes had to make wise decisions always. He'd colossally failed in that endeavor thus far in his life. Perhaps he was overlooking a chance to reset his course.

Nash scowled down at the pair. "You're making it so I have to come below and speak with you," he whisper-shouted.

"Indeed I am," Lilias said, laughter in her tone.

Nash drummed his fingers on his window. The girl was pesky and smug and made him unexplainably want to laugh.

"If you don't come down here this instant, I'll command my hounds to bark."

He couldn't tell if she was threatening him or teasing him, but feeling more lighthearted than he had in a long time, he shot back, "You wouldn't."

"She would," Owen confirmed, a blob in the darkness. "And her hounds will listen because she fixed them just like she wants to fix you. They are loyal to the death."

Devil take it, but Nash's curiosity lit up like a bonfire. "Did she fix you, too?" he asked Owen, suddenly unreasonably, ridiculously hopeful that this girl he did not know could make him feel something other than self-loathing.

"No," Owen promptly answered, "but she's working on it. She says tonight is the night I'll discover my inner courage. She's going to teach me to swim."

And just like that, Nash saw an unexpected path to redemption. Owen clearly had a tendre for Lilias. It dripped from every word he spoke. If Nash could help Owen get the girl, perhaps he wouldn't hate himself anymore. He'd failed Thomas, but he could help this boy. Nash's nostrils flared at the possibility.

Lilias had absolutely known she'd be able to breach the

walls Nash had erected around himself. Well, maybe she had not known *for certain,* she relented as she stood shivering beside him on the bank near the water. She did not really know him yet, after all. But she wanted to. She'd practically been fixated on him since meeting him in the woods four nights prior.

She blamed the obsession on two things. First was her love of Gothic romance novels. Nash was mysterious, just like a Gothic hero, and absurdly handsome, and she could admit to herself that she'd fantasized once or twice or a thousand times about being the heroine in a book with a gentleman who looked like Nash.

Second, and she'd only confessed this to Owen in a weak moment and sworn him to secrecy after she'd appallingly blabbed her secret, she *did* have a need to try to fix broken animals and people. The compulsion had been with her a long time, ever since her father had started drinking after he'd gambled a great deal of his money away. If her memory served her, she'd been nine at the time. She'd tried to help him by asking for nothing, for trying to make things last, but she'd not been able to fix his problems in the end. He drank himself to death, or at least that's what she'd heard the doctor say from her eavesdropping position crouched at the other side of her parents' closed bedchamber door.

"Why do you wear a kilt? Are you Scottish?" she asked as they stood on the riverbank.

"I'm half-Scot on my mother's side, and I wear it to annoy my mother. She thinks her family wild barbarians."

Lilias had done things to annoy her mother in an attempt simply to get her attention after her father had died, but it had not been successful. Her mother was too sad to be annoyed. "Does it work?" she asked.

"Not so far. She hasn't said a word. It's as if she doesn't even notice."

"I'm sorry," Lilias said, her chest squeezing for him. Her mother seemed to at least notice when Lilias was doing something irritating; she just didn't care.

Nash didn't respond. One of his boots clopped against the dirt, followed immediately by the other. Her awareness of him, the broad chest that strained against his white shirt, and the long bare legs she could see because he was wearing a kilt gave her a thrill that was entirely new to her. She'd read about such reactions women had to men. Her novels were filled with such things, but she supposed she had not truly believed that such tremendous emotion was real.

But heavens! It was like an ocean in her chest when Nash chucked off his overcoat and dropped it to the grass. Owen mimicked Nash, and the roiling waters inside her settled. Poor Owen looked like a pup compared to Nash, but she'd never let on so as not to hurt Owen's feelings. Friends did not do such things to each other. They bolstered each other up; they did not tear each other down.

She stole one last glance at Nash while he had his attention on the water. He had a fine noble nose, strong lips, a square jaw, and chiseled cheekbones. He leaned suddenly toward the water. What was he doing? She glanced to where she thought he was looking. He must have been trying to decide the best place to show Owen how to swim. Moonlight shimmered off the river, and it seemed to glitter off Nash's skin as he rolled up the sleeves of his shirt and revealed powerful forearms. She wished he'd strip his shirt off, but she knew it was too much to wish for. She also knew she *shouldn't* wish for such a thing, but the knowledge didn't stop the yearning.

Her awareness of him felt electric, the way the air before a storm sometimes felt as if it could prick you. It didn't matter that he hadn't spoken more than a sentence since appearing in the garden and telling her in a gruff voice to lead the way. All he had done was greet Owen and tell him that he looked to be the sort of man who would easily pick up swimming. Then he'd patted each of her hounds on the head and told them they were good boys. Those two things confirmed her instinct that Nash wanted friends, despite his words to the contrary, whether he realized it or not.

With all these thoughts in her head, she bent down to remove her slippers, but before she could do so, Nash's voice washed over her from above. "What are you doing?"

It seemed obvious to her, but in her experience—admittedly only with her father—a man's powers of observation often needed spectacles. So she brought herself upright and pointed down at her feet. "Taking off my shoes so I can teach Owen to swim."

"Do you have parents?" Nash's tone was incredulous.

Before she could answer the question, he launched another at her. "Do you have a chaperone?"

She opened her mouth to respond, but another question came at her like a bullet. "How the devil did you get out of your house unnoticed? You'd be ruined if anyone caught you with us." He shoved a hand through his wavy hair. "One of us would have to wed you." His left hand took the place of his right to tangle through his thick, dark hair. She wanted to touch that hair, but thankfully, she refrained. He glanced to Owen. "Had you thought of that?"

Owen answered with a shake of his head as Lilias stood there in mute fascination. Nash scoffed. "Of course not. Are you prepared to wed this girl?" He pointed at her, and she found she still could not speak. Owen apparently did not have the same affliction. He opened his mouth to respond, but Nash cut him off just as he had done to Lilias. "I don't know how I ended up out here. I—"

"I do believe the woman in my house is my mother," she interrupted, certain he was about to leave them and she desperately did not want him to go. "She claims to be, anyway. And if she's not, well, then—" Lilias set her hands on her hips as she imagined one of the heroines in her books would do when giving someone a set down. "That would be shocking. It would inspire loads of questions. Such as, what did she do with my mother?" Lilias tapped a finger against her chin, another Gothic heroine move. "Hmm... I do look like her, so I think it's safe to say that she *is* my mother, and we can conclude that I do have a parent," she finished cheekily.

Nash's lips parted in obvious astonishment, and she did not bother to repress her smug smile. Finally, it was she who was rendering him speechless. She offered a quick prayer of thanks to God for her elephant-like memory and then said in a scolding voice, "My father died this past year." She notched up her eyebrows to let Nash know that now was the appropriate time for him to feel remorse for his unthinking question.

Instead, he turned to Owen and asked, "Is she always like this?"

Owen nodded, his mop of blond hair falling across his right eye.

She would have been incensed by Nash's question, which implied there was something wrong with her, except his tone held unmistakable admiration. She grinned. Finally, someone who had an appreciation for people who refused to conform! She allowed herself one moment to savor this before she launched back into the task of volleying answers at him just as quickly as he'd shot questions at her.

"I *did* have a chaperone, Miss Portsmith, but I only had her for a short while. My papa didn't believe in chaperones. He had a free spirit stuck in an earl's stuffy life."

When Nash laughed, she grinned and kept going. "Mama drove Miss Portsmith away with unreasonable demands—Miss Portsmith's words, not mine—but I must confess, I was not sad to see her depart. I didn't particularly like having someone watch my every move and want to accompany me everywhere, but I do think my sister, Nora, could use a chaperone. She's only nine, and she's quite a handful already." She took a breath, certain Nash would tell her to be quiet or some such thing, but a smile teased his lips. He appeared to be following her every word. Another tingling thrill went through her. "I get out of my home down a convenient tree." She pointed to the trousers she'd borrowed from the stable master's son, Lucas, so she could climb down the tree at her bedchamber window and teach Owen to swim with ease.

"Thus the trousers," Nash said, seemingly amused. He pressed his lips together in a knowing smirk.

She returned the look. "Yes. I'm rather a good climber. My father encouraged me, to my mother's dismay, when I was younger. I don't suppose he ever considered I might use the ability to leave the house at night when I was not supposed to. Or maybe he did." She shrugged, pushing back the sadness of her father's loss, which was always at the edges of her happiness. "I can go about rather freely since my father passed, my chaperone fled, and my mother—"

She stopped herself from confessing that her mother took laudanum nearly daily and locked herself in her room for most of the days and nights. Even Lilias had boundaries of propriety she would not cross, and one did not confess such scandalous secrets. Well, at least not until one knew someone better.

He arched lovely, dark, expectant eyebrows at her.

"And my mother's preoccupation since my father's death," she added lamely.

"I see," Nash said, his deep voice filled with understanding, and she truly felt he did understand. Somehow he knew what she had not said, and in that moment, it seemed as if an unspoken bond formed between them.

"I've been wondering how you flitted about the countryside with me," Owen piped up, breaking the spell.

Lilias offered her friend an indulgent smile. He had not asked, not once since she'd met him, and it had always bothered her. She didn't know why, but it seemed he should have at least asked. Nash had asked. It made her want to sigh happily.

"As to being ruined," she continued, wanting to finish answering Nash's questions with the hope that eventually he'd answer some of her own, "you two are our nearest neighbors. The others are so far away that being seen in your company and then ruined is hardly a concern. So don't fret that you might have to wed me."

"It's you who would need to fret if you had to wed me," he responded, then chuckled.

But to her, the laugh was forced. It covered the truth of his words. He found himself unworthy of marrying. How fascinating. He was most assuredly a Gothic hero in the making.

"I feel I'll make an excellent husband," Owen blurted.

"Of course you will," Nash replied.

Nash's kind words to Owen were quite endearing but not yet true, and it would not do for Owen to fool himself. "You'll make excellent husband one day," she assured her friend with a friendly pat on the arm. "But you are only five and ten summers," she added.

"I'm the same age as you!"

She nodded. "Yes, and I'm not ready to wed yet, either."

What she didn't say was that he needed to become a lot less stuffy before he tried to find a wife. Romantic heroes were not supposed to be so concerned with propriety. Though, to be fair, she knew Owen's obsession with being proper had to do with the fact that his mother had run off with their horse trainer. Lilias suspected Owen was trying to make up for his mother's shocking lack of decorum by having so much of his own.

"I do believe I've answered all your questions," she said to Nash. "Shall we get started teaching Owen to swim?"

"Why at night?" Nash asked instead of agreeing to begin.

She bit her lip, not wishing to admit the truth of the matter, but there didn't seem to be hope for avoiding doing so. "Several reasons. One is that I cannot very well strip down to my unmentionables in front of the two of you to teach Owen to swim."

"I'd say not!" Owen exclaimed.

Nash, however, shockingly said, "I've seen girls in their unmentionables before."

"Well, of course you have!" Owen guffawed, which irritated her.

Apparently it irritated Nash, too, for he scowled at Owen, but she pressed her lips together on intervening. He'd been the one who wanted to shock Owen. It served Nash right that Owen had readily thought him a rogue.

But she did need to ensure he understood that just because she did not care for the fact that girls were bound by different rules than boys were, she did have a proper upbringing and plenty of self-worth. "I am not the sort of girl who will be showing anyone but my husband my unmentionables," she stated, giving him what she hoped was a warning look like the one her father used to give her when he'd lost patience with her antics. It had been rare, but it had occurred.

"That's obvious," Nash said.

She frowned, unsure whether it was a compliment or not and if he thought that a good thing.

"What are the other reasons?" he asked.

"I thought if we surprised you, you might be intrigued enough to come."

"You're quite honest, aren't you?" He sounded as if he was not used to such behavior.

"I don't see the point of being otherwise. Now…" Though the conversation was fascinating, the night was slipping away. "Shall we start?"

"*I* shall start," Nash replied. "You'll sit there." He pointed at the grass.

"I shall not!" she said hotly.

"You will or I'll leave and not help at all."

"But it was my idea to teach Owen to swim!"

"It may have been, but you are a girl." She opened her mouth to protest, but he continued. "And I have enough honor that I cannot, will not, allow you into dangerous water at night. You could catch cold. You could slip and twist your ankle. You could be bitten by a snake. I would never forgive myself if something happened to you."

That was the most gallant thing anyone had ever said to her. She couldn't even muster the outrage to protest again, nor the wish to show him what an excellent swimmer she was. She ought to be irritated, she supposed. He wanted her to sit on the bank while he taught Owen to swim, after all, but she could not find a hint of the emotion in her. He had not said he didn't think her capable; he'd said he wanted to protect her. Warmth filled her, and she had the most embarrassing desire to sigh at him.

Instead, she simply nodded. "I suppose someone should keep watch."

"Yes," he agreed quite readily, sounding relieved, and she half wondered if he had thought she'd argue. "You will make an excellent guardswoman."

So for possibly the first time in her life, Lilias did as she was told and sat while Nash taught Owen to swim. He was kind and patient, and he was an excellent instructor. In no time, he had Owen with his head underwater, stroking his arms and kicking his legs. And as the grand finale to the night, Owen swam for five strokes to Nash. Lilias jumped up in her excitement, caught her foot on a tree root, and fell face forward onto the dirt, twisting her ankle in the process.

She cried out in pain, and before she could even right herself, Nash was there, grabbing her by the forearms and then helping her up. "Are you all right?"

In the moonlight, she could see the outline of his strong jaw, his head tilted toward her, his eyebrows raised. His hands were cold from being in the water, but she didn't mind one bit. "I'm fine," she said, not wanting to admit that her ankle was already throbbing.

"Thank God," Owen said, coming up behind Nash.

When Nash released her and she put all her weight on her ankle, she almost fell down again. Nash caught her by the elbow and tugged her to his side, where he encircled her waist to hold her up. She had never felt protected like that in her life.

"You can't walk home like this," Nash said.

She hated to be helpless, but he was right, and the idea of him carrying her was not one she minded. She was really warming to it when he turned to Owen. "Can you carry her?"

Lilias felt her jaw drop open, but before she could recover from the sting of him not wanting to do the deed himself, she was being pushed gently out of Nash's strong embrace and into Owen's hands. Owen awkwardly slipped an arm under her leg as she protested, and he ignored her. He got her up against his chest, took two steps, and promptly tripped, sending them both flying forward, but Nash somehow managed to stop them from falling.

"I'm sorry, Lilias," Owen said, and she could hear the misery in his voice.

"I'm sure she's quite heavy," Nash assured Owen, to her astonishment and irritation. "She looks it." And then he jostled her out of Owen's grasp, into his own, and gripped her under her legs while bringing her into the crook of his other arm and against his very solid, wet chest. "Which way?" he asked her.

She pointed, still vexed with him. Owen gathered their things and then fell into step behind them as they made their way through the dark woods to her home. When they got to the road that led to Owen's home, he handed Nash's things to her, and then Owen bade them an awkward farewell, as if he did not want to depart.

"Let's meet tomorrow," she told Owen. "We'll work on your swimming again."

"We can meet at the bridge," Owen said, and to Lilias's delight, Nash agreed, though he did sound a trifle reluctant.

Once Owen departed, Nash strode along toward her house for a moment, and Lilias racked her mind for a way to ask him about his family that was not too intrusive. She'd seen a family portrait on one of her visits, and there was a boy and young girl in the painting who had to be his siblings.

"Do I truly look heavy?" she asked, unable to think of a better way to start the conversation.

"No. You look perfect, and you're light as a feather." His compliment would have made her smile, except he sounded irritated, and he picked up his pace, as if he wanted to be rid of her. At this rate, they'd be at her house in no time.

Blast. She wanted to learn something about him.

"Then why did you tell Owen I looked heavy?"

He paused, glancing down at her. In the moonlight, she could just make out his face and see his eyebrows arch. "Sorry about that. I didn't consider it might hurt your feelings. I was trying to ensure that Owen was not embarrassed if he couldn't carry you."

Her chest tightened at his words. "You're quite nice."

"No. No, I'm not, Lilias," Nash replied and started walking once more. Silence stretched for a long time, and as her home came into view, Nash said, "But Owen seems to be truly nice. He reminds me of my brother."

"You have a brother?" she asked, refusing to feel guilty about not mentioning the portrait she'd seen.

"Not anymore." His clipped tone did not invite questions, so she bit her lip as he set her on her feet. He took his belongings from her, silence stretching and nearly killing her, and then he slowly put on his shoes. When he finally stood, she thought it likely he'd simply leave, but he said, "He died last year."

His words stole her breath, and for a moment she recalled the image of the light-haired boy in the portrait. "Oh. I'm terribly sorry. How did he die?"

"He drowned."

The pain in Nash's voice pierced Lilias's heart. She

inhaled a long, steadying breath as her own grief over the loss of her father rose to the surface. "Is that why you decided to help me teach Owen to swim?"

"Yes." He cleared his throat. "How will you get back into your house unnoticed?" he asked, changing the subject.

"The tree I used to get down."

"With that injury?"

"I'll manage." Her ankle ached terribly, but she didn't want to admit it—nor did she want him to leave yet. "It's very selfless of you to help Owen."

"No, it's not. I'm hoping to get something out of it," he said. "Where's the tree?"

She pointed to her bedchamber, and he put an arm around her waist and helped her over. "What do you hope to get out of teaching Owen to swim?"

He slid his arm from her waist, but his fingers lingered on her arm, as if to ensure she was steady before releasing her. Nash Steele, the Marquess of Chastain, as she'd discovered from his butler, was a protector whether he knew it or not. His touch disappeared, and she felt the loss of it all the way to her toes. They stood in silence for several breaths, and she was beginning to think he was not going to answer her.

Finally, he said, "Redemption."

The word was low and throbbing. It caused an ache in her gut. "For what?" she whispered.

Again, they stood in silence, this pause longer. An owl hooted from a tree above, and her dogs, who always slept in her bedchamber, began to bark in response. Lights started flickering in the window to the right of her bedchamber. *Nora. The ninny.* She was afraid of every little sound, and soon she would wake their mother.

"What do you wish redemption for?" she urged him,

her heart pounding with the knowledge that she had to hurry and make her way up the tree to the safety of her bedchamber.

A sigh filled the space between them. "My brother's death," Nash finally said. "I killed him."

She could not have heard him correctly. "You said he drowned."

"He did," Nash replied. "But I was the reason he was on the ice. My selfishness killed my brother. So you see, Lilias, I am not nice."

Before she could point out that someone who wasn't truly a good person would not even be worried about whether they were good or bad, her window slammed open and Nora leaned out with her nightcap still on. "Lilias Honeyfield, I see you down there in the moonlight, and in a minute, Mama will, too. I'm going to wake her. Then you'll be in the soup, as you deserve for never taking me with you!" With that, her sister disappeared from the window.

"You've been caught now," Nash said. To her pleasant surprise, he sounded regretful, which could only mean he wanted to see her again.

She waved a dismissive hand as she grabbed a tree branch. "Nonsense. It would take the house coming down around my mother's ears to wake her. The laudanum—" Lilias bit her lip on the slip as she struggled to pull herself up the tree, but her ankle hurt something dreadful. "Give me a push?" she asked, not knowing what else to do. Eventually her mother *would* wake up if that tattletale Nora shook her long enough.

"I'm sorry about your mother," Nash said, his hands coming to her hips. His touch shot heat through her. "Is she ill?"

"No," Lilias said, shocked at the husky sound of her

voice. She cleared her throat. "She's sad since my father's death." And though she did not wish to leave Nash, she had to, so she tugged herself up as Nash hoisted her. She finally got a hold on the sturdy branch, and her foot found a good knot in the tree so she could make her way to the next branch. She turned and looked down at Nash. His head was tilted up to look at her, and his hands were on his hips.

"You'll still come to the bridge tomorrow, won't you?" she asked.

"Yes, I promised I would."

Relief flowed through her, but then she had a worry. Would he mention what she'd said about her mother to Owen? Truly, she didn't want anyone to know. She wasn't even sure why she'd told him. "About my mother—"

"I'll keep your secret."

And he thought he wasn't good... He was perfect. Never mind she'd only spent a few hours in his company, but he was wonderful. And she was going to mend him so he could be hers.

The fall went along in the dreamiest of manners. Lilias, Nash, and Owen met every day for Owen's swimming lessons. When Owen finally mastered swimming, she feared Nash would not meet them anymore, but that tragedy was skirted when Owen asked Nash to teach him how to fish. The three of them spent September together with Nash instructing them both on the finer arts of fishing—she begged to be included—and the process continued into October when Owen asked Nash to teach him to fence and to ride better. Lilias was already an excellent rider, but as she again did not want to be excluded from Nash's instruction, she pretended she wasn't.

Nash seemed to have taken on the role of older brother to Owen, but he didn't talk about it. She could not bring it up, though, because it was never just the two of them, and she didn't want to reveal what he'd told her in confidence about his own brother. He was gruff and grumpy at times, but he had honor and a fiercely protective side.

By the start of November, Lilias knew three things for certain: she was hopelessly in love with Nash, she wanted time alone with him, and the only way to get him to herself to find out if he felt the same about her was to seize the day. With that in mind, she sat at her desk and penned a note to Nash asking him to meet her at the bridge before the appointed time she, Owen, and Nash were supposed to rendezvous that evening. She was going to teach the boys about the constellations, which was something her father had taught her in one of his tentative moments.

Just as she was signing her note, her door swung open and Nora stood at the threshold with a grin on her face and letter in her hand. Lilias frowned at the interruption. "What do you want?"

"A rather stuffy footman brought this round for you, but I'm not inclined to give it to you."

Lilias jumped up and lunged for Nora, but her sister was faster on her feet than Lilias was. Nora dashed down the hall into her own room, slamming the door behind her as she went.

Lilias was halfway down the hall when her mother screeched, "Be quiet, girls! I've a horrid megrim, and I got no sleep last night."

"Sorry, Mama," Lilias called back, feeling guilty that she was actually glad to hear her mother had not slept well the night before. That meant she'd likely retire to bed early tonight, making it easier than usual for Lilias to leave the house without being noticed. Not that it was overly hard in the first place.

Her momentary pleasure turned sour as she tiptoed toward Nora's room, intent on taking her sister by surprise. It actually did not feel so grand that her mother never noticed that Lilias sneaked out of the house. In fact, at times, her mother almost seemed to forget that Lilias existed, except she had mentioned just yesterday that Lilias needed a new wardrobe to go to London next Season. Mama intended to introduce Lilias to Society to marry her off and get one daughter out from under foot. Those words had pricked.

Lilias sniffed and shoved her injured feelings away. Mama was overwhelmed and melancholy, as she had been since Papa died. Lilias reminded herself not to take it personally. After all, Mama ignored Nora, as well. Regardless, Lilias did not want to be clothed to be wedded off. She'd already found the man she hoped to eventually wed, and she'd done that in a pair of borrowed trousers.

She grinned to herself as she flung her sister's door open. Nora screeched and jumped off her bed, but Lilias tackled her and they both fell onto the bed in a fit of giggles. "Give me my letter!" Lilias demanded, laughing.

"What shall I get in return?" Nora asked through bursts of her own laughter.

"What do you want?" Lilias made a grab for the note.

"Your cloak," Nora said abruptly.

Lilias stilled. She knew the one Nora was talking about without having to ask. Papa had purchased her a fur-lined cloak before he'd died. It had been the last gift he'd ever given her. After he'd gambled away so much money, presents had been scarce. He'd promised Nora one, too, but that had not come to fruition. Lilias had been feeling rather guilty now that the weather was so cold about having the cloak when her sister did not, so she had not worn it yet, which also made her feel bad since it had been a gift from her father. This was the perfect solution.

"All right," she said.

"Truly?" Nora's blue eyes popped wide.

Lilias smiled and held out her hand for the letter. "Truly, dearest. Just be certain to take good care of it."

"Agreed," Nora said and relinquished the letter.

Lilias hugged her sister before scrambling off her bed and returning to her own room to read the note.

*Dearest Lilias,*

*My father has business in London that he requires me to attend to with him. I'll return in a sennight. Don't teach Nash about the constellations without me tonight. Oh, and let him know where I am. Also, I want to learn to dance. Will you teach me? Father says I'll need this skill in London eventually.*

*Your friend,*
*Owen*

With a grin, Lilias folded the letter, put it in her drawer, and tucked the one she'd written to Nash beside it. She tapped her fingernails against the glossy dark wood of her writing desk. Tonight, she'd be alone with Nash. Finally. And if he showed even an inkling that he felt for her as she'd come to feel for him, that was all the hope she needed.

Nash trod through the moonlit woods toward the bridge

where he was to meet Lilias and Owen without really noticing anything around him. His thoughts were on Lilias. In fact, she'd been all he could think about since he'd first hoisted her up into the tree the night he'd started teaching Owen to swim. It seemed as if the harder he tried not to think about her, the more he did.

And he shouldn't allow it. It wasn't even because of Owen. Nash had completely misjudged Owen's feelings toward her. His friend had told him a month ago, after a swim one afternoon when it was just the two of them, that he was going to find the perfect wife one day—a woman who respected the rules of Society and behaved with proper decorum. That certainly was not Lilias. Owen also had told Nash that his mother had scandalously run off with her horse trainer, so Nash understood what drove Owen to want propriety in a wife. Nash wasn't glad it had happened to Owen, but he couldn't ignore the relief he had felt knowing that Lilias was not who Owen was looking for. Owen had become his friend, but Lilias had become more than that. Exactly what, he wasn't quite sure. He'd been trying to fight it. Whatever it was, he knew he didn't deserve it, but it was impossible to fight the happiness she inspired.

He strode along the path thinking of her, shoving branches out of his way. When he glanced toward the bridge, he saw her. She stood in the moonlight, her hair glistening in the rays, her head tilted back, presumably looking at the stars. He looked around for Owen, and when he didn't see him, Nash picked up his pace in anticipation of a few moments alone with Lilias. When he was very close, her dogs—who were surrounding her—started barking.

"You brought the dogs?" he called.

Normally, she didn't.

She turned toward him, white teeth flashing in the dark as she grinned. "I left them outside in anticipation of coming tonight. I didn't want to be alone while I waited for you." Before he could ask about that, she said, "Hush," to the dogs, who immediately quieted. She made a shivery sound on the heels of that statement.

He frowned, coming to stand beside her on the bridge. He touched a hand to her threadbare cloak. "Is this all you wore out here tonight?"

She shrugged. "It's all I have. I had a fur-lined cloak, but my sister didn't, and she's been taking long walks out of doors lately, so…"

"So you gave her your cloak?" he asked, taking off his overcoat and settling it on her shoulders.

"You don't have to give me your coat," she protested, but he noticed the way she tugged the lapels together. It made him feel good to ensure she was taken care of.

"I know," he replied, his voice rough with the emotions he was repressing—the ones that scared him. "Where's Owen?"

"He's in London. He sent me a note this morning and said to tell you he'll be back in a sennight. He also asked me not to teach you about the constellations without him."

"Oh," Nash said. They were alone, after all. "I—" He should leave, but he couldn't make himself say so. It was the right thing to do, yet the words would not come.

He was aware of everything about her all at once. She smelled like a lily. Did she know that? Her head came precisely to his shoulder. She hummed when it was quiet, just as she was now doing. It made him think silence scared her.

Yes, he should most definitely leave. She didn't need to be tangled up with him, and yet, when he turned toward her and she, too, was facing him, it was as if there were an invisible string pulling them together.

"Why do you hum when it's quiet?" he asked.

A beat of silence passed. Then two. Then three. He should not have asked. "I'm sorry."

"No." She swallowed. "I hum to stay happy."

"You'd be sad if you weren't humming?"

She shrugged. "Possibly. Things have been gloomy since my father died. Actually, even before then." Another beat passed. "My house used to be loud, cheery. Now it's so very quiet. My mother insists upon it. So when I'm not there, I sometimes hum." She paused again. "If I tell you some secrets, will you keep them?"

"Yes." The word flew out of his mouth without thought, and in that moment, he realized that he'd die before ever willingly betraying her. She had found a way into his darkness, and she might be the only thing that could penetrate it with her light. He wanted that so much.

"My father gambled away almost all his money before he died. We are basically penniless. We still live in our home by the grace of my uncle."

The news made him want to throttle her dead father for leaving her so vulnerable. "I'm sorry," he said, trying to keep his feelings from permeating into his tone.

"Don't be. Money doesn't make happiness."

"I know that to be true. My family's miserable."

"And wealthy," she said, her delicate hand coming to rest upon his arm, something no perfectly proper girl would ever do. No, Lilias Honeyfield would never be the sort of girl to follow all the rules, and Nash had never been so glad about anything in his life.

All of a sudden, he knew what he wanted. He wanted to protect her from those in Society who would look down upon her for her lack of conformity. He wanted to protect her as he'd failed to protect his brother. Someday, he could offer that to her with his hand. His family was wealthy, titled, and had land. His father was a duke. Nash would one day be a duke. He could offer her every protection, and she could give him light.

Internally, he shook himself. Who was he to think such things? He had no right after what he'd done, and yet—

"Nash, what happened with your brother?"

It was the one question he always dreaded. Nash tried to pull his arm away from her, but she grasped him.

"I told you already," he said. "I killed him with my selfishness."

"Tell me exactly."

He sighed. "My brother was born sickly. He looked up to me, and I was supposed to protect him, watch over him. And I did. But no matter how much I gave, my parents wanted me to give more. I was to let my brother win at anything I did with him, and I followed that order. Always." Nash paused and swiped his hand over his face. "I was to stop speaking when he spoke, and I did. I was to give him things of mine that he wanted, from toys as children to pistols as we got older, and I did. I wanted to go on a grand tour with my uncle, and they said no since my brother couldn't go because of his health. And one day, my brother asked me for one more thing, and I did not grant the favor he requested." He paused again and looked to the ground as shame rolled over him. "I chose to be selfish, and that selfishness killed him."

"What did he ask for?" she asked.

"It doesn't matter." The guilt roared in his ears.

But it did. Still, he didn't want to see the look on her face if she knew. It would be the same look his parents had given him when he'd told them that his brother had asked him to ignore the tutor's daughter, who had been flirting with him, because Thomas liked her and wanted a chance with her, but Nash had ignored his brother's request. Helen had flirted with him, and he'd encouraged her selfishly. The worst part was that Nash had not even truly liked her. He'd simply wanted to think of himself first for once.

"We can all be selfish sometimes, Nash. It's a human quality."

"I was supposed to be his protector," Nash replied, refusing to let her grant him forgiveness when she didn't even know the whole truth. "My brother was furious with me when he realized what I was doing. He charged me on the ice, the ice cracked beneath him, and he fell through." Nash swallowed the knot in his throat and forced himself to look up. "I couldn't save him."

The tears rolling down Lilias's cheeks shocked him. "I couldn't save my father, either," she said. "I tried."

Nash gently wiped away her tears, then took one of her hands in his, glad she was not going to press him for all the details. "Tell me."

"He was different," she said, sniffling. "A dreamer. A writer. But his parents forbade him from pursuing 'such folly.' I think that's why he encouraged us, me and my sister, to do as we wished. I think that's why he did not place the usual boundaries upon us that most girls of the *ton* are required to live and die by. Mother despised it." Lilias let out a laugh at that, partly bitter, partly understanding. "He sent a story to a publisher once." She bit her lip, then spoke again. "I'm not supposed to know that, but I do."

He didn't ask how. She was clever, this girl. He could picture her with her ear to some door. "My mother told him not to do it. She was fearful, I think, of what would happen if his story got accepted."

Nash nodded, understanding. It was odd to him how people in their set frowned upon work, especially if one got paid.

"It didn't get accepted," Lilias continued, "and he started drinking and gambling. And then—" She waved a hand in the air, and he could feel her helpless despair. "He simply slumped into his plate one night and was dead."

She was crying softly now, and he put his arms around her and drew her close. Her head came under his chin, and her soft body pressed along the length of his. A tremor of awareness went through him unlike anything he'd ever known. He wanted to take the sadness from her.

"I tried," Lilias continued, her voice muffled. She turned her head, pressed her cheek to his chest, and slipped her arms around his waist. He felt her fingers lock behind his back. "I tried to save him, but I couldn't. And so now—" she paused and tilted her head back to look at him "—I try to save other things."

Owen. Her dogs. Nash. Did he deserve to be saved? He didn't think so, but she did because she was a dreamer like her father. She was rare and precious, and she needed someone far better than he was, and yet he found himself leaning toward her, drawn to her goodness, drawn to every single thing about her, from her smile, to her dimples, to the way her hair always looked in lovely, wild disarray, to how she didn't follow a single dictate that ladies of her upbringing were supposed to. He pressed his forehead to hers, telling himself that if she drew back, he would understand. But she didn't, and he was filled with hope. Her breath mingled with his, sweet and enticing. He wanted to kiss her. He'd never wanted anything more in his life.

Bringing his hands to her back, he brushed his lips to

hers ever so gently to give her time to pull away, to tell him to stop. When she moaned, searing need rushed through him, but he reined it in. He didn't want to frighten her. He slid his hand up the perfect curve of her spine until his right hand held the slender column of her neck, and his left hand came to her lips. He ran his thumb over her mouth, and when she moaned again, he traced the soft fullness of her lips with his tongue. He'd never felt anything so good in his life.

He had to feel her heat, taste her goodness. He parted her lips with his tongue, half expecting her to stop him, but she tugged him closer, and as his own need mounted, she kissed him with a hunger and a sweetness that made him feel completely alive and as if redemption was possible with her.

"Lilias," he said, breaking the kiss, wanting to tell her the things in his head. "God, Lilias. You make me feel—"

"Lilias! Nash!" Owen burst through the trees before Nash could react. Owen came to an abrupt stop, his jaw dropping and silence descending. As Lilias and Nash scrambled apart, Owen's gaze stayed on Nash, narrowing.

"What are you doing here?" Lilias exclaimed.

"Shall I leave?" he asked, his tone sharp.

"Don't be ridiculous!" Lilias burst out, her voice sounding a tad high to Nash. "I, well, I was sad about my father, and Nash was simply—Well, he was simply—"

"Comforting her," Nash supplied, knowing there was nothing else to be said. They'd had their arms entwined about each other, after all, their faces a hairsbreadth apart.

Owen moved toward Lilias and past Nash, scowling at him. A slight suspicion arose that Nash didn't even want to acknowledge.

"Lilias, why didn't you tell me you were sad? I'm here

for you," Owen said, slipping his arm around Lilias's shoulder.

The urge to throw Owen's arm off her astonished Nash with its intensity. And when Lilias dipped under Owen's arm and away, Nash could not suppress the gladness.

"I need to go home," Lilias murmured. "I, well, I don't feel well."

"I'll walk you," Nash and Owen offered at the same time.

She shook her head, and Nash said, "We'll both walk you."

"No, I'll see you two tomorrow." She turned, took a few steps away from them, then turned back. "Owen, what happened to your trip to London?"

"My father took ill. He's abed, but I had to wait to be certain he was going to stay there before slipping away."

Lilias nodded. "I see. So you won't be going to Town anytime soon?"

Nash glanced at her, hearing an odd hitch in her voice. Hopefulness? Maybe he was only hearing what he wanted to hear.

Owen shook his head. "I doubt it. He wrote his solicitor to conclude the business on his behalf."

"I see." Nash could not mistake the disappointment he heard in her voice, and when Owen tensed, Nash did, as well, and his niggling suspicion grew tenfold.

"Tomorrow, then," she said, whistling for her dogs to follow, and then she left Owen and Nash as if there were something chasing her.

When she was totally out of sight, Owen turned to Nash, his irritated expression apparent, even in the moonlit night. "Race me."

Nash frowned. "What?"

"Race me," Owen repeated, his voice hard.

"What are we racing for?" Nash asked, that suspicion now nearly choking him.

"The right to court Lilias."

And there it was. A swift punch of unwanted truth to his gut. For one moment, he was robbed of the ability to speak, but then he finally found his voice. "I thought you said you wanted a wife who would behave properly and never go against Society rules."

"Of course I said that," Owen growled. "I didn't want you to know I liked Lilias, but I do. And you do, too."

He did. God, he did, but it was as if he were standing on that ice again and Thomas was before him. He could put Owen's desires above his own as he had failed to do for Thomas. There wasn't ice under Nash's feet now, simply solid ground, but he was going under anyway, drowning fast. "What you saw was two friends, nothing more." The surface was gone, as was his hope.

"I think she likes you," Owen said, his voice glum. And before Nash could respond, Owen added, "I know about your brother. My father heard in Town the gossip of what occurred."

All the air left Nash's lungs.

"Tomorrow, I'll challenge you to a race, Nash," Owen said. "Who knows, perhaps I'll win and Lilias will finally see me."

Nash swallowed the desire to declare that Lilias was his. She was not. He did not deserve her. "I'm certain you'll win," Nash replied, meaning it. He would not race his hardest.

Owen nodded and left Nash standing in the woods alone.

Nash couldn't say how long he remained there, but the

sun came up eventually, and when he made his way home, he vowed to himself not to be the thing that drove Lilias and Owen apart, no matter what the cost to himself.

<hr />

The next morning, Lilias hurried to meet Nash and Owen for their morning ride. She'd overslept because she'd had such trouble getting to sleep the night before. Every time she had closed her eyes, she would recall every detail of Nash kissing her. She hated to wish Owen away, but wish him to London, she did. Yet, when she came to the clearing where they always started their ride, he was there, and she felt guilty for the disappointment that filled her.

She glanced around the clearing, not seeing Nash, and then he came over the hill and jumped over a fallen tree that, to her, looked nearly impossible to clear. Nash reached Owen at the same time she did.

"You ride dangerously," Lilias chastised Nash, though she was secretly amazed.

"I ride the way I live," he said, his voice so solemn her breath caught and worry blossomed.

"You should be more careful," she said. If anything were to happen to him, she would be devastated. "But I will say, you are the best horseman I have ever seen."

"I believe I'm now better," Owen said. His tone was boastful, and his expression irritated, like a petulant child.

Lilias bit back the wish to retort, realizing Owen must be feeling as if he were in Nash's shadow. She was certain no boy would wish to feel that way. Owen scowled at her. She placed a placating hand on his arm. "You are a fine horseman. I—"

"Race me, Nash," Owen demanded, shrugging off her

hand. "Let me prove I'm better. Unless you are afraid to?" It almost sounded like a taunting challenge. She clenched her teeth at the foolish pride of men.

"Owen, no," Lilias said, certain he'd be embarrassed in a race against Nash.

"Yes," he clipped.

"Nash—" she tried.

"If he wishes to race, I cannot, as a gentleman, decline."

"Then don't be a gentleman," she fumed. But it was hopeless. Before she knew it, they took off, leaving her behind as they raced back toward the fallen tree Nash had just jumped.

Lilias held her breath, watching, admiring Nash's form and hoping Owen did not make too poor of a showing. To her shock, Owen pulled ahead of Nash and started to lengthen the distance between them. But then Nash seemed to gain ground as they moved like lightning toward the fallen tree. Her heart began to pound as they drew closer and closer to the tree, but to her relief, Nash pulled his horse to the right, away from the tree. She assumed Owen would do the same. But just as she was exhaling, her mouth slipped open as Owen jumped the tree and his horse came tumbling down on the other side, pinning Owen underneath.

# Chapter One

**London, England**
**1837**

*G*uilt was a funny thing. Though the initial onslaught of it could set the course of one's life, when one lived with it for so long, it eventually went unnoticed, like a shadow. That was, until something made one take note, like the sun overhead and a glance down to see the outline of oneself in startling perfection or like a man who used to walk perfectly straight suddenly leaning on a cane and walking unevenly toward the offender who caused the injury.

Nash Steele, the Duke of Greybourne, raised his brandy and took a long drink. It slid down his throat, easing some of the knots as he waited for the Earl of Blackwood to make his way across the Persian rugs in White's gaming room. The sound of Owen's irregular footsteps scraped across Nash's eardrums in the mostly deserted room. It was well before the hour that most of their peers frequented the club, but when Nash had contacted Owen to let him know he had returned to Town, Owen had written back quickly, asking Nash to meet him here.

The belongings that had been with Nash at Oxford and then Scotland these past seven years hadn't even made it up to his bedchamber before he had hurried out the door to meet Owen. Luckily, Nash's mother and sister were not at home when he'd arrived from Scotland so he'd been spared explaining why he was rushing out so soon. To explain the call of guilt, he would have had to tell them of the day Owen had been hurt, and that, Nash would not do.

Owen made his way past the large fireplace and to the table in the back corner where Nash was sitting. As he approached, Nash noted the grim set of his friend's mouth, and fear twisted inside him. He sat forward, his pulse spiking. "What is it? Is it Lilias? Is that why you wrote that you needed to see me today?"

Owen motioned to the server standing nearby to indicate he'd have the same drink Nash was having, and then he pulled out his chair, balanced his cane against the table, and said, "Yes."

Nash chest squeezed. "Is she hurt?"

"No," Owen said easily, his gaze flicking momentarily to Nash before he looked down at his hands, which were now resting intertwined on the table. "I wanted to see you in person to ask you not to contact her now that you have returned to Town."

"I wouldn't," Nash replied, his words harsher than he had intended, but everything about Lilias had always made him passionate. "You know I wouldn't. So why this meeting? Why this request? Have I not refrained from contacting her for seven years, as you asked of me the day after your accident?"

He could recount going to see Owen the next day with perfect clarity. Owen had been in his sickbed with a crushed leg and had looked at Nash with such pain in his eyes.

*You'll win her if you stay,* he'd said. *You cannot help yourself. You saved her in the water that day, and she thinks of you as a character in one of those nonsense Gothic novels she reads. She thinks you honorable.*

The way Owen had said it, as if they both knew it were

not true, had been seared in Nash's memory, and Nash had feared Owen was right. Lilias *had* bestowed upon him some ridiculous qualities of a character in a book, a man he was not. So he had left without so much as a goodbye to her. It had felt as if he'd reached into his chest and ripped out his heart. He'd stayed away after that—mostly. He'd seen Owen through the years, and they had written letters. Nash knew Lilias and Owen had spent all their time together in the Cotswolds, and Owen had sometimes written about the things he and Lilias had done together.

She had stayed with Owen every day after his accident. Owen had told him about how she had always been there when he awoke, how she had held his hand while reading to him. She had helped Owen push himself to walk and, eventually, had taught him to dance, even with his limp. That had filled Nash with a jealousy that had kept him up many nights, imagining holding her in his arms and twirling her around, making her laugh.

As Owen's glass scraped across the table and he picked it up, Nash focused on the man. "Have I not kept my promise not to come between you and her?" His head throbbed with his frustration.

Owen's mouth tightened. "You have. It will just be harder not to see her here in Town at balls and such than it was in the Cotswolds, where there was no reason for the two of you to interact."

Nash's fingers curled into a fist under the table. There was no reason for him and Lilias to interact because he had ensured she would not want to speak to him. He'd only responded to one of her letters after he'd departed and that had been to tell her to quit writing him.

He had purposely avoided her for seven years, only going back to the Cotswolds once a year and being very careful whenever he ventured out. He'd seen her twice by chance in those years, and both times had made him feel as if someone had plunged a knife into his gut. Once, when she'd ridden past their property on her horse, and then again last year, after Christmas, when he'd seen her walking with Owen past their home. It had taken all his will not to thunder down his stairs, throw open his door, swallow the distance between them, and rip Owen away from her. They'd been walking so close that their arms had been brushing. It had left Nash shaking.

"How long do you wish me to avoid her?" he finally asked.

Owen tugged on his neckcloth. "Well, I had hoped to be wed by now, but I feel sure it's coming soon."

Owen might as well have punched a fist through Nash's chest. "Oh. So you've asked for her hand?" He sounded supremely uninterested, which was good.

"Not yet." Owen's mouth pinched. "I, well, she has been so independent, and I wanted to give her time to realize that she needed to settle into her lot as a woman."

Nash felt a tic start at that statement, but he bit back any comment. Lilias's "lot" was not his concern. "And you feel she has settled?" He felt as if he had choked out the question.

"I think she is very close to giving up her girlhood notions that women can flaunt all rules of Society, and I worry that your reappearance could remind her of a time she was recklessly independent," Owen said.

Nash gritted his teeth at that news, though he himself had worried what trouble her independent nature might bring her.

"I think she sees how loyal I am to her, how I have been there for her," Owen continued. "I know how she feels about me, of course."

That sentence took Nash back to four years ago when Owen had written that Lilias had told Owen she loved him. The news had sent Nash into the first of many women's beds. Initially, he'd done so in hopes of forgetting Lilias entirely, and when that hadn't worked, to just forget her for a while. The brief moments never lasted, though. She always returned to his mind and his heart, tempting him to simply drift back to her. But it wasn't real. She would not think him so wonderful if she knew the truth of what he'd done to Thomas and to Owen.

"Yes," he agreed, because what else was there to do? "It's good that you know that. I'm certain it's been hard to wait for her." Though Nash would have waited a thousand lifetimes if there had been any way for him and Lilias to be together.

"It's not hard because I have always known she would eventually be mine."

The image of Nash's hands around his friend's neck startled Nash. *Christ.* He shoved his chair back, not wanting to be here. Owen glanced at him in surprise. "I'm sorry," Nash said. "I just recalled that my mother has invited guests for dinner."

"That's fine," Owen said with a wave of his hand. "If you do happen to run into Lilias, it might be best to treat her with cool regard. No sense in stirring up a past that does not matter."

Was Owen referring to finding Lilias and Nash in each other's arms? No, Nash would not want to stir up those memories any more than they already stirred themselves up within him. The damn things refused to stay buried.

The rogue had returned.

Lilias Honeyfield stood outside Nash's home in Mayfair, her fist raised to grasp the knocker on his gleaming dark door. The clop of hooves on the busy lane hummed in her ears as memories assaulted her. Seven years' worth of memories, to be exact. Seven years of longing, of hoping, of hating and loving. She was exhausted, and she wanted to put an end to it all. As horribly embarrassing as this would likely be, she had to do it. Yet, her gloved hand did not move. It stayed hovering just out of reach of the shiny brass door knocker.

She couldn't make herself do it. She was a founding member of the Society of Ladies Against Rogues, for heaven's sake. She was a pioneer of stealthily doing things forbidden to women. For more years than she cared to recall, she had managed to avoid being forced to wed someone she didn't care for. She was a strong woman, and yet, she was frozen with fear of what was to come, of what might have been, of discovering it had all been the fanciful imagination of a girl who had read—and still did—far too many Gothic novels.

She had been in love, and she had been almost positively certain that Nash had felt the same, but she hadn't gotten the chance to find out. He and Owen had raced, Owen had fallen, his leg had been crushed, and he had been left with a permanent limp. And before the dust had settled, Nash had fled without a word.

She could still recall in numbing detail going to his house to see him, to cry with him over the horrible accident that had occurred, to take his hand and lead him to Owen's home so they could sit with him until he was strong enough to get out of bed. She had pictured them helping Owen learn to walk again, and maybe someday to run and ride, but that was not to be.

Nash's mother, a woman as cold as the River Eye in winter, had answered the door and told Lilias that Nash had left that morning for Oxford, which had apparently been scheduled all along, and that she did not know when in the foreseeable future he would return.

Lilias had been dumbstruck that he had left Owen in such a state, but then she considered Nash's past with his brother, and she knew in her heart that guilt had driven Nash away. Still, she had thought he'd return. Not the next day, but certainly before seven years had passed. She'd been sad, then angry, then numb, but through it all, hope had remained. She was happy to say the hope was fairly dead now, but this—confronting him face-to-face, seeing him, looking him in the eye—was what she needed to put her love for him in the grave where it belonged.

Owen thought her mad. She knew it. For years he'd been telling her to move on with her life and forget Nash. Even Nash had written her and told her to do the same. The last letter she had written him and the one he had written in response, the only one he'd ever written despite the numerous letters she'd sent to him at school, was seared in her mind and on her heart.

*Dear Nash,*

*This will be the last time I write you. I know I said that in my previous letter, but this time I mean it. Owen's accident was not your fault. Your brother's death was not your fault. You are my best friend, and you are... Well, I thought perhaps we might... I miss you. I miss you horribly. Please write. Please come visit. Please don't just disappear from my life. You are good. I know you said you weren't, but I know in my heart that you are. I know you are hurting. I know you need me. You said I make you feel—What?*

*Please write me back this time.*

*Lilias*

*Lilias,*

*Please don't write to me anymore. I've met someone else. And I'm not hurting. I'd have to feel to hurt, and I don't feel anything.*

*Nash*

Lilias inhaled a deep, steadying breath. It had been that last line—*I'd have to feel to hurt, and I don't feel anything*—that made it so hard for her to give up hope. She'd believed that what had begun between them was something special, a love story for the ages like those she read about in her books, and not just the fanciful imagination of a lonely girl on the cusp of becoming a woman. She had not confessed that to anyone but Owen. She had not even admitted her real feelings to her closest friend, Guinevere.

Owen was her closest male friend. Well, her only one really, and he had known Nash's goodness just as she had. Bless Owen. He had dried her tears and been there for her as she tried to mend her broken heart, but it would not quite heal. She'd assured him at one point that it had, and he'd simply patted her shoulder and told her that in time it would, that eventually, Nash would return to England, she would run into him, and she would find that her heart did not flip in her chest. Her breath would not whoosh out of her lungs. Her lips would not tingle in anticipation of another kiss as perfect as the first one he had given her.

And this was it—the moment seven long years had led her toward. She finally grasped the knocker and struck it, feeling as if she were holding the weight of her entire future.

Within a breath, the door opened and a butler adorned in silver and navy livery stood at the threshold. "May I help you?"

The question was polite, as was the look he bestowed upon her down his long, hawklike nose. He was a well-trained butler indeed. He didn't even blink his dark brown eyes or show a hint of surprise that she was alone, standing at the doorstep without a companion.

"I'm here to see Lady Adaline." Guilt tugged at her that she wasn't really here to call upon Nash's younger sister. She did like the girl, who had been presented to Society this Season. Lilias had made a special point to meet Lady Adaline, compelled to do so for mostly selfish reasons at first. She had hoped that in getting to know Adaline, she might learn information about Nash. It embarrassed her to think upon now.

She'd scarcely heard a word about him since he'd left seven years ago. She knew he'd gone to live in Scotland at one of his family's estates after Oxford—Owen had told her so—but Owen didn't seem to know much more since he and Nash rarely corresponded. She had overheard his sister say that Nash had not had any serious intentions toward any women and that she'd likely get married before her rogue of a brother did. Lilias had promised herself that she would not think it was because he was longing for her, but the promise was ridiculously futile.

She also knew, as everyone in the *ton* did, that Nash's father, the Duke of Greybourne, had recently died. She reminded herself to call him *Greybourne* and not *Nash*. No, she'd need to call him *Your Grace*. He'd likely not be anticipating such conformity from her, but times had changed a bit. She had to think of her sister and mother and not just herself.

The butler cleared his throat, snapping her attention back to him, and she noted him staring at her hand expectantly.

She knew what he wanted: a calling card. But she did not have one. Even if she had not been in a state of shock upon hearing the announcement from Guinevere's younger sister Frederica that she'd seen Nash in Town that morning, even if she hadn't rushed straight here from the SLAR meeting at the home of Guinevere and her new husband, the Duke of Carrington, Lilias would not be in possession of a calling card. She and her mother had run out, and Mama had said they must wait to ask her Uncle Simon for funds for more. It was scandalous to her mother to be without a calling card. It was ridiculous to Lilias, but it was a fact of life in the *ton* that she should have a calling card to produce, and not having one would mean there would be those bored, vapid sorts who would treat her like a leper.

She arched her eyebrows. "I'm without a calling card, but I am Lady Lilias Honeyfield."

She'd had doors shut in her face before for such boldness, but the butler stepped to the side. "Come in, my lady, and I'll let Lady Adaline know you're here."

Lilias entered, her heart nearly pounding out of her day gown as she moved across the threshold and into the grandeur of Nash's Mayfair home. The entrance hall looked as she'd imagined it might through the years. The floors were a gleaming black-and-white marble, which the butler's shoes tapped against as he walked, and marble pillars stood on either side of the interior hall like soldiers guarding the family within. The floors in Lilias's own, much smaller townhome were dull and chipped. The whole home needed repair, but there was no money to do it, and her uncle had not offered.

They paused, and the butler took her wrap, and as he left her to set the wrap aside, she gazed into the dining room, which was just barely visible. A beautiful marble fireplace was the centerpiece, and it was accompanied by crystal sconces and a breathtaking, shimmering chandelier. She imagined Nash sitting there across from his sister and mother. Were they close? She did not even truly know. He had not talked of his parents much except when he'd told her how they'd expected him to watch over his sickly brother and let him win at things. She was sure they'd only wanted to protect his younger brother, though they had done so at Nash's expense.

When the butler returned, he said, "If you'll follow me to the parlor."

Lilias nodded, though a sudden thought struck her. If Nash was not with his sister, which he very well likely might not be, how would she manage to see him? She racked her brain to think of some excuse she could use, but she need not have for there at the bottom of one of the grandest staircases she'd ever seen stood Nash and Adaline, talking animatedly. They did not notice the butler, nor her, and Lilias took the opportunity to drink him in. The picture he presented stole her breath.

The kilt he wore instantly brought a smile to her lips. Did he still wear it to annoy his mother? Had he managed to get a reaction from her over the years? His calves had become even more titillating over time, if that were possible. They were the calves of a man who was not idle. Age had served him very, very well, the devil. The images that filled her head as she stared at his bare legs would have shocked the bawdiest of sailors. She forced herself to look upward and inched her gaze over his long, sinewy legs, up over his slim hips, and farther still to his chest, proportioned to make an artist weep. She finally stopped at his broad shoulders, which looked like the perfect place to rest her head and listen to his the rich timbre of his voice.

He waved a hand in the air as he spoke to his sister, and Lilias followed the motion, noting that his bottle-green coat was clearly the work of a master tailor. His cravat was untied and hung down his chest, as if he'd recently jerked on it in irritation. His hair, still just as gleaming, dark, and thick, made her want to thread her fingers through it as she had longed to do so many years before. He had a darker shadow of stubble on his beautiful face than she remembered, but it only lent him a more rugged appearance. He stopped talking suddenly as Lilias and the butler passed the window that put them midway to the staircase. Nash looked toward them, and for one breath, he appeared so exquisitely happy to see her that all the years of missing him, hating him, loving him, yearning for him did not matter. Nothing mattered but him.

"Lilias." There was a faint tremor in his voice, as if some deep emotion had touched him. She felt it in her bones.

"Greybourne, how do you know Lady Lilias?" Lady Adaline asked, studying him rather intently.

The question did something to him, something that made Lilias come to a shuddering halt. His gray eyes, which had been clinging to her, became hooded. His face became impassive, but his stance was rigid. He glanced at his sister. "She is our neighbor in the Cotswolds. I met her when we first moved there." He chucked his sister's chin in a loving, protective gesture that made Lilias's chest squeeze. "You never met her, Adaline, because Mother always had you in some sort of etiquette lessons."

"Well, that explains that," Lady Adaline murmured, looking as if she were thinking about something. "Lady Lilias, I'm so glad you have called!" She came toward Lilias, shiny black curls bouncing against her slender shoulders incased in expensive blue silk, and arms outstretched. She grasped both of Lilias's hands, and Lilias had to force herself to look away from Nash, who turned toward the window as if there were something fascinating in his garden. Lilias checked—nothing there, just flowers. They certainly were pretty, but not fascinating.

He was uncomfortable. He was avoiding looking at her. Fear pricked her that what had kept her in knots for years, the memories that had made her unable to properly give attention to any other man, had been a fantasy of her overactive imagination. But she could have sworn he'd been glad to see her, even if only for a moment. Or maybe she'd only seen what she wanted? That prick of fear became more of a stab with an annoyingly sharp invisible knife.

"Don't mind Greybourne," Lady Adaline said, and Lilias, who realized she was staring at Nash, jerked her gaze away from him and back to his sister. Lady Adaline waved a dismissive hand. "He's practically a hermit."

"Adaline." Nash spoke but a single word, but it was forceful, as was everything about him.

Lady Adaline turned scarlet but notched her chin, and Lilias recognized the seeds of a determined woman in the younger girl. "It's true," Lady Adaline muttered and leaned close to Lilias as if to tell her a secret. "Do you know, in all of his years at school and living in Scotland, he only ever came home once a year? And only to the Cotswolds, never to London."

Lilias's eyes flew toward Nash and crashed into his stormy gaze. His look was easy enough to read now—

barely controlled irritation. His fists were clenched, his jaw was tense, and his gaze was narrowed.

"Adaline, cease talking," he warned.

"I shall not," the young girl said in a mutinous tone. "I daresay you never even knew your childhood friend came to the Cotswolds once a year, did you, Lady Lilias?"

"Adaline, Lady Lilias does not care about my comings and goings."

But she did. Oh, how she did. And he knew it. She saw it on his face, which for one flash of a second, held embarrassment and remorse.

*Nash had been to the Cotswolds. Seven times.*

Heat flooded her face. She was possibly the biggest fool to ever live. An expansive hole appeared in her chest.

"I can see you didn't know," Lady Adaline continued. "He practically hid in the house every time he came, as if he were avoiding someone."

*Dear God. It could not get worse!*

Lilias wished the ground would open and swallow her up.

"Adaline!" Nash thundered and started toward them.

But Adaline continued. "He only ventured out to see his friend Owen, and even then only at night. It's all so very—"

"Mother is calling you," Nash interrupted.

Lady Adaline frowned. "No, she's not. She—"

"Is calling you," he ground out. "So go to the parlor."

The girl bit her lip but nodded. She released Lilias's hands, offered an apologetic smile, and departed.

Lilias stood before Nash, trembling. Her emotions swung wildly between embarrassment, anger, and agony. She knew she ought to keep her mouth closed, but she didn't care about what she ought to do.

"You came back to the Cotswolds, and you avoided me.

And Owen knew." She sounded pathetic, but she would not let that stop her. There was no room for pride when true love was involved. She wanted to pummel his chest, but she at least had enough self-restraint not to do so.

"Do not blame Owen."

The four words held no hint of remorse or apology. But they did hold impatience, as if he wanted this to be over—or more precisely, wanted her to be gone. For one moment, she considered holding her tongue, doing as practically any other woman would do and simply take her leave and give him a reprieve, despite how he had treated her, how he had made her think he was worthy of being a hero when he was really the villain of the worst book she'd never read because it did not exist. The errant thought to write a book and make him the villain came to her mind. It would serve him right.

"I will deal with Owen later." She wanted to weep with relief when her voice came out sounding strong. She wouldn't weep, of course. Not in front of Nash. She was used to having to be strong even when all she wanted was, for once, for someone to protect her, to watch over her. But not just any someone...

*Foolish.* Her head was filled with stuffing and nonsense. There was no one to watch over her but herself. Nash was not her Gothic hero.

"I asked Owen not to mention to you when I came to visit," he said.

"Why?" Her heart pounded so hard that her chest hurt.

Nash looked distinctly uncomfortable. "Because it served no purpose for you to know I was there."

"I thought we were friends. Real friends." She could not bear to say out loud that she had believed they were going to be more. "You said—" She swallowed, wishing she didn't need to ask the one question that had burned in her mind all these years. But if she didn't ask it now, she'd never forgive herself for being so weak. One moment of embarrassment could not break her, but if she knew she'd let something special, something wonderful slip between her fingers because of pride... Well, that would drive her mad.

"The night we were alone, you said I made you feel—" *Thump. Thump. Thump.* She took a deep breath to calm her heart so she could hear him when he answered. Why was she pushing? Why wouldn't that hope totally die?

He looked startled for a moment, but then his dark lashes lowered to almost fully conceal his eyes. When he looked up again, whatever emotion he might have been feeling was unfathomable to her. She wanted to scream.

"I don't recall the conversation." His voice was even. Flat. And yet she could see him clenching and unclenching his teeth by the way his jaw moved.

"You are a liar." Her mother would have simply expired on the spot if she'd heard Lilias now. Thank heavens no one was around.

He flinched at her accusation but did not deny it. For some reason, that made her glad. At least he acknowledged his fatal flaw. His right hand came up to thread his fingers in his hair, just as he'd done years before. "Lilias, I don't remember the conversation because whatever I was going to say was not important enough to me to remember. I told you I am not a good person."

She nodded, feeling as if every emotion she possessed was lodged in her throat. "Yes, yes, you did. I daresay I'm more inclined to believe you than I ever was before."

"Is there some other way I can help you, Lilias?"

The question was asked as if she were a stranger, as if they had not shared the secrets of what shredded their hearts. "You said that you were not hurting, that you'd have to feel in order to hurt, and you felt nothing. But everyone feels," she said, arching her eyebrows, demanding him to challenge that.

"Yes," he said to her shock, "they do. I did contact Owen. I did feel very bad."

"But you did not feel for me," she whispered, understanding finally sinking in.

His lips pressed together in a hard line, and then he jerked his hand through his hair. "I felt as a young man would for any pretty girl who showed interest in him. But not as you wanted me to feel. Not... Not—"

She'd never seen him flustered. It was an astonishing sight. He'd never seemed as if he could be made to feel uncomfortable. He'd seemed utterly confident always, but he was uncomfortable now. She would have let him drown in it, but she was going under with him.

"You needn't say more," she said. "I understand." He had not loved her. He'd made her fall in love with him, but all she'd done was inspire a fleeting desire to kiss her. How appalling that she was so foolish that she'd wasted seven years pining over something that had never even existed.

"Your Grace," she managed to get out with a semblance of, well, *grace*. "Please tell your sister I came here at the behest of my friend the Duchess of Carrington to invite her to the ball she and the duke are hosting." It was nonsense, but she had to say something. She had to try to save a tiny shred of her pride. She'd explain to Guinevere, and her friend would understand.

Nash's gray eyes held skepticism at her claim. Of course they did! It was poppycock, and he likely knew it, but at least he was not going to mention it.

"Shall I get my sister?"

"No. I suddenly don't feel well." With that lie—goodness, they were flying out of her mouth today—she gave him the time and location. It wasn't at all proper to invite him to Guinevere's ball. The invitation should have been sent by Guinevere, but Guinevere would forgive her. And as she spoke the last word, the butler materialized as if he'd somehow known it was time to see her out.

She exchanged goodbyes with Nash as one stranger to the other, each syllable that tumbled from her lips increasing the ache in her stomach. When the door closed behind her, and she was alone in the bright light of day, she grabbed her side and barely resisted the urge to double over. Hot tears pricked her eyes, but she blinked them away, determined to hold them back until she was in the privacy of her home.

She inhaled a ragged breath when the door behind her creaked open. Before she could even turn to see who it was, Nash said, "You forgot your wrap."

His voice washed over her, sounding as inviting as she had dreamed. She frowned as she slowly faced him, caught between warring desires of wishing him away and wishing him near. *This was madness!* She'd loved him for so long, she didn't yet know how to hate him, but she would not make a fool of herself anymore. She arched her eyebrows as she stepped toward him to retrieve her wrap. "Thank you. I'm sure you could have simply sent your butler after me."

She grasped the wrap, her fingers brushing his, tingling coursing through her at the warm feel of his skin against hers. She pulled back her hand, but he grabbed it, surprising her. Their eyes locked, and in his, remorse burned. "I'm sorry, Lilias."

If she'd been the same woman she was when she'd raced over here, she would have imagined he was trying to tell her something, but she was not that woman anymore. The part of her that had held out hope that her love story with Nash was still to be written was gone. They had no story. They never had. He was not trying to convey anything other than the fact that he felt pity for her, and that blessedly made her livid, which was far better than feeling crushed.

"You needn't apologize. You did tell me you were not a good man." With that, she snatched her hand from him in a most unladylike manner. "I was the one who was too silly to listen." She turned on her heel, prepared to make a grand exit where the scorned heroine leaves the hero standing gaping after her, but as she started away, footsteps thudded behind her.

She stopped and whirled toward him with a glare. "What are you doing?"

"I see you do not have a carriage."

"My, aren't you observant. But that does not answer my question. What. Are. You. Doing?"

He smiled. He *actually* smiled. And it was blindingly beautiful. Hating him was becoming easier by the second. Whyever was he smiling at her? He needed to stop instantly.

"Stop smiling at me." When he accommodated her immediately, it was even more vexing. He had not once been accommodating since she'd met him. He did not need to start now, not when she was planning to hate him forever. "Stop being accommodating."

He arched twin perfectly formed, dark, thick eyebrows. Everything about him was annoyingly perfect, except his heart.

"Do you want me to smile or not?" he asked, amusement in his voice.

She served him what she knew from experience with Nora and loads of practice in the looking glass was her best scowl. "I want you to tell me why you are following me."

"I cannot very well allow you to walk home by yourself. That would not be very honorable of me."

"Ah yes, you and your honor," she snipped. It was his blasted supposed honor that had first made her tumble into love with him when he'd made that little speech by the stream so many years ago about not allowing her to aid him in teaching Owen to swim because she could have been hurt. He was honorable, she begrudgingly acknowledged. Which also meant he was good. She begrudgingly acknowledged that, too. What he was *not* was besotted with her, and he had told her as much. Plainly. Years before.

She felt like such a fool. Again. "I order you not to follow me." She prayed he'd listen. She wanted to cry, and she absolutely could not do so with him at her heels like a guard dog.

"I'm not the sort of man to follow orders, Lilias. Just as you are not the sort of lady to follow commands."

"You know nothing about what sort of lady I am now," she snapped, though what he'd said was true. She had never been good at following commands. She blamed that on her father. He'd always said his biggest regret in life was following the course for his life that his parents had demanded instead of the one his heart had wanted.

For one moment, Nash looked as if he might argue, but then he simply nodded. "You are quite right, but that does not change the fact that I am going to ensure you get home safely."

"Do as you wish," she grumbled. "But I vow I won't speak a single word to you."

She could have sworn his lips started to tug upward into

a smile, but he very quickly schooled his features into the most serious expression. "I'd be disappointed if you did."

She opened her mouth to insist upon his telling her what he meant by that, but she promptly snapped it shut, realizing that such an action would break her just proclaimed vow to herself. She whirled away from him, started toward her home, then changed course to make her way back to Guinevere's home on Picadilly. She needed a shoulder to cry on.

"Where are you going?" Nash asked from behind her.

The desire to tell him it was none of his business nearly burst from her, but she pressed her lips together, determined not to speak to him.

"Lilias, this is not the way to your home."

She almost tripped at the realization that he knew where her home was. They were not in the Cotswolds any longer. So how did he know such a thing? For a man who'd been away for seven years and had never been to her family's home in Mayfair, Nash should have no notion which way her townhome was. Had he made it a point to discover where she lived?

*Stop it.* She would not allow herself to live in a fantasy any longer. Seven years was quite enough.

She squared her shoulders and strode forward as fast as her swishing skirts would allow. When she reached the steps of Guinevere and Carrington's townhome, she thought to simply march up the steps without a goodbye, but it occurred to her that by behaving as she was, she was letting him see how much his rejection had hurt her. She would not be such a fool as to tell herself he did not know she had liked him. At least he did not know she loved him. Oh, she still did. She couldn't simply turn it off. But she would smother it until it no longer had life.

She forced a smile to her lips that made her cheeks hurt, turned, and offered a curtsy. She came up and—

*Was that admiration she saw in his eyes? Stop. Stop. Stop.*

She really needed to sit and think upon why she kept imagining things in regard to him so that the next time she saw him, she'd see what was really there and not just what she wanted to see. "Thank you for walking me home."

"This is not your home." His smile could have melted the thick ice of the River Eye in winter.

Blast the man. He had her mind in a swirl. She gritted her teeth. "Of course not," she said sweetly. "I was testing you to see if you knew where I lived."

*Do not ask him. Absolutely do not.*

"How do you know this is not my home?" she asked, arching her eyebrows expectantly and cursing herself for the inability to control her tongue.

"Because this is the Duke of Carrington's home," Nash said, surprising her.

She frowned at his knowing Guinevere's husband and that he managed to dash yet another bit of hope that he may have inquired as to where she lived. She absolutely should have known better. "How do you know Carrington?"

"From Scotland," Nash replied, but he sounded rather evasive.

Heat burned her cheeks as a realization set in. "Am I to assume you already had an invitation to his ball?"

A nod confirmed her worst fear.

*Oh, the devil.*

She lifted her chin, refusing to shrink like a violet. She was no flower. She was a rapier of a woman, and one day the loss of her would cut him to the quick, just as his loss cut her. She swore it in this moment, even as humiliation burned her. "You let me stand there and lie." Another nod. How mortifying. He'd likely stood there pitying her.

She clenched her teeth so hard, she thought she heard one crack. She would not bother to try to explain away the lie. He could not truly know she'd come to see him, but he likely had guessed. "Good day, Your Grace," she said with as much civility and pride as she could muster.

"Good day, Lady Lilias." His tone now matched her formalness, which infuriated her for no good reason other than anything he did in this moment would anger her because she was so embarrassed.

She turned, raised the brass knocker, and muttered under her breath as his footsteps faded behind her. "May you fall on the way home and break that too perfect nose."

## Chapter Two

It was painful how much he still desired the proud woman who muttered wishes for him to break his nose. How was it possible to still want her so much after so long? Nash paused on his trek home. He ached. His damn body physically ached from the restraint he had shown not to touch her. God, how he had wanted to…

Everything about her whispered to him to hold her, to make her his. Her flaxen hair was still in wild waves, her eyes still a shade of brilliant blue that did not exist on this earth. Her eyes made a cloudless summer day seem dull. They filled him with ridiculous happiness and hope. He had not seen her since last Christmas when he'd gone home to the Cotswolds and watched her from afar, as he did every time he returned there, but he had not been truly in her presence in seven years. He'd forgotten just how alive he felt when she was so near he could reach out and touch her. She still smelled divinely of lilies, too.

He stepped to the side as two young ladies passed him, each smiling and sending him inviting looks. He nodded cordially but did not engage them. Their feverish giggles trailed after them as they walked away, silk skirts swishing.

Nothing. He felt nothing. Not even desire in the moment. They certainly did not awaken that inner instinct to protect and possess, make his chest tight, cause yearning to put an ache in the pit of his gut. No woman had ever made him feel that way but Lilias, and damn, but she still did. He'd recognized just how much after the first words she'd said to him: *You came back to the Cotswolds, and you avoided me.*

Lilias had always spoken so bluntly. It was as if someone had forgotten to relay the cardinal rule of being English to her—say what you are supposed to, not what you truly feel.

His father had lived by that rule until he'd drawn his last breath, and his mother still did. Neither of them had ever actually said his actions had killed Thomas. They'd offered nothing but silence and an almost total withdrawal of emotions. And they'd not asked him to return home more than the requisite once a year for his father to update him on the affairs of the dukedom. Even the letter his mother had sent about his father's death had been as cold as the frigid air of the Highlands in winter. She had advised him to come home to take up his duties or people would gossip. There was no mention of love, forgiveness, or sadness over her husband's loss, just worry about what people might say.

So here he was. He'd known he would come face-to-face with Lilias, but after his talk with Owen yesterday, he'd planned to do all in his power to avoid her for as long as possible as Owen had asked. He owed Owen that.

It was his fault Owen walked with a limp. He had let Owen challenge him to that horse race all those years ago, and he'd told himself he'd let Owen win so that Owen would look good in Lilias's eyes. He could and would do for Owen what he should have done for Thomas—that's what he'd told himself. But then they'd been racing and Nash's thoughts had gone to impressing Lilias himself, not putting Owen first. It was the second most shameful memory of his life.

He tugged a hand through his hair as he entered his

house and brushed past the butler. He made his way to his study, poured a drink, and sat down. Lilias's image immediately filled his mind in blinding vividness. The craving he'd long had for her had not diminished one damn whit. It was a dark and dangerous thing that threatened to consume him.

She should not have come to his house. He gripped his glass, his thoughts crashing into each other. Why had she come? To see Adaline? That's what Lilias had said, but what was the nonsense about the invitation to the ball? No, she'd come to see him. Had she waited seven long years to confront him? A bark of desperate laughter escaped him. He somehow was not surprised. He'd hurt her. She'd thought them real friends, and he'd betrayed her. His glorious girl.

Perhaps she'd felt a small bit of the emotion that he'd felt, still did, for her, and she had simply wanted the closure he'd never given her? Perhaps she'd wanted to set things straight between them for Owen's sake, as she likely knew she'd wed Owen. Most likely, she wanted him to understand that if he still felt anything for her, it could not be. He didn't know. His mind wasn't working properly.

He felt haunted, and he was—by her. She was the ghost that would not die in his mind or heart. He poured another drink and prayed for no dreams of her tonight.

---

"No."

Nash's mother sat across from him in his study the next day and arched her dark eyebrows at him. "Nay?" She repeated the answer he'd just given her with definite incredulity. "I never ask anything of ye."

That was not quite true. She frequently asked for more

pin money for new gowns and baubles, but he gladly gave it. She did not, however, ask for his company. Ever.

"Ye live yer life as ye wish. Ye cling to heathen ways." She flicked her hand at the kilt he wore.

He resisted the urge to laugh. There was nothing heathen about wearing the kilt of his mother's clan. She just didn't like it because her stuffy friends would not like it. They thought themselves better than the Scots, so his mother liked to conveniently forget that she *was* a Scot. Just as she'd conveniently forgotten his existence until it had become inconvenient.

"I need ye to go to the ball," she said.

"No." He could not go to Carrington's ball. Lilias would be there. He didn't trust himself around her. Yesterday, when he'd realized she had walked to his house alone, he'd dashed out the door to see her safely to where she wanted to go. That was not his duty. *She* was not his duty. At the very least, he could have had his footman accompany her or his coachman take her, but that would have required forethought, and Lilias stole that ability from him simply by being near. He needed to keep a good distance between them until she was wed, and he could finally put her on the shelf where she belonged, the high one where precious things went so some fool didn't come along and break them.

His mother scowled, opened and closed her mouth several times, and then said, "I have not wanted to ask this of ye, but—"

She paused, and damn it if he did not find himself leaning forward as an eager boy of seventeen would have instead of the man of five and twenty he now was. He knew better. She was not going to offer a chance to finally be forgiven, a way to redeem himself, and yet...

"What is it?" he asked.

"I need ye to watch over Adaline. I've tried, but she is clever and refuses to listen to me about the dangers of unscrupulous men. She flees her chaperone at balls and most assuredly avoids me. Ye are the only one who can control her with yer father gone. I've no notion why ye are refusing to go to this ball, but ye must put yer sister's welfare above yer feelings."

*And if I do this, will you finally forgive me?*

He didn't ask it, though he wanted to. For one, he'd do anything for his sister, whether it meant his mother could finally forgive him or not. But the other reason was he was quite sure he would not want to hear how she answered the question. Sometimes it was better not to know how someone might answer a question. Like the one he'd replayed in his head a mind-numbing number of times in which he confessed to Lilias that he'd kissed the girl he knew his brother liked and that he'd not allowed Owen to pull ahead of him in the race because Nash had been too busy trying to impress her himself: *What do you think of me now, Lilias?* He'd never ask the question; he didn't want to know the answer.

"Will ye attend the ball or not, Greybourne?" His mother's lips pressed together in a line of annoyance.

*Greybourne.* His title. Never *Nash*, the name she'd given him. Always cold. But he owed her for what he'd done to Thomas.

"I'll go," he said with a sigh. He'd simply have to stay away from Lilias. Of course, that could be difficult if he encountered her with Owen. If that occurred, he'd be pleasantly cool. He looked at his mother. He'd learned from the best.

"If Mama saw you in that gown, she'd have fit," Nora said, pursing her lips at Lilias.

Nora was correct, but her mother was abed with another deep melancholy. It was the third time this month that Mama's sadness had been so great that she'd told Lilias to attend a ball without her. Her only parting motherly advice had been to "please secure a husband."

Lilias eyed herself in the crimson gown she'd borrowed from Guinevere. It was cut daringly low, and the rich color of the silk would make her stand out. It was perfect. This was the new her. A woman who was no longer a fool, who no longer believed if she loved Nash enough, he'd love her in return. He was not some hero from one of her books. He would never protect her and cherish her, and she would forget him. But before she really strove to do that, just once she wanted him to see her, to desire her, to perhaps even question what he might have let slip through his fingers.

After tonight, she would be good. She would follow the rules of Society and find a proper husband to ease her mother's burdens and to set a good course for her sister's future. She'd been selfish long enough.

"Lilias, did you hear me?" Nora demanded.

Lilias took one more look at her hair before answering her sister. It was down and in slight disarray. She patted it, but it was fairly hopeless. She had no skill with putting up her hair, and they could no longer afford a lady's maid, not that the one they'd formerly employed had been any good with hair, either. Finally, she turned to Nora. "I hear you. Mama won't see me. She's abed."

Nora gave Lilias an exasperated look. "I said, what are you going to offer me for keeping this—" she motioned to Lilias's attire "—a secret."

"I'm out of trinkets to give you, Nora." Lilias's escapades at the Cotswolds had cost her nearly all her things, including her ribbons and lace.

Nora grinned. "You should behave, then. I'll take a ride in Owen's coach in the park," she said, eyes twinkling. "At the fashionable hour."

Lilias scowled at her sister. "Your lust to be part of the fashionable set is going to cause you heartache when you make your debut." That pretentious lot would never accept Nora with her lack of funds.

Nora tossed her blond curls over her shoulder. "When I wish for your opinion, I'll ask for it. If you will not convince Owen to do this, then I'll tell Mama about your gown."

Lilias gritted her teeth. Nora could be a real pain, but she did love her. "I'm not speaking to Owen," she said, matter-of-fact. And she wasn't sure when she would do so again, but it was none of her sister's business. He had lied to her. He had kept Nash's presence in the Cotswolds through the years a secret, and he'd even visited with him. The betrayal cut deep, even though the logical side of her mind knew Owen had been trying to protect her feelings. He'd likely seen what she had refused to: Nash would never love her.

"Perhaps the Duke of Carrington can drive you in the park with Guinevere at the fashionable hour?" Lilias suggested.

Nora scowled. "That won't do. It must be a handsome, eligible man so that the other girls my age will see me and be green with envy. When Mama lets me debut next Season, I'll be the talk of the *ton*."

"You certainly will," Lilias quipped, realizing how hypocritical the words she was about to say were. "But it will not be the sort of talk a young lady trying to make a good match would wish for."

Nora gave her a look that told Lilias her sister thought her as much of a hypocrite as Lilias thought herself. A flush heated her face. "I was not trying to make a match," Lilias huffed. "I thought I'd found the man I would wed."

"And now?" Nora asked, sounding fascinated.

Lilias realized she had not done a good job at all of setting a proper example for her younger sister, and tomorrow she would start doing so. For herself, she honestly didn't care very much, but for Nora and for her mother, she had to try. "And now," she said, "I see that 'true love' is more apt to occur in Gothic novels than real life." Saying the words made her very depressed, but she needed to accept reality.

"But how am I to be envied, then?" Nora wailed. "We have little money. My gowns will be old. And you will be on the shelf, which will make my prospects even worse!"

Lilias stiffened. "Thank you for your confidence, Sister, in my ability to secure a husband. I've had offers, if you recall."

"I recall," Nora said, arching her eyebrows. "I also recall you finding something wrong with both men, though they were handsome, titled, and wealthy. It was very selfish of you. I do believe you are part of the cause of Mama's melancholy."

Lilias opened her mouth to defend herself but promptly shut it. "When did you get so wise?" she asked instead, shame burning her cheeks.

"Not long ago," Nora said with a giggle, "after I discovered your hidden hoard of Gothic novels and read them. Very informative!"

"Don't bother with them, Nora. I have firsthand experience that real life is nothing like a novel. Not everything turns out as you dream it will."

## Chapter Three

"I like what you've done to the gown," Guinevere whispered as Lilias came to stand beside her where the duke and new duchess were gathered with some of their guests. Carrington was telling a story, and Guinevere was smiling fondly at her husband.

Lilias glanced down at the daring bodice she had modified at the last minute after speaking to her sister. She'd pinned a flower at the low V to cover the tops of her breasts the plunge had exposed. She decided just enough was left to show Nash what he'd let slip away but not so much to make tongues wag.

"Do you really think it's passable?" she asked in a low voice, meeting her friend's guileless green gaze.

Guinevere nodded, then cut her husband a pleading look, which slightly baffled Lilias until Guinevere took her by the hand and led her away from the guests. It wasn't the done thing to step away from one's guests simply because another had arrived, but Guinevere was now a duchess and, therefore, was afforded much leeway by the *ton*. Her friend greeted people as she wove through the press of bodies and made her way to the edge of the ballroom by the terrace doors. There was a scattering of tables on the right side, which held but one elder woman who looked to be napping, and potted plants to the left of the doors.

"Do you see that woman over there?" Guinevere asked,

tucking a strand of her chestnut hair behind her ear.

"The one at the table with the gray hair? Who appears to be sleeping?"

Guinevere nodded. "That's Kilgore's aunt. I've borrowed her."

Lilias frowned. That sentence raised so many questions, she hardly knew where to start. "Does your husband know that you've 'borrowed' your former suitor's aunt? The suitor your husband detested?"

Guinevere smirked. "First of all, you and I both know Kilgore was never truly courting me."

Lilias nodded. Guinevere had told her all about how the Marquess of Kilgore had only been pretending to court her because he'd lost land in a card game and the man who held it had wanted Kilgore to stop Carrington from wedding Guinevere. That man, who happened to be Carrington's half-brother, had wanted Guinevere for himself. Guinevere had also told Lilias how she was nearly completely sure that Kilgore was in love with a new SLARS member, Lady Constantine Colgate.

Lilias didn't know how inclined she was to believe that, though. Kilgore didn't behave like a man in love. He had a different woman on his arm every week, and the rumors about his affairs in the *ton* were legendary. But Kilgore certainly fit the description of a Gothic hero with his dark good looks and brooding and mysterious nature. He was a rogue of the first order. Everyone knew that there had been a wager placed on the betting books at Whites Gentleman's Club some years ago that Kilgore could not seduce four specific ladies. Two of the women were wed, and two were young, unmarried ladies. Guinevere had been on that list, as had Lady Constantine. If the rumors were to be believed, Kilgore had seduced all the women but Guinevere. It didn't matter if it was true or not; Lady Constantine was all but ruined. Of course, Lilias now knew that Kilgore had, in fact, seduced Lady Constantine, and the poor lady had fallen in love with him only to have her heart broken.

But that was all Lilias knew of the matter. Lady Constantine refused to speak more on it, and it was a rule in SLARS that they never made members speak of things they did not wish to. "So has Carrington forgiven Kilgore, then?"

Guinevere nodded. "He has, but he won't say exactly why. I believe Kilgore made some sort of confession to him, but try as I might, Asher will not divulge what it was or explain what happened. His honor can be tedious at times." Guinevere grinned.

Lilias felt a pang of jealousy that her friend had gotten her hero, but she buried the useless emotion. She was happy for Guinevere. Her friend had certainly endured her fair share of heartache on her road to true love.

"And why have you borrowed the sleeping aunt?"

They both looked at the woman whose head was still down on her forearm. "I borrowed her for you," Guinevere pronounced.

Lilias frowned as she looked at her friend. "Whatever do you mean?"

"I overheard some harpies commenting on your lack of chaperone, so…"

Lilias bit her lip. "I had hoped no one would take note."

Mama had hired chaperones now and again since Papa had died, but they never stayed. Lilias had thought it was because of Mama's moods, but lately she had begun to wonder if there was something else involved.

Guinevere snorted. "A vain hope in this set of people who long for someone to cut down. Have your family finances worsened?"

Lilias didn't take offense to the question. Guinevere was her dearest friend, and she knew Guinevere was trying to help. The only person she'd ever admitted it to had been Nash. "No more so than we've had for years."

"Oh, Lil," Guinevere said, squeezing her hand. "Why didn't you say something?"

Lilias thought about the question for a moment. "I suppose for several reasons. I was a bit embarrassed, and I suppose not acknowledging the problem almost made it feel like it did not exist. That way I could go on in my fantasy." She really did need to have a frank talk with her mother.

"About Greybourne being your hero?" Guinevere asked, studying her with concern.

"How long have you known?" Lilias asked.

"Ever since you came to Town and we met, and you told me about meeting him and all about the time you spent with him in the Cotswolds. And then when I told you I knew him from Town and you questioned me for days, it was fairly obvious. What was that? Seven years ago?"

Lilias nodded, feeling more the fool. "I must turn my attention to truly finding a match."

"Is that why you came to the house yesterday and asked to borrow the gown?"

"No." She quickly told Guinevere about rushing over to Nash's after Frederica's announcement in the SLARS meeting the day before that she'd seen Nash in Town. "I was coming to cry on your shoulder, but then, well, it was all so embarrassing to realize I'd pined for him for seven years and he does not care for me at all. I thought he had not come back to the Cotswolds because he was hurting over what had happened to Owen and blamed himself, and it turned out he had come back and seen Owen, just not me. He didn't care enough to see me. And I have a horrid suspicion he might have been avoiding me because he suspected I had developed a tendre for him."

"So the gown is to make him see other men desiring you, which will make him regret what he did?"

Lilias bit her lip. "Yes. It's foolish and vain, I know. It's rather smarting to have all your pride stripped from you. I'd like a shred back. I daresay he seemed to be pitying me yesterday. I cannot leave it like that. I cannot allow him to think he has the power to devastate me." Though he did.

Determination and ire set on her friend's face, and then a mischievous grin turned up the corners of Guinevere's mouth. "I know just the man to aid you in showing Greybourne he is already utterly forgotten by you."

"Who?" Lilias asked. "I don't want to use any man, so it must be one that—"

"Do not vex yourself," Guinevere interrupted, waving her hand. "Kilgore has just entered the ballroom, and I know of no other lord better suited to playing the besotted suitor with a devilishly wicked flair than Kilgore. I vow to you, Greybourne will not leave this ball tonight with any reason to pity you."

The words were exactly what Lilias wanted but did not offer the comfort she was hoping for. She would, she realized, trade pride for love if given the chance, but Nash had not given her such a chance, nor even the smallest reason to hope he would. So tonight would be about pride, endings, and moving on. It was not as she wanted it, but it was how it was.

<hr />

Nash spent the first hour of the ball trying to keep his sights on his sister. It wasn't until Adaline was finally dancing with a man who looked to be as harmless as a flea that Nash leaned against a column to relax. And of course, in that moment when his guard was down, he saw Lilias.

It was like being struck in the heart by a thousand arrows. The ground beneath him shifted, the air charged with a strange current, and his chest tightened as if a band had been placed around it. He could not look away. He was trapped by years of repressed longing. He was a fly in the web that was sweet, wonderful, untouchable Lilias.

She was a vision of sin with her blond hair flowing uncontrolled, evoking the desire to lay her on his bed and spread her flaxen tresses around her bare shoulders. Couple that with her ruby-red gown, which stirred the throbbing yearning to put his hands on the dips of her waist, and he could not stop his physical reaction to her. He went hard as a stone, and a feral instinct to stride through the crowd and rip her out of the arms of the man who was currently holding her too damn close pulsed to life within him.

Where the devil was Owen?

Nash jerked his focus away from Lilias to scan the annoyingly crowded ballroom. He roamed his gaze quickly over the guests, dismissing them as fast as he took them in. *Fop. Lecher. Drunkard. Mother on a hunt for a husband for her daughter. Bored husband with an even more bored wife. Widow searching for a lover.*

And Carrington, his longtime friend.

Nash pushed away from the column, and with his attention divided between his sister and Lilias, who luckily were dancing near each other, he strode across the ballroom toward Carrington. Carrington would be able to tell him who was dancing with Lilias and possibly where Owen was. He had not seen him all night, and that had been fine with Nash—until now. He'd assumed Owen was somewhere in the ballroom cherishing Lilias, protecting her as he damn well should be, and that was not something Nash had any wish to watch. He would rather gouge out his eyes than stand by observing the two of them together. He needed time. A couple hundred years ought to suffice.

As he threaded through the crowd, bursts of conversation and muted laughter came to him, but he pushed it all away, considering what to say to Carrington.

Carrington was the one person Nash trusted completely to be discreet, and Nash needed discretion now. Four years of friendship had begun with Carrington observing a man pickpocketing Nash's coachman in a boisterous inn in Scotland and the same night had ended with Nash taking a bullet in the arm meant for Carrington. He'd been shot by a member of a pickpocketing gang the two of them had fought, and the evening had led to Carrington telling Nash that he owed him a life debt. Nash had never called in the marker, but tonight might be the night.

He could feel interested gazes upon him as he continued through the heated press of bodies. He didn't care to stop and be cordial. He knew he should, but it was taking all the strength he possessed to stay away from Lilias, so whomever he offended could go to the devil. As he drew closer to Carrington, his friend's wife appeared by his side and whispered something in his ear.

Damn. Nash could not ask about Lilias without drawing her curiosity. Carrington may wonder why Nash was inquiring about Lilias's dancing partner, but he would not ask Nash about it. It was an unspoken code among men, but Lilias's friend would undoubtedly poke about if he inquired about her.

"Greybourne," Carrington said as Nash approached. His friend's tone seemed rather cool, but perhaps it was Nash's imagination. What he did not imagine was catching Carrington's wife discreetly elbowing her husband. What was that about?

Carrington cleared his throat as he caught his wife by the elbow and angled his body to cover the gesture, but it was too late. Nash had seen it. "I'm glad ye changed yer mind and came to the ball," Carrington said. "Ye remember my wife…"

She offered him a polite, albeit seemingly forced, smile. "I told you, darling. I've known Greybourne since we were much younger. I'm surprised you are not dancing, Greybourne."

"Are you?" Nash glanced away for a breath and located his sister dancing very near him. He should have turned back then, but he found himself searching out Lilias once more to ensure she was not being mauled by the man she was dancing with. When he looked back to the duchess, he had the distinct feeling she'd been watching him. "I beg your pardon," he said. "I was ensuring my sister is still safely on the dance floor."

"Hmm," the duchess said, the sound dripping with disbelief. "You appeared to be scanning the ballroom for someone other than your sister, given I noted you looking at her as she is right there." The duchess tilted her head toward Adaline. He could see why Lilias was friends with Carrington's wife. She was bold like Lilias.

"I was actually looking for Blackwood," Nash said smoothly, using Owen's title instead of his familiar name.

"Oh," the duchess replied, her mouth parting in a surprised O.

Beside her, Carrington tried to cover a chuckle with a cough without much success.

His wife elbowed him good, and she did not bother to

disguise it. "I believe I saw him near the terrace doors caught by Lady Tindall and her daughter, Lady Camille. The woman is in search of a husband for Lady Camille, and I think Blackwood is her prime candidate."

"Surely the woman must know she's wasting her time," Nash muttered, looking toward the terrace doors and finding Owen leading a frail girl away from it and toward the dance floor with an unhappy look on his face. Nash noticed that Owen was walking without his cane, but the uneven gait was there and guilt pricked him.

"Why would she be wasting her time?" the duchess inquired, frowning at him.

Did the woman not know that Owen had been courting Lilias and that Lilias had told Owen she loved him? Nash recalled what Owen had said yesterday about Lilias being so independent, and Owen wanting to give her time to settle into her lot. Was that what the duchess was referring to? Did she know something? Such as Lilias confessing she did not wish to wed Owen? *Oh, happy thought.* No. Devil take it. That could not be allowed to make Nash happy.

"As far as I know, Blackwood has not offered marriage to anyone," she said, studying Nash.

Was that it? Was she vexed on Lilias's behalf because Owen had not made his intentions clear enough to Lilias?

"But the night is young," the duchess continued, surprising Nash. "Why, at balls such as this, shocking offers are given all the time. Take, for example, my dearest friend Lilias and the man she's dancing with, the Marquess of Kilgore. He may be a renowned rake, but Lilias is so beautiful, so warm and special, that I wouldn't be surprised if Kilgore declares himself for her this very night."

"The devil you say," Nash bit out before he could stop himself.

He saw the swift look that was exchanged between Carrington and his wife, and Nash supposed he'd offended her somehow with his crude statement. But he didn't give a damn. All he cared about was Lilias. He found his gaze on her again. The marquess had his hand on Lilias's back, too low for propriety and for Nash's liking. What the devil was Owen thinking letting Lilias dance with a rake?

Nash wanted to be involved with aiding the match between Lilias and Owen as much as he wanted to be at this ball. Not. At. All. Penance was bloody trying. If he thought he could live with himself without staying this course, he'd deviate off it now. Owen needed to take the reins and tell Lilias exactly how he felt and that he wished to wed her immediately. The time was now! Before she slipped out of Owen's grasp. Owen was, as usual, too busy worrying and not doing enough seizing of the moment. He'd have to have a talk with his friend as soon as he was done dancing.

The thought of speaking to Owen about how to secure things with Lilias made him want to toss back several dozen drinks, and as a footman passed by with a tray of champagne, Nash grabbed two flutes and downed them in succession without pausing. And then, because the anger stirring inside him was starting to feel uncontainable, he drummed his fingers on the crystal, imagining it to be the rake's face.

Behind him, Carrington cleared his throat, and Nash forced his gaze away from Lilias and back to the duke and duchess.

Carrington was staring at him with a speculative look while his wife was smirking as if she'd discovered a titillating secret. Their behavior was both annoying and odd. "Tell me what you know of this man Kilgore," Nash said, throwing caution to the wind. He might raise the duchess's curiosity with his questions, but that did not mean he had to explain himself.

"He tried to seduce my wife away from me before we were wed." Carrington's face grew dark, but his wife laughed. Nash frowned at her reaction. One would think she would not want to raise her husband's ire.

"He kissed me twice," she said. "Once at a ball. Just. Like. This. One."

"Excuse me," Nash said, shoving the two champagne flutes he was holding at Carrington.

The moment Carrington grasped them, Nash was turning, locating Owen to drag him over to Lilias and then changing courses when he could not immediately find his friend. Nash had not tortured himself for the last seven years for some rogue to end up with Lilias. And he sure as the devil wasn't going to stand around watching the rake seduce Lilias while Owen foolishly danced attendance on some marriage-minded mama and her daughter.

He once again made his way through the crowd, but this time, he was stalking. He was practically upon Lilias and Kilgore when it occurred to Nash that he had completely forgotten about the main reason he was here—Adaline.

"Damn and double damn." But a glance around the ballroom revealed Adaline was now standing with Carrington and his wife. That was rather surprising but very, very convenient. And then the oddest thing happened. The duchess raised her hand and waved at him, as if she'd been expecting him to look for his sister. He didn't have time to consider it, though, because in that moment, Kilgore danced Lilias right in front of him, and when the man actually raised his hand to Lilias's cheek and brushed his fingers down the perfect slope, Nash could only see red.

## Chapter Four

"Thank you, dear," Guinevere whispered to her husband.

Asher's lips came immediately to her ear. "Ye're lucky I can understand yer signals. For a moment I was not sure what ye wanted me to do."

Guinevere grinned. "You caught on rather quick."

A grunt was his answer. The force of it sent his warm breath over her ear and caused gooseflesh to rise on her neck.

"Guin, do ye think it wise to interfere with Greybourne and Lady Lilias?"

Guinevere wanted to answer, but every stealthy woman knew not to talk private affairs in public if someone was too near. To her left, the Duke of Greybourne's sister stood now chatting with Frederica, whose gaze met Guinevere's for one brief moment. Understanding, the kind that could only be between sisters who had shared secrets and well-meaning schemes since the day they were old enough to plot, passed between Guinevere and Frederica. As if Frederica had been given some magical signal—because of course she had—she took Lady Adaline by the elbow and exclaimed she must make the acquaintance of their other sister, Vivian. And off they went. One of one thousand problems solved.

Now Guinevere could focus on her husband. "I don't

see how we cannot interfere. I am certain she loves him. I know firsthand that trying to forget the one you truly love is hopeless."

Guinevere didn't need to use Lilias's name; Asher would know to whom she was referring. They'd discussed Lilias last night after her friend had left with the borrowed gown. But Asher did not know what Lilias had told Guinevere about her plan to forget Greybourne after she regained some of her pride tonight. Nor did her husband know that Guinevere had asked Kilgore to aid her friend.

Asher frowned. He was the only man she knew who could look positively alluring when frowning. "I'll defer to whatever ye wish, *mo chridhe*, but can ye explain to me what has occurred between yer concocting this plan to make 'our friend' see what he's lost and just moments ago when ye adeptly manipulated 'our friend' onto the dance floor to interrupt the dance?"

Guinevere glanced toward Nash, whose entire attention was focused on Lilias, and the look of yearning and fury on his face stole Guinevere's breath. And as for Lilias, Guinevere saw her friend's eyes widen when she noticed Greybourne approaching, and the longing on Lilias's face was unmistakable.

"Greybourne occurred," she whispered in her husband's ear, breaking her rule so there would be no confusion. "It was in his voice when he spoke of her just now. It was in the way he stared at her as if she were the very thing he needed to survive."

"I didn't see or hear that," her husband said.

She waved a dismissive hand. "It's there. We need to draw it out of him. Simply telling her what I saw and heard will not do. She's quite determined to move on. He hurt her immensely yesterday. *Again*. I think she's been waiting for seven years to confront him."

Asher slipped his arm around Guinevere's waist and drew her against the length of his body. She wanted this for her best friend—for her to be in the arms of the man she loved, not simply a man she would wed to do her duty. Then Asher scandalously nuzzled Guinevere's neck, and she let him. She didn't care if people whispered about them.

"We'll need to let Kilgore know ye've set a rabid hound on his heels," Asher said in a low voice in her ear, amusement in his tone.

Guinevere snorted. "He deserves it for his obstinance in not admitting that he loves Lady Constantine." When silence met her statement, she met her husband's eyes. "Did he admit as much to you?" she demanded for the hundredth time.

"Ye know very well I cannot discuss what's been told to me in confidence, but I'll advise ye again not to pursue trying to make those two a match. It's not going to happen."

"Because he's stubborn?" she prodded, but her husband simply smiled at her. She loved his honor, but in this moment, it was a hindrance to progress. Silence again was his answer. "Fine," she finally said. "Will you at least help me with the other couple in question?"

He arched his eyebrows. "Didn't I already?"

"Well, yes, but this is likely the beginning. You must tell me if our newly returned friend comes to you and admits any feeling toward a particular lady in a lovely, daring, ruby gown. I fear she'll go and get herself betrothed before I can uncover the truth."

"Men do not readily admit feelings, *mo chridhe*. Especially a man like the one in question."

"What sort of man would you say he is?" she asked,

genuinely curious how one man would view another. She saw Greybourne as cold and withdrawn and, well, of course, utterly handsome. She had known him when his twin had been alive, and Greybourne had not been nearly as withdrawn then, but he always had been serious, as if he carried a heavy burden.

"Darling?" she prodded when Asher did not answer.

A beat passed, and then he said, "Broken."

She sucked in a sharp breath and kissed her husband right in the middle of their ball. It was unheard of. It was scandalous. Tomorrow they'd be on the tip of gossiping tongues. The besotted, vulgar duke and duchess. She didn't care. "You're brilliant!"

Asher grinned, and her heart skipped. "I like to think so."

"Tomorrow we must find out exactly what it is that broke our friend, though I imagine it has something to do with his brother's death."

Her husband's dark eyebrows dipped together in confusion. "And then ye propose we try to fix him?"

She laughed at that. Her husband was brilliant, except when it came to matters of the heart. "Of course not, darling," she said, squeezing his very solid waist. "That will be Lilias's job," she whispered.

"Will she know it?"

Guinevere rolled her eyes at her husband. She could not help herself. "Of course not, darling. Do keep up."

## Chapter Five

One rule. Nash had made one unbreakable rule for himself in regard to this ball tonight: stay far away from Lilias. And now he'd made an exception to the rule. Of course he damn well had. He was not a bloody idiot. He was a man who made contingency plans. If he had to get near her, say, for instance, Owen approached him with Lilias in tow or he ended up in a group she was in, he would be polite and cool. He would not under any circumstance whatsoever touch her.

And yet…

He'd failed to consider what he'd do if he needed to protect her. He'd not considered to what lengths he might go, rules he might break. But as he approached Lilias and the man who dared to take such a liberty as to brush her cheek and place his hand too low on her back, Nash understood with utter clarity to what lengths he would go—*any*. And he knew what rules he would break: *every damn one of them*. If he were a king, Lilias would be his kingdom, and he'd do whatever it took to protect her. But he had to do it without breaking his vow to Owen. If he did, he would not survive the guilt. If he did, his heart would be just as black as his mother acted like it was. He would be officially unredeemable.

"Kilgore, I'm Greybourne. Pleasure to meet you," he said by way of greeting as he sidled up next to them and stuck his foot in front of the man, forcing him to come to a halt.

"Greybourne, what are you doing?" Lilias demanded.

What the devil could he say?

"Blackwood needs you." It was the one thing he knew for certain would get Lilias to follow him and leave this man behind.

"Is he all right?" she asked, already breaking away from Kilgore and moving toward Nash. Concern was etched on her face.

"Yes, yes," he replied, taking her by the elbow to get her away from Kilgore, whom he shot a warning look, one that he hoped relayed that he would gut the man if he did not stay away. "I, well, let's just go find him to see what he wants," he said, not waiting for her to agree.

He gripped her gently, amazed that an elbow could be so enticing. His body was throbbing with awareness of his fingers on her warm skin. It was a good thing he'd never get the chance to touch her anywhere else. He'd likely devour her with how much he wanted her. He should release her now, but it would be just like Lilias to dash away from him.

He scanned the crowded ballroom looking for Owen but still saw him nowhere. Bloody typical. What should he do now? A glance over his shoulder showed that louse Kilgore stalking them. Nash increased his pace, propelling Lilias before him through outraged dancers and matronly mothers standing at the edge of the dance floor, and onward until they were through the terrace doors and outside in the crisp night air under the bright twinkling stars Lilias had once promised to teach him about. And they were alone. He would not look at her. He would think of a brilliant lie to compel her to stay here while he went to fetch Owen and ordered the imbecile to offer his hand to Lilias this very night.

Nash's feet didn't move, but his gaze did, right to her full lips and then upward, torturously slowly, until it felt like he stood in Hell instead of outside on a cool winter night. He wanted to kiss her. His gut told him he'd never want anything more. He wanted to feel her lips on his one more time. This was definitely hell, and he was the proper imbecile, not Owen. He'd led her out here into the fiery pit of temptation.

"Nash?" She looked at him questioningly in the achingly beautiful, frank way only she possessed. "Why are we out here? I thought we were going to find Owen."

"We are." His brain felt slowed by her. She made time stand still. If only she could reverse it right back to the day he'd betrayed Thomas.

"You are not moving," she pointed out. Then she gasped.

Why was she gasping? Her warm breath fanned his face, and he stilled, cold fear going straight through him. He'd leaned his head down close to hers. So very close. Nearly face-to-face, a wicked hairsbreadth. He could not control his own body when it came to her. No. That was wrong. He could.

"Stay here," he choked out but still didn't move.

The questioning look on her face became more pronounced, and then her lips parted as if she were considering something. Possibly him? Possibly his intentions?

*Let her move away.*

But she seemed to press closer, or maybe his feverish brain imagined it. Good Christ. It didn't matter. Seven years of lust and yearning gripped him in a vise.

"Nash." His name was the softest, sweetest caress from her lips. "Did you bring me out here to be alone with me?"

Behind her, the terrace door opened. Owen stepped out, and sanity crashed back into Nash like a wave. "Don't be ridiculous," he said, enraged at himself and regretting the harsh words the minute he spoke them. He saw her flinch, but he turned away, muttered a greeting to Owen, and fled the terrace like a coward, like the hounds of Hell were chasing him. And if Hell's hounds were guilt and longing, then they were on his heels snapping with their razor-sharp teeth.

He swallowed the distance between himself and Owen, intent that his friend knew to do the deed and intent that Lilias not hear Nash instruct Owen. As they passed, Owen turned his face to Nash, and Nash said in a low voice, "You must make your offer tonight. That man Kilgore is sniffing after Lilias."

---

Standing there watching Nash walk away, Lilias could not fathom how she'd set out tonight to show him what a fool he was, and instead, she had proven herself a fool once more. She hated love. She never wanted to be in love again. Why had she thought he was looking at her as if he wanted to kiss her? Why could she not keep her mind in reality instead of letting it drift into fantasy? She wished her aunt had not bequeathed her collection of Gothic romances to Lilias when she'd died. Lilias placed the blame for her disastrous romantic entanglements squarely on her dead aunt's shoulders.

Or maybe it was simply her? It was true that she'd had two offers of marriage, but neither of those men had known her. They'd liked her pretty face. She'd never had an offer or even a hint of flirtation from a man she knew well. Nash did not count because she'd only imagined he was flirting. Not even Owen—sweet, hapless Owen—had ever flirted with her. Not that she wanted him to. She didn't think of him in *that* way, but still, it would be nice not to be standing here now questioning if perhaps it was her personality.

If it was, that was a grave problem. She could alter an old gown to fit the current style, but her personality, what made her who she was, she did not have the first notion how, or the wish, to change that. As Owen came to stand before her, she was struck with the extreme desire to know the truth, and who better to ask than Owen. She shelved her anger at him for not telling her about Nash's visits. That, she would address later.

"Lil—"

"Owen," she accidentally interrupted. "Oh, I'm sorry. You go first. Nash said you were looking for me?"

Owen appeared momentarily startled, but then he said, "Yes. Yes, I was, but you go first, Lilias."

She sucked in a deep breath for courage. "Is there something wrong with me?"

He frowned. "What? No. You are perfect."

Drat. His answer did not reassure her at all.

"You're obligated to say that," she muttered.

"No, I'm not."

"You are," she replied with an emphatic nod. "You are my best male friend; therefore, you do not see the flaws that every other male who knows me must see."

Owen's bewildered look became a furious one. "What other males know you? Kilgore? I'll kill the man! Has he—"

"Do quit acting like an incensed brother," she snapped.

"What?" Owen sounded aggrieved and shoved a hand through his blond hair, disheveling what was normally in perfect order. "I'm not anything like your brother."

"What a thing to say," she gasped, all the emotions of the last day overwhelming her. "I thought we meant something to each other."

"Lilias." Owen surprised her by awkwardly, albeit sweetly, cupping her cheek. "We do. I'm sorry. Let's not quarrel over a silly misunderstanding."

She nodded, grateful, and pressed her palm over his, her heart thudding as she thought once more about Nash. "Owen, am I odd? Do you think I drive men away with my quirkiness?"

"Are we speaking of anyone in particular?" His voice was hard, and he sounded suddenly so angry that she knew he understood she was referring to Nash. She would not say it, though. That would get them into another quarrel, and at this particular moment, she'd rather not admit that Owen had been correct all these years when he'd told her to forget Nash because he had long ago forgotten her. Owen had said Nash would break her heart if she let him, and Owen had been right. Her heart was shattered.

"No," she lied. "I had thought by now a man would have realized I was the woman he'd been longing for." That was as close to the truth as she was willing to get tonight.

"Ah, damnation, Lilias. I... Well, hell..."

And before she knew what was occurring, her best friend, the man she thought of like a brother, yanked her to him and covered her mouth with his. Shock stilled her for a moment, then utter dismay, but before she could react, gasps filled the silent night, followed by a bevy of excited chatter.

---

"I will live in exile as a spinster," Lilias said over her

mother's wailing.

Her mother whirled toward her, the excessive noise finally, blessedly stopping. Yet Lilias's ears still rang. She supposed she should expect no less since Mama had been weeping very loudly since Lilias had been forced to wake her last night and tell her what had occurred at the ball. Lilias was ruined. In fact, her ruination was so complete that she felt she'd given new meaning to the word. She couldn't have just been discovered in a compromising embrace by anyone. No, certainly not. She'd been found with Owen's mouth sealed over hers by not only Lady Adaline, but by Lady Adaline's closest friend, Juliette Blanche, and her father, who everyone knew owned one of the cruelest scandal sheets in London. There was no hope to conceal the incident, and if she'd held the faintest fantasy that there might be, the scandal sheet she now held, which had just been delivered and on which hers was the very first story, dispelled that ludicrous notion.

Her mother paced back and forth, wringing her hands. "Blackwood is a good man. He will come to offer you his hand. I'm sure he simply did not have the chance to do so last night."

No, he had not. She'd fled the ball and come straight home. She'd left him standing on the terrace calling her name. She still could not believe Owen had kissed her. It was a tragedy beyond reckoning. She had lost the man she loved and the man she'd always counted on as a friend in one night. Would he come? She prayed he did not. Or maybe she prayed he did and that he'd say he'd been impulsive, that he'd acted to simply make her feel better about herself. She did not want to hurt him. She did not want to be capable of hurting him. It left her reeling to think it was possible to hold such power over him and that she'd never seen it, never even suspected it. Her stomach cramped to think perhaps this was exactly how Nash thought of her.

"I cannot wed Blackwood," she said again.

Her mother turned to her and looked at her as if she had sprouted two heads. "You can and you will."

"Mama, no! I do not love him. I—"

Her mother grabbed her by the arm in a shocking, viselike grip. Mama had never touched Lilias in anger in her life. "Do you think you are the only consideration?" she hissed.

Fear shot straight to Lilias's heart, and Nora's face popped into her head. "No," she whispered. "I know this could affect Nora's ability to make the best match." She was drowning in guilt over that.

Mama gave her a little shake. "If only it were that simple."

The fear in Lilias's heart spread everywhere. "Whatever do you mean, Mama? Are you speaking of our finances?"

Her mother grasped Lilias to her bosom suddenly and squeezed her tight, a sob escaping her. "We have *nothing*, Lilias. Your father left us with nothing." Another sob burst from her. "No," she cried out, shoving Lilias away, Mama's face twisted in a pain that hurt Lilias's heart. "That's not quite true. He left us in debt—enormous debt—that I have been struggling to repay because the people he owes are unrelenting and unscrupulous! He died owing four gaming hell owners in the worst part of Town you can imagine!" Her mother pressed a hand to her flushed cheek. "And those men… Those men don't care about laws or that we did not create the debt. They only care about getting their money." Yet another sob ripped from Lilias's mother, and Lilias flinched. "He left a huge debt to two very unsavory

Irish brothers who run an illegal whiskey business at the docks." Tears filled her mother's eyes. "The things they threatened to do to us if I don't pay them..." Her mother shuddered. "Your father was not in his right mind near the end. He could not have been to leave us so vulnerable."

Lilias felt her jaw slip open. "I cannot believe it." The room seemed to spin around her.

Mama took Lilias by the hand and led her to the settee, dragging Lilias down with her into the cream-colored velvet cushions. "I discovered it several months after your father died—or rather the horrid men started calling upon me, threatening me, and demanding I pay them or else they would harm us, or take us and sell us!"

Lilias did not understand, and her head was aching fiercely. "If we had no money at all, how did you afford all those restorative cures in Bath?"

Mama sighed. "I was not in Bath taking restorative cures. I lied. I was away selling my jewels, our art, your father's guns, our silver. I worked out yearly payment plans with these men and every year when the payment came up to the men your father owes, I had to go away and sell things. I could not do it here lest I be discovered, and we were ruined. Those men... Well, they arranged for me to meet buyers. But I have nothing left to sell, and there is still so much debt."

Shock pricked Lilias and then deep guilt. She had not even noticed the silver being gone, and when she'd remarked on the art, her mother had told her that looking upon it made her sad, so she'd taken it down, and Lilias had simply believed her. She had been so self-absorbed. "Oh, Mama. All this time I thought you were melancholy—"

Her mother forced a bright smile. "Well, I was. Truly, in the beginning. But there is nothing like the threat of bodily danger to force someone to make a choice, and I have chosen you girls."

Lilias bit her lip. She had been utterly, utterly selfish. "What shall we do? Perhaps we can beseech Uncle Simon—"

"No, dearest," Mama interrupted. "Your uncle refused to aid me when I confessed all to him."

Lilias supposed she should have guessed that, but she had hoped if he knew the trouble they were in, he might have helped. "I'm surprised he's aided us this long," Lilias murmured, her mind spinning with what they could possibly do.

Mama scoffed. "He has not aided us. Not once. He allowed us to stay in the house in the Cotswolds and use this home because I gave him a payment, as well."

Lilias knew instantly what the payment was. Her aunt had always coveted her mother's wedding ring. Her gaze went to her mother's finger where she used to wear that ring, which had belonged to Lilias's grandmother. It had been set with a rare diamond. "Your ring?"

Mama nodded. "But now he says that payment has been exhausted, and he wants us out."

A coldness settled deep in Lilias's gut. Nothing was as she'd thought. All this time she'd been waiting for a man who did not even want her while her mother had been trying desperately to keep them alive. "Why didn't you tell me?"

Her mother stroked a hand down Lilias's head. "I didn't want you to worry, and I wanted you to wed the man you loved."

Lilias sucked in a breath. "You knew?"

Her mother nodded. "I heard you talking to your father at his grave about the Duke of Greybourne one day. Do you think he might rescue—"

"No." Lilias stopped her mother before she could finish the sentence. "Greybourne does not care for me as I had foolishly allowed myself to believe. He'll not be rescuing me. Our only hope is Blackwood." She could hardly believe she was saying it, and she didn't know if she could actually go through with it. "*If* he comes and offers, I'm sure it will be merely honor that compels him."

At her mother's questioning look, she quickly explained about her conversation with Owen on the balcony last night. "So you see, Mama, Blackwood is my dear friend. I am certain his kiss was impulsive and merely an effort to make me feel better."

"And if it wasn't?" her mother asked, the hope in her voice obvious.

Lilias's gut clenched tight. She could not be selfish. She could not say she'd rather be alone and ostracized from Society than wed to a man she didn't love and ruin his chances at finding his own true love. But she pressed her lips together on saying any of that. Her mother and sister came first; their safety was in jeopardy, and if Owen extended an offer, she would speak to him, possibly discuss terms where he could wed her and have a mistress, a woman he truly loved. Lilias and Owen could possibly be husband and wife in name only. Marriages of convenience occurred in the *ton* all the time. Except this marriage would only be convenient for her. She wanted to crawl into her bed, under the counterpane, and never come out.

At that moment, a knock came at the parlor door. "My lady, the Earl of Blackwood is here to call upon Lady Lilias."

The look of utter relief on her mother's face made Lilias feel as if the weight of the world had just been dropped upon her shoulders.

"Bring the earl here," her mother replied, and then she

turned to Lilias. "You should know, we only had the butler as part of the payment for the house. Your uncle plans to take him from us immediately."

"Don't fret, Mama," Lilias vowed. "I will make it right."

After gushing greetings at Owen and shooting Lilias a beseeching look, her mother retired from the parlor and gently shut the door, but Lilias knew good and well that her mother was undoubtedly standing on the other side with her ear pressed to the mahogany.

"Owen, I'm so sorry that I drew you into a scandal. I—"

"What? No! I kissed you, Lilias. I'm sorry. So very sorry. You know how I hate scandal."

She did, which was why she had forced herself to start with an apology; for her mother's and sister's sakes, she could not muck this up, as much as the thought of wedding Owen made her stomach twist into knots. Owen closed the distance between them to stand directly in front of her. His green gaze, so different from Nash's stormy gray one, locked with hers. "I've waited forever to tell you this, Lilias."

*Oh no. No, no, no.*

She didn't want to hear what he was about to say, though she should be falling on her knees with relief. It was almost somehow worse if he was going to say what she suspected. It made her feel like an utter fraud.

"I, well, to my utter shame, I have not been able to summon the courage," Owen continued. "I was afraid, I suppose, that you'd say you could never love me, that you'd reject me."

She swallowed the moan that rose up in her throat. It

was worse than anything she'd imagined.

"I love you, Lilias."

Her heart thumped a ruthless beat of guilt in her chest that she could not say she loved him in return.

"I have loved you for years," he went on. "I think since practically right after I met you."

Then it hit her. Was that why Owen had not told her Nash was in the Cotswolds? Because of Owen's feelings for her? Or was it simply to protect her?

It hardly mattered now. Dear God… Why, why could it not be Owen that she loved? Or why couldn't Nash have loved her?

Owen was looking at her expectantly, and she knew he wanted a response, but her tongue was thick and her mind offered no words. "Lilias, do you remember the day Nash and I raced, and I had my accident?"

She nodded.

"I did that for you… To impress you."

The magnitude of her foolishness, of how he felt for her, was crushing. If she had known years before, she would have told him it was hopeless. She would have told him to forget her. She cringed. Just as Nash had told her. And what good had that done? She had gone on loving him anyway for seven long foolish years. Her heart plummeted to her feet.

"The limp means nothing to me if you are my wife. The pain I live with has been worth it if I win you in the end."

Her gaze flew to his right leg and then the cane he was using today. He did not use it all the time, but he normally did after a ball. She could have prevented the accident, if only she'd realized why he had raced Nash. She would have told him then and there that winning a race was not the way to win someone's heart. Her chest squeezed.

"Lilias." He took her hands in his, and all she could think was that they felt so different from Nash's. Whereas Nash had large hands, Owen had smaller ones. Whereas Nash's fingers were like sturdy branches, Owens were long and slender. She knew what was coming as his gaze seemed to delve into hers, and she did not feel anticipation or happiness, only dread and sadness. "Lilias, will you wed me?"

She knew she had to say yes—for her mother, for her sister—but her treacherous, selfish lips would not form the word. The parlor door banged open in that instant, and her mother fairly stumbled in, a horrified look upon her face. Nora was behind her.

"I'm sorry, Mama," Nora sang, and Lilias understood that Nora must have leaned against their mother and caused them both to fall into the door, which hadn't been shut firmly.

"Lilias, have you accepted?" Nora asked, the picture of wide-eyed innocence and poverty with her too small gown that had a hem trailing and was approaching threadbare.

"Nora," Mama chided, looking as if she was about to faint, looking exhausted with dark circles under her eyes.

How had Lilias been so blind to what was really occurring with everyone around her? How could she say no?

She could not.

## Chapter Six

"Good morning, Nash!"

The skip in Owen's step as he happily waltzed into the study and past Nash's butler was like a dagger in Nash's heart. So the deed was done. Owen had obviously asked Lilias to wed him, and she must have said yes.

"I take it you are betrothed," Nash said and quickly cleared his throat. His voice sounded shaky. Why was this so damned hard to speak of?

"Yes," Owen replied, a rather smug look coming to his face. He half sat on the edge of Nash's desk, grinning like a peacock. "I can't tarry. I have a great deal to do today, but I wanted you to hear it from me and give you my thanks for all you did to assist me in getting the girl I love."

Nash knew he needed to reply. Owen was looking at him expectantly, and so Nash wrestled with his mind, which felt sluggish, to come up with a suitable response, but it was hard. So very hard. He imagined congratulating Owen, but the thought curdled on his tongue. He imagined punching him in his irritating smile. Nash gripped his desk on that idea. In the end, all he could manage was, "Excellent."

"Yes. Yes, it is," Owen crowed. "I don't mind telling you now, but I had created fears in my head that did not exist. I had thought perhaps she might turn me down because I'm not overly exciting or that she held some ridiculous girlhood tendre for you that would have been roused by your reappearance."

Nash wasn't sure if he groaned or laughed at Owen's words, but he'd done something. Owen was looking at him quizzically and took in a hissing breath. "I'm pleased to report I had worried over nothing. She kissed me last night on the balcony, and she was beside herself with joy this morning when I called upon her."

Nash did not feel like himself. He was in some other man's skin, a man who had to respond, to act happy, to be affable. He forced a smile to lips that felt brittle. "I'm glad." *Glad that Owen has to depart soon.* "Where is it you need to be?" Time could not move Owen in that direction fast enough. Nash tried to swallow, but his throat no longer worked. He was parched, dry inside. The life was being sucked out of him.

"Oh, here and there," Owen said, rising. "I'll see you soon."

Nash managed a grunt as Owen made for the door, and it was damn lucky Owen did not look back and say anything else. A single thread of restraint held Nash in place at the moment, and when his study door shut, he shoved back his chair, made for the wall, counted to one hundred to ensure Owen was far enough away, and then he began to beat his fist against the wall until the pain in his hand overshadowed the pain in his chest.

<hr />

"I didn't know ye frequented my club."

Nash scowled but turned in his chair at Carrington's voice behind him. "This is my first visit since you told me of your partial ownership in it," Nash replied, then picked up the drink that had just been delivered to him and downed it in one gulp.

"Mind if I sit?" Carrington asked, sweeping a hand toward the empty chair across the table.

Nash was not in the mood for company, especially a man wed to Lilias's best friend, even if Carrington was Nash's friend, as well. The duke was bound to mention Lilias, her ruination, and the subsequent gossip. It had taken him all day since Owen's visit to get himself under control. He felt like a caged lion, which was why he was here imbibing.

He still could not manage to feel pleased for Owen and Lilias, though he should, given what he'd set out to do had been accomplished. He may have failed his brother, but he had not failed Owen. Nash had proven to himself that he could be painfully selfless. He should feel somewhat redeemed, but instead he felt damned. A blackness was swallowing him, and God help him, he wanted to let it, but he had responsibilities.

When Carrington cocked his eyebrows at Nash, he realized he had not answered his friend's question. "If you wish," Nash replied, raising his hand toward a serving girl standing by one of the fireplaces.

Carrington mimicked the gesture as he pulled out the empty chair and sat, eyeing Nash's wrapped hand. "What happened to yer hand?"

"It met a wall," Nash replied flatly.

Carrington cocked an eyebrow at that but wisely did not ask. "I hear Blackwood and Lady Lilias are to wed."

Nash's teeth instinctively clenched as the serving girl came to stand by their table. He tapped the side of his glass to indicate he'd have another of the same while Carrington placed his order. When the girl left, Nash forced himself to answer. "Yes, Owen told me this morning."

Carrington's gaze touched on Nash's wrapped hand once more, then met Nash's eyes, probing him. "My wife was verra surprised Lady Lilias agreed to wed him."

Lilias's image popped into Nash's head unbidden. Her full-lipped smile. Good God, why could he not forget that smile? It teased and tormented him. Nash tried not to react to his own roaring memories or Carrington's news. "Was she?" he said mildly, fighting back a frown with such fierceness that his temples throbbed. "Why would her friend agreeing to wed the man who has her heart surprise your wife?" He was pleased with how bored he sounded and that the girl was returning with their libations. He could use his drink as a distraction, lest Carrington see something on Nash's face that he did not want the man to bear witness to.

"I had a wager with myself whether ye'd take up the bait I threw out," Carrington said, his voice smooth as a polished rock.

Damn Carrington.

"I inquired only out of politeness," Nash retorted, feeling surly. "You wouldn't know about that, though. You were raised in Scotland, where manners are not taught. You are in the heart of England now, my friend, and it's polite to respond to people's leading statements."

Carrington scoffed. "Ye never did that in Scotland. Ye ignored me."

"I adapt to the expectations of my surroundings," Nash replied, forcing a smile.

"As I was saying," Carrington continued, then took a swig of his drink before completing his sentence, "my wife was surprised."

Nash let silence fall between them. He had no intention of rising to the bait again, no matter how much he wanted to.

"Are ye not going to ask why?"

"No." But if Carrington didn't offer the answer anyway, Nash might just use the man's perfectly tied cravat to strangle him. "A cravat does not suit you tied like that. I could rework it for you." He did not hide the veiled threat in his tone.

Carrington laughed. "I'd like to see ye try. But as I wish to return home soon, I'll just get to my point."

"That would be bloody amazing. This conversation is fast becoming tedious."

Carrington flashed a grin. "Guinevere was surprised that Lady Lilias accepted Blackwood's offer because she does not believe her friend loves the man. Guinevere feels Lilias must have been compelled to accept him so that she could aid her mother and sister financially."

The drink Nash had picked up fell from his hand, hit the table, and sloshed liquor over the dark wood. The glass tilted onto its side with a rattle.

Nash didn't move. He was too stunned, but Carrington did. He righted the glass before it spilled completely, then met Nash's gaze. "I know of yer history with Lady Lilias. Guinevere told me."

"There is no history but a brief friendship." It was a bloody lie. He worshipped her.

*I vowed not to interfere. But if she doesn't love Owen... If she's wedding Owen only for her family's sake...*

"Shut up," he hissed to himself.

"Pardon?" Carrington said with a frown.

Good Christ. Nash swiped a hand over his face. He was going mad. Thoughts of Lilias were stealing his sanity.

"Nothing. It's nothing," he muttered.

It didn't matter why she'd accepted Owen's proposal.

He could not allow it to matter. He had to stick to his damn bloody vow. He had to put Owen first. The yearning hammering him taunted him to do otherwise. He could not talk about them anymore. If he could, he would leave London again, but his sister needed to be taken in hand.

"Why are you here and not with your wife?" he asked, hoping Carrington would go along with the change of subject.

Carrington looked contemplative for a moment, and then he leaned forward. "My wife is in a secret society for women," he said, voice pitched low. "The Society of Ladies Against Rogues. SLAR."

"How interesting," Nash murmured, not really caring. He cared about nothing but Lilias. It was maddeningly awful. Sitting here, he felt dead inside knowing she would be wedding Owen, knowing it was his penance to allow it.

Carrington scrutinized him for a moment, as if he realized Nash's mind was elsewhere. "My wife started the society after I hurt her greatly. Interestingly enough, Lady Lilias is also in SLAR. It's made up of women who either have been ruined by a rogue or have had their hearts broken by a rogue. Or both."

Struck, he opened his mouth to demand more information and then promptly shut it. No. He could not ask. He could not. The desire to do so, though, clawed at his throat. Had she joined the society because of him?

*Impossible.*

A hammer started in his head, banging his skull and rattling his composure. She had once believed him to be a man he was not. She had not known his secrets. Was it possible she had felt the endless depths of what he had felt, what he still felt? No. Damn it, no. He could not allow himself to go there. Yet, his mind went like a moth to flame.

Was it possible? The question echoed in his head, becoming his heartbeat. Even if it was, he was not the man she had thought he was. She didn't know the things he'd done. She wouldn't wish ever to be with him if she knew. She was wrapped in pureness and loyalty and honor. He was wrapped in wickedness.

"In fact, Lady Lilias is a founding member," Carrington said, studying Nash. "She and my wife."

"Why are you telling me this?" Nash was a blink away from getting up and leaving. He'd never known information could be so much torture.

"Ye asked."

"I asked you," Nash said, struggling to keep ahold of his composure, "why you were not with your wife."

"And I'm telling ye."

He leaned hard against the back of his chair, feeling as if the world were collapsing in on him. "Do you mind getting on with it?"

"Ye look as if ye want to pound on something," Carrington said in answer and with a slight smile. "Bad day?"

The desire to do just that rose dark and powerful within Nash. "You found me drinking alone, did you not?"

"Point taken. I'll just leave ye to it, then."

Nash had his hand on Carrington's arm before he'd even realized he'd moved to stop his friend. The reaction was instinctual, and thankfully, Carrington did not protest. Instead, he offered Nash a triumphant look that sounded a warning in Nash's mind.

The man slowly sat, and Nash released him. "My wife is on a mission," Carrington said. "That's what her society does. They task themselves with preventing rogues from ruining unsuspecting women."

Nash frowned. That sounded as if it could be dangerous. "Do you not worry for her? Should you not be with her?"

"She no longer goes on any dangerous missions without me. It was a vow she made to me once I learned about the society."

Nash blew out a relieved breath. He couldn't even think of Lilias in danger. "Very wise of you to require such a vow. I imagine the other ladies did not care for that." He was thinking specifically of Lilias, but of course, he would not say so.

"I don't think they loved that my wife would not be joining them, but they've not voiced any displeasure to me."

Nash leaned forward, his pulse ticking upward. "Do you mean to say the other women in the society—What did you call it?"

"The Society of Ladies Against Rogues. Or SLAR, as they refer to it."

Nash nodded. "Do the other women still go on dangerous missions?"

"They do. They need a good man to take them in hand, but ye'd be surprised how hard some women can be to control."

No, he wouldn't. He knew Lilias and how independent she was. "Surely they don't go alone?"

"I go when I can, but take tonight, for example... I had an engagement to attend, so Lady Lilias went down to Satan's Den on a search and rescue mission without me."

"Satan's Den?" Nash couldn't breathe. It was one of the oldest, most notorious gambling and pleasure dens in one of the most notorious rookeries, St. Giles. "You cannot be serious. You cannot be sitting here telling me that you allowed Lady Lilias to go to such a dangerous place alone."

"I cannot control a woman who is not any relation of mine."

"I'll kill you if anything has happened to her," Nash said, rising, losing his grip on his control, which had been rapidly slipping. He was already considering the quickest way to get to the rookery.

"Nothing happened," Carrington said.

"How would you know?" Nash roared.

Carrington studied Nash for a long, silent minute. "She sent word that all went well before I came here. Mission accomplished. But it's interesting to hear that ye would wish to kill me if she was injured."

Nash slumped down into his chair. He'd been played by Carrington. He finished the last bit of his drink and stared at Carrington, waiting to hear what the man had really come here to say.

His friend's gaze softened in understanding and pity. "Ye should tell her how ye feel about her."

"No." There was really no point denying it now. "She is betrothed to my friend, and regardless of what your wife might think"—whatever excuse for her betrothal his mind tried to torture him with—"I've reason enough to believe she wants to be." Nash had bloody well practically orchestrated the deed, though he'd not been behind her being ruined. That had been chance. Though, what if she'd not been found on the terrace kissing Owen? Would she still have accepted his offer?

*Yes, you bloody fool.*

She'd been the one to kiss Owen, after all. Owen had told him so.

"I'll tell ye from personal experience that what we men believe a woman is thinking and feeling is rarely correct. They are wonderfully mysterious."

"Lilias is not my mystery to solve. She is Owen's." Carrington looked as if he wanted to protest so Nash played the only card he could to ensure the man did not interfere. "I want my life debt, and I want it in the form of you not telling your wife what it is you think you know about how I feel. I feel nothing." That was the second time he'd claimed those exact three words in his life. When he'd written them to Lilias, he had meant he felt empty when she was not near him. He meant the same thing now.

"Ye—"

"Ah, ah, ah," Nash said, wagging his finger at his friend. "No questions. No arguments. Only compliance. That is the heart of a life debt, yes?"

Carrington's eyes drew to slits. "Aye. Damn it. My wife will likely sleep in another bedchamber for at least a sennight when I refuse to speak of tonight."

Nash rose. He had to get away from his friend before Carrington tried to change Nash's mind. "I'm certain you'll work it out." He pushed his chair back and paused, considering the problem of Lilias and the missions. "SLAR?" he asked, pitching his voice low. "You said it was a secret society?"

Carrington nodded.

Nash could not stand by and do nothing, say nothing, while Lilias went on dangerous missions. "Do you think Owen knows about the society?"

Carrington shook his head. "I know he does not. Only husbands are supposed to know, and I just broke my vow telling ye."

"You have to tell him," Nash bit out.

"Sorry, my friend. I'm doubting myself now that I told ye. Ye I trust to keep this secret. I do not know Owen well enough to say he will do the same, and Guin would kill me."

Nash nodded. He'd have to tell Owen tonight, but think of a way not to implicate Carrington. The thought of any harm coming to Lilias chilled Nash.

---

Guinevere scrambled to her knees when the door to her and Asher's bedchamber opened and Asher strode in. "Well?" she said excitedly. "Did you find him?"

"Aye." Asher sat on the bed, and Guinevere scooted up behind her husband and slipped her arms around his waist. "Did you tell him of Lilias's dangerous missions but not tell him how we always have Merckle following out of sight but close behind?" Guinevere did not like keeping it a secret that, upon learning about the society, her husband had insisted on employing a man to guard all the women from a distance, and she'd had to concede after Asher had made such a convincing and descriptive argument of what could happen to the women in places like the rookery. It was then that she'd realized how naive they'd all been.

"I told him, as ye verra prettily requested, and I omitted the part about Merckle as we agreed," Asher said, his response disappointingly short.

"How did he react?" she asked, nearly bursting to know. Their plan—hers and Asher's—had been to discover how Greybourne felt about Lilias, and if he cared for her, which Guinevere was now convinced he did, she would tell Lilias. Guinevere was certain Lilias was wedding Owen due to pressure from her mother, though Lilias had not said as much. She had not said much of anything, actually, which was not like Lilias at all. Just as Asher's lack of response was unlike him. "Darling, did you hear me?"

One of Asher's boots dropped to the floor, followed a moment later by the other. "I heard ye."

Guinevere frowned at her husband's broad back. "Do you think he might start following her?"

"I couldn't say."

"What do you mean?" she demanded, becoming a trifle irritated. When Asher did not answer her, she scooted around him, into his lap, and threaded her arms around his neck. "You are acting very oddly."

A strained look came to her husband's face. "I know. And I'm sorry."

She kissed him on the lips to show him she loved him, even with his evasiveness. "Does Greybourne care for Lilias or not?"

"I couldn't say."

"Asher!" Guinevere said, her irritation spiking. "Whatever are you about?"

Her husband let out a long sigh. "A life debt. I'm about a life debt, which Greybourne has called in this verra night."

"And that means?"

"It means that whatever was said between me and Greybourne tonight will stay between the two of us."

Guinevere scoffed. "Darling, that's all you had to say." She giggled when her husband looked astonished.

"Ye're not vexed with me?"

"Of course not, darling. By Greybourne demanding this life debt from you—you really must explain that—it tells me everything I need to know without you saying a word. Greybourne would not have demanded such a thing if he did not care for Lilias and wanted to ensure you said nothing to me so I'd say nothing to her!"

Asher's response was to seal his mouth over hers for a long, drugging kiss. When they broke apart, he said, "Ye are the most brilliant person I have ever known. One of the most devious, as well," he added, kissing her again.

"So you will not interfere?" It was her turn to kiss her husband, but she started at his neck and worked her way upward to his lips in a fashion she knew he loved.

When she drew back, he said, "With what?" in a thick voice.

"With my helping the two of them come together."

"Guin," Asher said, nuzzling her neck, "what do ye have in mind?"

"Well, I cannot very well tell Lilias what I think since I have no proof, and you won't give it to me with Greybourne's own words, but I *can* make sure she goes out on missions, and you could happen to mention them to Greybourne so he feels inclined to follow her. Then, perchance, fate will take over."

"Ye're playing with fire, Wife."

"Then it is a good thing," she murmured, slipping her night rail off her shoulders, "that I have you to keep me from getting burned."

## Chapter Seven

Nash knew it was a mistake coming to Serafina's home the moment she opened the door. Still, he pushed himself forward with the rendezvous his sometimes partner in pleasure had requested with the note she'd sent him. He was determined to purge Lilias from his mind, if not once and for all, then, God willing, for an hour of mindless coupling.

Serafina was a widow Nash knew from Scotland who had a home in London as well. She was extremely wealthy in her own right, with a castle near his family's there, and could do and live as she pleased. That was not necessarily a good thing, though, as the woman liked to indulge in drink and pleasure just as much as, if not more than, most men Nash knew.

She straddled him, her night rail bunching up on her thighs. "Yer mind is not here, Greybourne."

If she only knew what an understatement that was. His mind was on Lilias. He'd gone straight from the Orcus Society to Owen's, only to be informed by Owen's butler that he had left that very night for the Cotswolds. It seemed Owen's father had taken a bad fall, and Owen's presence was required at his country home immediately.

Serafina's hand slipped to Nash's crotch and settled there. She frowned. "Yer desire is not here, either."

"I'm sorry," he said, grasping her by the waist and hoisting her up and to the floor. He stood and reached for his overcoat in one swift motion. He was aware Serafina was pouting at him as he put on his overcoat, and when he was done, he faced her, trying to think what to say so her feelings would not be injured.

They'd been intimate several times before in Scotland. Serafina knew not to expect any sort of commitment from him, and she'd assured him she wanted none herself. She had been wed once, and she vowed once was enough for her. But she had made one stipulation, and that was that he be honest with her.

She stared at him and asked him bluntly, "Why did ye come here tonight, Greybourne? It's clearly not because ye were longing to be with me."

He tugged a hand through his hair. "I was hoping to forget," he admitted. "And there have been times you've been able to make me do that." Though the moments had been brief.

Forgetting Lilias seemed to be an impossibility. He wasn't certain why. He'd thought about it through the years but had been unable to come up with an answer. Was it because she'd been the only person he'd ever come close to telling about his brother? Was it because he'd seen in her eyes that she thought him better than he really was and it had given him hope that he could be that man? Was it because they'd never joined so he was left to wonder what it would have been like? Was it because he knew she was unlike any woman he'd ever met or would ever meet again?

Of course it was the bloody last one. He knew it. He just didn't damn well care to dwell on it. It could be one of the other reasons, as well—or all of them. Who damn well cared? The result was the same.

He didn't want any woman but Lilias—not truly. And

he could not have her. So what now? He was getting older. He needed to produce an heir, of which his mother had reminded him when he first returned to England. And for an heir, he needed a wife. The prospect left him cold.

*Another ducal duty.*

"Greybourne, did ye hear me?" Serafina demanded, her tone slightly exasperated.

He snapped his gaze away from the wall he had not even realized he'd been staring at. Serafina's green eyes were narrowed, and she was twisting a strand of her red hair around one of her fingers. "No, I'm sorry," he admitted. "What did you say?"

She placed a hand on his chest and glanced up at him, her gaze earnest. "I said, as long as I've known ye, yer mind has never been totally with me, but I have never seen ye like this. Am I to assume ye have encountered the woman Lilias? The one who truly holds yer desire? Does she live here in London?"

His jaw slipped open. "How do you know her name?" he asked, not bothering to deny the statement.

"Ye muttered it in yer sleep the one time ye stayed the night with me."

Good Christ. He talked in his sleep? That was a devil of a thing to discover. Thank God he'd never stayed the night with any other woman.

Serafina gave him a knowing look. "So, does she live in London?"

He nodded. Serafina lived her life with utter discretion, and he trusted she wouldn't speak of Lilias or of him to anyone. Besides, she was not part of the same social circle. Her husband had not been of the *ton* but a businessman who had a large share in one of the railroad companies. And the fact that her husband had not had a title and had worked for what he had kept the doors to the *ton* firmly shut to them. It was rubbish, but it was the way of things.

"Have the two of ye never—"

"No." He cut her off. He didn't need Serafina's help putting images in his head of him and Lilias flesh to flesh. He tortured himself quite regularly with images his own mind provided. "She's not the sort of lady to be intimate without entanglements."

"Then why not get entangled?" Serafina asked. "Ye clearly wish to."

He scrubbed a hand across his face and made a move for the door. "It's not that simple. She belongs to someone else."

"Ah. I'm sorry, Greybourne. But it's good to be the sort of man who does not take what belongs to another."

That's what he kept telling himself.

"Goodbye, Greybourne. I'll miss ye."

He frowned. That sounded like an end to whatever had been between them. He wished he felt something, but he didn't. "'Goodbye' as in this is the end of our time together?" he asked for clarification.

She nodded, came to stand before him, and pressed onto her tiptoes. "Aye. I do not like to take what belongs to another, either."

"What the devil do you mean by that? I don't belong to anyone."

"Silly, foolish man," she said while opening her bedchamber door. "Of course ye do. Yer heart belongs to her, whether ye wish to acknowledge it or not."

Her words stilled him completely. It was like light flooded his mind. *Damnation.* He couldn't deny the truth. It had never been about mere desire or worshipping her. It was much more. It was that dangerous emotion that drove a man to do unwise, dishonorable things just to be with the woman who held his heart in the palm of her hand. *Love*. It was more imperative than ever to keep a distance between himself and Lilias. Too much time near her and he wouldn't trust himself not to weaken, to say something he ought not say, to do something he damn well should not do, and that would be unforgivable.

Lilias almost ran Nash over with her horse and gig. It happened so fast she did not even have time to scream, but as the realization hit her, she began to shake. In her defense, it was very late, the fog swirled heavily, and she was exceedingly tired. Besides that, he'd dashed out in front of them. Nash was lucky that the light from the street lamp hit him directly or she most definitely would have killed him. Now *that* would have been a true Gothic romance.

*Heroine runs over hero who didn't love her.* In the unwritten tragic book that was her one-sided love story starring Nash, she'd be cast as a scorned murderess. Her heart thudded at the thought.

"What the devil are you doing out and about at this hour?" Nash roared, swallowing the distance between him and her very agitated horse. The horse reared, and Lilias's heart skipped several beats in fear for Nash's life—*again*—but he sidestepped the beast, grabbed the reins, and stilled the animal.

He looked magnificent, as usual, the rogue. He had on another kilt that showed his legs—heavens, they were lovely—and his cravat was undone, as well as the top of his shirt being yanked open. She could see a light dusting of hair on his chest, and her fingers tingled with the desire to touch him, and as the mist turned to a soft rain, a drop of water landed on his nose which made her want to wipe it off or even lick it. Heat flushed her at the thought.

She'd imagined when she might see him again at a ball, and she had planned to look much better than she likely did at this moment. She likely looked a mess. At least the foldable head of her gig was up or she would have looked utterly bedraggled, seeing as how she'd been to the rookery and back tonight in sporadic rain. *Twice*. She'd driven in the drizzle the first time to rescue a witless lady from the rogue who'd lured her there, intent on seduction, and then Lilias had been called out again unexpectedly by Frederica. It seemed a very damning scandalous confessions manuscript by a Society mistress was about to be published. One of the titillating chapters in the book happened to be about a marquess, Lord Quattlebom, who was having an affair not only with said mistress but with a young unwed lady, a Lady Katherine. Lady Katherine and Frederica were friends, and she had cried to Frederica about her problem. Frederica had taken it upon herself to accept the mission and go out alone to confront the mistress who had written the manuscript. There were strict rules against going on missions without anyone knowing and about accepting missions without a vote from the other SLAR members, but Frederica had broken those rules.

Then Frederica's carriage had been stolen in the rookery. A dirty, though devilishly cute, urchin boy had shown up at Lilias's home and told her Frederica was in need of her help and where to find her. Lilias had collected a dazed Frederica from a rather surly redhead, taken her home, and helped her sneak back into her bedchamber. Having done all that, she was certain her hair was in utter disarray. Not to mention her gown was soiled and torn from helping

Frederica up the tree to her window. And Lilias was missing a slipper. It had fallen off while climbing, and she had not been able to find it in the dark.

No, she most definitely did not look anywhere close to the picture she'd wanted to present: the woman he'd see and ask himself why he let her get away. Of course she knew she ought not let her mind go down such paths, but honestly, she tried and her mind refused to obey. It was a problem. A large one. Especially now that she was betrothed to Owen, a man who didn't make her mind go anywhere other than to fond memories of pleasant times with a good friend. It was all so depressing and final.

"Lilias, did you hear me?" he bellowed, making her scowl. "I asked what the devil are you doing out at this hour?"

"I heard you," she bit out, her irritation rising as she studied him. A suspicion arose. His untied cravat had not raised any inner alarms, nor had his being upon the lane at such a late hour. She knew men went to gaming hells and gentlemen's clubs late at night. It was the lip paint smeared on his cheek that made a hard realization hit her. He'd been dashing out on the lane from a woman's house—or the lady's bedchamber more likely. Lilias's stomach clenched. An illicit affair? Was the woman wed? Did it even matter?

*No. No, it did not.*

Nash had stolen her heart, albeit apparently not purposely, and he'd frozen it while she'd waited for him for seven long years. Although, again, not purposely on his part. Then he had crushed it when she'd seen him at his house, and again on the terrace. Honestly, there should not be even the tiniest portion of her heart left to break, but she vowed she heard a crack as she stared at that lip paint.

"It is none of your concern what I'm doing out," she

said and tried to snatch her reins away.

But he held firm and scowled up at her. Even scowling, he was a sight to behold. Firm, full lips. Chiseled jawline. Arched brows that displayed his annoyance perfectly. "You are my concern," he shot back.

Her heart squeezed, though she tried to stop it. The concern he spoke of was not the sort she had longed for, and now that she was betrothed, it would be devastating in an entirely different way if she were to learn Nash did indeed care for her. The situation was intolerable. She almost wished he'd go back to Scotland. *Almost.* She could not quite make herself truly wish him away. She supposed she must enjoy the torture of being near him.

Really, her thoughts were most inappropriate. She had to take herself in hand and get home quickly. She could not chance being seen out at night alone, nor with Nash. Either discovery would destroy Owen, not to mention endanger their betrothal and her mother's and sister's well-beings.

"We have absolutely no ties to each other anymore," she said, yanking on the reins again to no avail, "so I am *not* your concern."

"You are wrong," he said, the words making her hope soar. "You are betrothed to Owen, which binds us."

Her hope plummeted. *Again.* She prayed it stayed down permanently this time. It was a futile hope at this point, anyway. "Let go my reins! If I'm discovered with you, the scandal will set London on fire."

"I'm more concerned about your being out alone than a possible scandal, Lilias. Besides—" he glanced up and down the empty lane "—there is no one out and about at this hour."

"Besides men returning to their homes after trysts with lovers," she snapped, eyeing him. Silence fell. Blast him.

"Who is she?" The soft words tumbled from her lips before she could stop them. She was mortified, but she did not take the question back.

"No one you know," Nash supplied.

Fury and hurt rose up in her throat to almost choke her, but she managed to speak. "Let go of my reins at once, or I will scream so loudly that I will wake this neighborhood."

"I thought you were concerned about causing a scandal," he said, his tone challenging her bluff.

"I was," she replied, infusing tartness into her voice. "But I've decided a scandal would be preferable to one more minute with you."

*There.* A knot clogged her throat that she could not swallow.

"Why so hostile, Lilias?" he asked, gazing at her with his thickly lashed beautiful eyes as if he were concerned. He had liar's eyes, she decided uncharitably. And the fact that he sounded genuinely perplexed made her even more livid. He'd broken her heart without ever really knowing it. He had not even thought of her enough to realize he'd had the power to crush her. That should offer comfort to a reasonable person, but she was feeling decidedly unreasonable.

She couldn't say any of that, though. She needed a believable excuse for her anger. "I am hostile, *Greybourne*, because men always act as if they have the God-granted right to tell a woman what to do, even when the man in question—" she paused to let the first part of what she'd said sink in "—has no right whatsoever. I am not your sister. I am not your mother. I am not your friend. I am not your betrothed. I am nothing to you."

He moved in a flash, springing from the street, and landing at her right on the ledge of her gig to clasp her wrist. His hold was firm but not harsh. Everything else about him, however, was an invasion. Smoldering heat from his fingers singed her. His scent—brandy, horse, and smoky wood—assaulted her, making her curl her toes. She sucked in a greedy breath. His size made her want to know what it would feel like for him to cradle her, hold her, protect her from the mess that was her life. She found herself leaning toward him when she should be pushing him away. Their faces were suddenly so close that his sharp inhalation whispered in her ear and his exhalation wafted over her lips. Gooseflesh rose all over her body, and an ache sprang up deep in her womb, making her clench.

"There has never been a second since the moment we met that you were nothing to me. You are... You are—" If he didn't finish that sentence, she could not be held responsible for what she did to him. Her heart pounded so hard her ears rang. "I—That is, *you* shall always be remembered fondly as...as...the girl who broke my nose."

Ire flared within her, and she shoved him straight in the chest as hard as she could. She shoved with all her disappointment, and it was quite a lot. She caught him unawares, and her actions surprised her, as well. His eyes widened, and he fell backward, unfortunately righting himself when his feet hit the ground and the puddle that had formed as he'd stood there splashed up around his boots. She scowled that only his boots had gotten wet and muddy. He really did deserve to land on his arse.

"Lilias—"

"Do not," she said, seething, "call me by my given name ever again. It is Lady Lilias to you. Being remembered fondly for a brief period we spent together seven years ago gives you no right whatsoever to question me or tell me what to do."

The rain grew a bit harder and the fog seemed to thicken, which fit her dark mood, and she was enjoying immensely that he was still in the rain. He'd not tried to sit in the small seat beside her, and she'd not offered.

For one brief moment, with Nash's face tilted up to look at her and the lamplight illuminating his expression, she would have wagered every coin she had, if she had any, that he looked as if he was in misery. As if her words had crushed him.

*Impossible.*

She was seeing what she longed to see, or *had* longed to see, and not what was true. She squeezed her eyes shut for one breath, determined to stop portraying him as the man he had never wanted to be for her, and when she opened her eyes and brought her gaze to him once more, his dark eyebrows were slanted as he frowned.

"You are correct, *Lady Lilias*. I have no right whatsoever to ask you what you are doing out and about at night. Alone. Nor do I have any right to demand you go home and never go out unchaperoned again. But I am certain Owen will be interested to know."

She forced out a derisive scoff, though his words were fairly true. Once she was wed to Owen, he would practically own her, and if he chose not to wed her because she was doing things he did not approve of, things would be dire for her family, indeed.

The fog seemed to grow even thicker, swirling and curling around Nash, and the rain became yet harder, tapping like a drum against the foldable head.

"If you go home now and vow to me that you will stay there at night from now on, I vow to you not to tell Owen."

"I vow I'll stay home," she lied, though what she really wanted to say to the conceited man was to go stuff his cravat in his mouth. It wasn't as if he was going to lay in wait outside her home and watch to ensure she kept her vow, and Owen was in the Cotswolds to see after his father, so for now she was free to do as she pleased. And she planned to take full advantage of that freedom as long as she could.

"Am I excused now, *Father?*" she bit out between clenched teeth. She could not say more. She wanted to. Oh, she had a great deal she wanted to say. Such as if he loved her, they could have gone on these late-night missions together. She was positive it would have been the sort of adventure that would have excited him. Nash and propriety had never been intimately acquainted, which was probably one of the reasons she'd fallen for him so hard and fast. Her soul had recognized a kindred spirit. The older Owen became, however, the more tightly he wrapped himself in propriety, and honestly, it had been one of the only things that ever made them fight. She could tolerate him being so restrictive with himself, but she had detested when he made mention of the things he thought she ought not do.

She feared she and Owen would make each other miserable. She feared he would eventually forbid her to work with SLAR. It would be impossible to go on missions and hide them from him. She feared she would never love him as she should, but what could she do? What choice did she have? The man she loved did not love her. He loved ladies who painted their lips and invited him into their homes to do God only knew what. She would not imagine him doing *that* with anyone else, nor would she allow herself to imagine a life with him ever again.

He stepped aside and waved a hand for her to go. "Straight home, *Lady* Lilias, and no more outings. Or remember, I'll tell Owen."

"May your tongue rot off," she muttered and then reached far forward to grab the reins Nash had taken from her that were now dangling from the horse. She grunted when her stays cut into her waist as she struggled to secure the reins, and just as her fingertips grazed the leads, her gown, which had been hopelessly torn at her right shoulder during the tree climb on Frederica's behalf, ripped even more and slipped off her shoulder. She gasped and made a grab for the reins, trying to get a hold of them while tugging up the right shoulder of her gown. She was so busy with these two things that she didn't know Nash had moved until her gig dipped.

She looked up to find him standing on the ledge of her gig once more, his face a hairsbreadth from hers once again, but his eyes were narrowed. He brushed the hand away that was fumbling at her right shoulder and tugged her gown up himself. Everywhere his fingers touched, he left a path of heat on her skin that sent her pulse into a desperate gallop.

"Who did this to you?" he demanded, his voice vibrating with unmistakable rage that so shocked her, she could not form an immediate proper reply. In that pause, Nash came fully onto the gig, his arm sliding over her shoulder and tugging her into the rock wall that was his side. Iron and heat—that's what Nash was made of.

Confusion washed over her. The rage in his voice sounded greater than what would belong to a man who merely cared for a friend's lady. Perhaps she was merely hearing what she had longed to hear for so many years.

"Shh, don't fret," he said, his hand suddenly moving from her shoulder to stroke her head.

Good heavens, his hand sliding down the rounded slope of her skull felt divine. She wanted to curl into him like her cat Tabitha did to her when she would pet the feline. But what did he mean *don't fret?*

"Why did you not say something?" he asked, a faint tremor in his voice. "Were you afraid?"

Well, of course she wasn't, but she found she wanted to hear what he would say next, so she kept her silence.

"Give me the man's name, Lilias. And if you don't know his name, tell me where you saw him, what he looked like." Nash's hand had stopped stroking her head.

*Pity, that.* Though, how tightly he was now holding her and the way both his arms were encircling her, as if he was going to protect her from the world, felt wonderful. Too wonderful. Longing sprang forth hot and throbbing. She had to move away from him, break contact before she did something unthinkable. She set her hand on his thigh to push him away, and the unbridled power she felt under her fingertips made her shiver.

"It's going to be all right," he said, his voice now low and soothing. "I will find the man that dared to touch you, and I'll kill him. I'll rip his heart out. I promise I'll—I mean, Owen will never let harm come to you again."

His impassioned words sent her pulse spinning in a direction she dare not allow her emotions or her mind to go again. He was honorable so he was angry that any man should act with dishonor, and that was that.

She shoved away from him, breaking his hold and put the little space she could between them on the small seat of the gig. "It was a tree, not a man. I climbed a tree and ripped my gown. Though I appreciate your neighborly concern."

She expected him to laugh or possibly lecture her on tree climbing or some such. What she did not anticipate was the fury that settled on his face as he stared at her. "You," he bit out, "need a keeper. You will get yourself killed carrying on as you do. Your mother has never been up for the task, and—"

"Don't you dare speak ill of my mother," Lilias bellowed, and this time when she shoved Nash, he did fall backward onto his arse where he belonged. She snatched up the reins before he righted himself, whistled at her horse to go, and proceeded to leave him behind her, as she should have done the day he'd left her without ever looking back.

But before she got too far, she heard him yell, "Stay home or else!"

※

Later that night, she lay awake in her bed staring at her ceiling. She'd long given up the notion that she would sleep this night. Nash was far too heavy on her mind, and guilt filled her heart and her head that Nash, not Owen, was in both. Owen, who had declared his love. Owen, who had told her that the pain he lived with from his limp was nothing if he had her as his wife in the end. Owen loved her, but Nash still filled every cell she possessed. She hated herself, and she hated Nash, too.

Yet, she didn't. She hated that she loved him, and that it was not a simple matter to forget him, particularly when he sounded so enraged on her behalf that someone might have harmed her. She rolled onto her side and punched her pillow. When he did things like vow to kill the villain and rip his heart out... Well, those sorts of words could confuse a lady, especially one prone to romantic leanings as she used to be. She was not going to be that sort anymore. An impassioned vow such as Nash's could make a lady think a man was harboring secret feelings for her. But not this lady, of course. She flopped onto her back again. She could not, under any circumstances, ask Nash if any of those scenarios might possibly be the case. Nor could she put herself in a situation where he might tell her.

She bit her lip as she stared once more at the ceiling. If Nash did love her, it would be worse to know, wouldn't it? She listened to her breathing for a long while as her mind wrestled with that question. Yes, it would be worse. She'd accepted Owen's proposal. They were to wed. But was it fair to Owen?

"Oh, for the love of God," she muttered and pressed her fingers to her aching temples. Was she so pathetic that she would twist the truth to suit her desires? She might be. The thought was not a pleasant one. She doubted she'd even see Nash alone ever again. She could see no reason why she would. It wasn't as if the chances were high that she'd encounter him in the middle of the night leaving a woman's house ever again. And who was that woman anyway? Tomorrow Lilias would—

*No! No!* She would not play the sleuth where Nash was concerned. It was none of her business, even if her heart wished otherwise.

## Chapter Eight

The next night, Nash hid under the tree outside Lilias's window and waited. He had a hunch that she was not going to keep her word. It was something in the way she'd so readily agreed to his demand.

Once he'd gotten home and was in his bed with time to think upon his encounter with her, he had concluded several things. First, a lady who had come and gone as she pleased for years because no one was properly watching her would not so easily relinquish her freedom. Second, Lilias undoubtedly knew Owen had been called from Town, so she knew that Nash could not immediately tell Owen her secret as Nash had threatened. And lastly, he had hurt her.

He had heard it in her voice and had seen it on her face last night, and the knowledge was a flowing pain in his veins that also made him question, once again, if her feelings for him had ever run to the depths his did for her. No. No. And yet... The possibility tormented him. He could not stop the thoughts. They burned in his head, consuming him. Considering what might have been if he'd never betrayed his brother, if he had not come perilously close to doing the same to Owen, if Owen did not love her, if Nash was truly the person she thought him to be filled him with an all-consuming, pulsing desire. He shook to battle against it. Perspiration dampened his brow and back, and his jaw ached from his clenched teeth.

All Nash needed to do was keep her safe until Owen returned, and if she tried to sneak out of her house again before that, he'd stop her. He'd attempted to pass the duty to Carrington, but the man had acted indifferent, as if it was perfectly acceptable for Lilias to be galivanting around London at night alone. It infuriated Nash that Carrington did not seem concerned, but what could he do? He could not force Carrington to do anything, so here Nash was.

The first hour passed uneventfully. In the second hour, she appeared at her window, and he watched it slide open. He thought about calling up to her to stop her foolishness, but he didn't want to chance waking her mother. As much as he thought her mother needed someone to wake her up to what Lilias was doing, Nash could not stand the thought of being the one to cause Lilias problems with her mother. He'd simply have to stand guard here every night until Owen returned to London, and then he was going to have to tell Owen about Lilias's little adventures so that Owen would demand she stop.

Lilias kicked one leg over her window ledge, giving Nash a view of her creamy flesh. He had to swallow a groan of desire. She sent her other leg over, and then the little hellion started down the tree, shimmying her body, which moved her hips in a way that made him think of how she might move them if he were on top of her, entering her. He hardened instantly.

He let her descend almost to the bottom before he spoke. "I said to stay home."

She stilled, gasped, and looked over her shoulder at him. "What are you doing here?" she demanded.

He ignored that obvious question. "I vow it," he said instead, mimicking the oath she'd falsely given him last night. Then he snorted. "You force me into a position where I have no choice but to tell Owen."

"Fine," she growled, then surprised him by dropping very nimbly to the ground. She landed with barely a thud, which told him Lilias had descended this tree often. More often than he cared to think about her endangering herself. She thrust her hands onto her hips and glared at him. "Tell him." Then she smirked. "But you will have to wait unless you plan to travel to the Cotswolds to do so."

By God, she was magnificent in her confidence.

"Now if you will kindly excuse me." She tried to sidestep him, but he easily blocked her path.

"I will tell him, Lilias," he said, sure she was bluffing about being unconcerned. "I'll tell him, and you know he'll demand you cease this. Owen is a proper rule follower, and he has never been the adventurous sort."

He hated when her shoulders drooped. The last thing he wanted to do was make her feel defeated. She glanced at him from under her lashes. "You are undoubtedly right," she said, sounding miserable, which made him feel worse. "He will very likely demand I stop my work with—"

Her words came to a halt, and she bit her lip.

"SLAR," he supplied, not sure why.

Her eyes widened. "How do you know about the Society of Ladies Against Rogues?" She sounded both outraged and wary.

"I have my ways," he replied. He did not want to tell her that Carrington had told him about it.

"Carrington," she said, her tone derisive. "It had to be him. You may as well admit it."

"I'll do nothing of the sort," he replied, rather than lying to her about it.

"If Carrington told you about SLAR, then he must have told you of the important work we do."

"He did," Nash agreed. He rather liked the idea of a group of women banding together to stand against rogues. He just did not like the idea of Lilias endangering herself.

"Let me ask you this," she said, her voice taking on a sweet note that made him suspicious. "What if it were your sister who was in need? What if the missive I received tonight was to aid Lady Adaline? Would you not want me to help her?"

"No. I would want you to contact me immediately," he replied, crossing his arms.

She crossed hers, as well. "What if I could not find you? What if a woman with no brother or father needs someone to protect her?"

"All women have fathers," he said, mentally cursing himself the minute the idiotic words left his mouth. "God, Lil, I'm sorry."

"Don't call me that," she said, her voice hard.

"You still wish me to call you Lady Lilias?"

She sighed. "You may call me Lilias. *For now.* Unless you give me reason to wish you to call me Lady Lilias again."

"Such as?"

"Well," she said, "such as trying to stop me from going where I need to go tonight."

"Lil—"

"Just listen," she interrupted. "Guinevere's sister Lady Frederica needs my help. It was her I was aiding last night, as well. There is a manuscript that has been written by a well-known Society mistress. It recounts all of the men she has bedded. In great detail. It seems some of her patrons did not pay her what they promised they would, and she wrote it with the intention of publicly shaming them."

"Seems fair to me," he replied.

"Well, I suppose," Lilias said, "they should have paid

her for services, er, rendered, but one of the men, a marquess who was her patron, also had an affair with a naive, unwed lady, and apparently, in the chapter about the marquess, the young lady's name is mentioned, along with the fact that the marquess had intimate relations with her. It's dreadful. She'll be ruined."

"Did you tell the mistress—"

"Mrs. Porter," Lilias supplied, thinking to keep the woman's identity secret if she could. "Yes, she knows. She was actually already very remorseful about writing the manuscript and had decided not to publish it. But she gave it to her brother, and he will not return it. I must obtain that manuscript before the brother and the publisher he's working with release it. Lady Frederica cannot get away from her home tonight, so it's up to me to ensure it does not get published."

*Lilias's big heart and admirable ideals will get her killed.*

The thought made him feel as if his blood had turned to ice in his veins. "If I help you obtain the manuscript, do I have your vow that you will quit your work with SLAR?"

"You'll help me?" she asked, her surprise evident.

"I don't see that I have a choice." He didn't say that the thought of her possibly being injured made him want to do all manner of unthinkable things. Such as lock her in her bedchamber and keep her there. *With him. In her bed. Preferably naked.* He swallowed his desire and fear for her. "I'll help you until Owen returns, but when he does, I'm going to tell him."

"Do as you must," she said with a flippant air, then waved a dismissive hand at him. "If Owen demands I stop, I will."

"You are a liar," he said, recalling her previous "vow" to stay home.

"That's rude," she replied. "But I suppose 'tis true in this circumstance. If you force a person into a corner, what do you expect? These women need me, and I'll not fail them. They need someone to help them, to protect them."

Good Christ. He understood now. She was trying to be for them what she had never had herself. It was perfectly clear now why she was a founding member of this society. It had nothing to do with him. It was because neither of her parents had truly made her feel protected. He was a conceited arse for ever entertaining the thought that it could be him.

"Fine. I'll accompany you on your missions to help these women until Owen returns, and then you are Owen's problem."

"Is that what you consider me?" The hurt in her voice was unmistakable. "A problem?"

"Yes," he clipped, afraid if he said anything else he'd tell her something that would give away how he really felt. She was rash, impulsive, impassioned, and wonderful. Of course, she *was* a problem, but he'd rather have a million problems like her that made him feel alive than the nothingness he normally felt. "But I will bear you somehow," he added, which would have been the perfect thing to say to keep a distance between them if his arm had not reached out without alerting his brain and his fingers had not brushed down the slope of her smooth cheek. It was perfect, just like her. He wanted to tell her how she made him feel. Instead, he said, "Where are we going?"

"The Orcus Society," she said without a trace of embarrassment or concern.

Nash's mouth slipped open. He knew a great deal about the place from Carrington, such as the fact that there were pleasure rooms there and men who did not deserve to even breathe the same air as Lilias. "How did you imagine you'd gain entry into the Orcus Society? You need to be a patron or be one of the women who—"

His words trailed off as she opened her cloak and revealed the seductive cut of a gown that would cause the scandal of the Season were she to wear it to any balls. She must have seen him staring at her delectable cleavage because she pulled her cloak closed once more. But it was too late. The creamy, round mounds of her breasts would be singed in his memory for the rest of his life. A ravenous need to touch her rushed through him.

Instead, he tugged a hand through his hair and forced himself to keep control. "You mean to tell me that you were planning on going into the club alone, and there you intended to pretend to be a courtesan?" It was unthinkable. Because if he thought too much upon it, then he would go mad with worry at how Owen would be able to protect her from herself in the future.

"I do not mean to tell you anything, but you've left me little choice. The answer is yes and yes, though. Now, where is your gig?"

"At my home. I could not very well drive it here and risk anyone seeing me and asking questions."

"You walked here just to watch over me?"

Something in her tone sounded odd to him. He could not place it so he simply answered. "Indeed. I owe Owen that."

"Yes, of course it's about Owen. Well come along, then. Let's get my gig."

He followed her as she strode to the lane behind her townhome to the mews, as if she had no fear that she'd be seen by her mother. Because, of course, she would not. He grasped her arm before she entered the stables. "What of your coachman and stable master? Will they not ask questions?"

"No."

"Whyever not?" he bit out. A proper stable master would.

When she simply shrugged, his temper snapped. "Does no one in your life put restraints on you for your own safety?"

Her eyes widened in the darkness, but away from the lamplight, the moonlight did not illuminate her face enough for him to judge if his outburst had revealed anything he did not wish it to.

"Why, Nash, I did not think you cared."

There was that something in her voice again, the something he could not quite place. But he didn't need to place it to decide he didn't like it. It was unknown, and he did not care for the unknown. "For Owen's sake, I care," he replied on the chance he had revealed himself to her.

"Owen," she said, the word a sigh. "Of course. You care for Owen's sake."

Did she believe him? He didn't rightly know, and he was certainly not going to ask.

Once they were settled on the seat and on their way, he instructed Lilias to pull the hood of her cloak close around her head. Nash didn't think they would encounter anyone on the streets this late, but he would not take any chances with Lilias's reputation.

Lilias, he noted, did her best to keep space between them, and that was fine by him. Just sitting beside her was torture enough. If they were touching, he couldn't be certain he could keep his desire restrained.

It occurred to him that she had not answered his question about the stable master and coachman, and he had an unwelcome suspicion that Carrington's wife might have been correct in her belief that Lilias was wedding Owen to take care of her mother and sister. And yet, four years ago she had told Owen she loved him. It did not make sense. He had to know for certain why she was wedding Owen.

*And then what?*

He slid his teeth back and forth, at war with himself. There should be no interference. He'd vowed not to come between Owen and Lilias, but that vow had not included standing by as she made herself a sacrificial lamb. That he could not do. He would not pursue her, but he could damn well not let her be forced to wed someone she did not love, to have no choice in the matter because of money. If she was wedding Owen simply to have her family taken care of, Nash could aid her and her family. He could give them money without acting on his own selfish longing for her. There had to be a way to do it without her knowing where the money came from.

He could give her the gift of freedom that money brought, though it would be a thorny gift as she would be all but ruined after the kiss with Owen and then also breaking their betrothal. He stole a look at her. Her cloak was threadbare, but her chin was lifted, and her shoulders were back. Her eyes were focused straight ahead. The Lilias he had known would value her freedom above a reputation the *ton* deemed ruined, and he could provide enough funds for her that even if she never wed, she would have a comfortable life, as would her mother and sister. Lilias's reputation would affect her sister's, but with time and an unexpected enormous dowry thrown at Lilias's sister, he imagined her chances of wedding well quite good.

He considered the possibility of how to give her the money anonymously. She would never take it, but he'd wager his useless life that her mother would. So the question remained: was she wedding Owen out of love or need?

As he guided the gig down the lane toward their destination, he glanced at her hands, which were folded in her lap. No gloves. "Where are your gloves?" he asked, already knowing. The ache for her nearly choked his ability to speak.

"What concern is it of yours?" she demanded.

"It's rather foolish," he said, making his tone purposely chiding, "to go about without gloves on a cold night. I didn't take you as someone to show such carelessness."

She turned toward him, glaring. "I am not careless! I've one pair of gloves, and I purposely did not wear them to keep them decent. No one where we are going will give a farthing if I have gloves on or not, so it is you who is the fool!"

She was quite right. He'd left her seven years ago knowing how desperate things were for her, and he'd selfishly never looked back because he feared his inability to control himself and not betray Owen. Yet, in the process, he had betrayed her. He had to make it right, even if she never knew it.

"I suppose you are correct that no one will care. Still, if you had planned to play a woman of the night—a *successful one*—I would have thought you might wear your best cloak and slippers." He noted the hole in the toe of her slippers, which made him want to take her directly to the shoemaker and have a dozen pairs of shoes made for her so that she never had to wear such shoddy slippers again.

When she did not respond to his prodding, except for her glare becoming more pronounced, he pressed further. "You look like a street urchin, not a sought-after courtesan.

I doubt they'll let you in the door."

"You insufferable beast!" she hissed. "How dare you! I'll show you when we are there. I'll show you that whatever fool of a man is at the door won't even notice my worn slippers and cloak. He will be looking at my br—"

Nash's gaze fell to her chest as silence descended. He could well imagine that no man would notice anything she had on; she was so very beautiful that she could wear a sack and still devastate one's senses. He was so busy thinking about it, that he almost ran off the lane before the turn toward the Orcus Society. He had to jerk the gig back onto the road.

"Ha! My point exactly!" she cried out, smugness in her tone.

Nash jerked his gaze to her face, and she smirked at him. He was, he felt, very nearly at the answer he sought. "I suppose you are correct," he said, ensuring his voice belied the fact that he really believed it to be so.

"What do you mean, *you suppose?*" she demanded with righteous anger.

He had to clench his teeth to keep from smiling. God, he'd missed this. Lilias had been the only woman he'd ever shared such easy banter with. This true back-and-forth of opinions clashing and trying to make the other person see one's side. She used her wits, whereas other women had either readily agreed with him all his life, even when he knew they could not possibly, or tried to use their wiles to convince him. He maneuvered the gig to the alley entrance of the Orcus Society where workers and any courtesans entered. Tonight he, too, would enter there to escort Lilias, his supposed courtesan, into the club.

He slowed the horse to a stop, then turned his full attention to her. "I mean, you do have *some* charms in your favor, but the smartest thing to have done would have been to truly dress the part of a successful courtesan and to have brought your coachman with you. Of course, these are all details I suppose only a man would think of. You ladies don't usually consider near as much as we men do."

*That ought to do the trick.*

He honestly wanted to chuckle at his brilliant word choice.

He was so busy congratulating himself for his superb acting that he did not see her punch coming. She whacked him right in the arm. He was surprised but immensely pleased she had a nice, solid punch. Though it would not stop a man built like him, it could make him question proceeding if he intended her harm. That moment of questioning could give her time to escape if she needed it. Not that she ever would. He was going to see to that. Somehow.

"For your information," she snapped while rubbing the hand she'd used to punch him, "I can assure you we ladies think just as well—no, better—than any man! I thought of everything you just mentioned, you insufferably arrogant man. These *are* my best slippers!" She lifted her foot, showing a sinfully enticing ankle and pointing at her foot. He could see her toes wiggling back and forth. She slammed her foot down.

On top of his.

"Damnation!" he let slip. "That hurt."

She smirked at him. "It was intended to. I could see the punch did not meet its mark. Your arms are entirely too muscled."

She thought him muscled? He could not stop the grin from spreading across his face, to which she rolled her eyes and then leveled him with a glare that would have shrunk a lesser man's ballocks.

"And this is my best cloak by far!" She eyed him with haughty disdain, but he knew it was only because he'd angered her. He wanted to wrap her in his arms and assure her it would be all right. That he would provide for her. Protect her.

Her sharp inhalation alerted him that she was not done with her dressing down that he richly deserved. "I would have brought a coachman, if I had one, but we are not all blessed with wealth like you, *Your Grace.*"

"What of your stable master? Why could he not have stood in as your coachman?"

"We no longer have one of those, either. You really should not speak of things until you are certain you have all the information, and if you cannot, keep your opinion to yourself."

It was the most blistering reprimand he'd ever received, and he loved it. He adored that she spoke her mind. His mother never did so, not directly. A murmur here. A look there. A total withdrawing of her love ever since Thomas had died. He loved that Lilias was so impassioned and not cold. He wanted to kiss her. Instead, he went in for the coup de grâce. "Your mother is shameful to pay so little attention to you and her household that both are in shambles."

Her eyes widened, her lips parted, and she reared back and slapped him. He saw it coming. He could have stopped her, but if it helped her keep her pride, he'd let her slap him a million times over. His cheek stung for it, but the sting made him ridiculously happy.

"My mother," she said, her voice quivering, "is worth a thousand of yours."

He didn't doubt it. He would have said so, but he needed Lilias to finish, to reveal the truth.

"She has spent the past seven years trying desperately to pay off the debts my father left us with. She has gone without, all the while letting us think she was escaping for restorative, luxurious cures to Bath when she was making trips to sell off her jewelry bit by bit to keep the ruffians my father owed from doing us bodily harm. And she had to endure groveling at my selfish uncle's feet to allow us to stay in his houses. So don't you dare talk about my mother. She is amazing. Yes, she may have a bit of a dependency upon laudanum when she is home, but I daresay anyone in her situation would."

"I imagine you are correct," he said quietly, though a black rage had come over him at the thought of unscrupulous men threatening Lilias and her family. And the notion that her uncle, her family, had not wanted to help them, had clearly barely done so, made him want to kill the man, but that would help no one. He kept the rage inside, and in a calm voice, he said, "Your mother sounds as if she has done her best."

"She has," Lilias whispered, looking down at her lap and wringing her hands. "But it is not enough."

He could only imagine with what Lilias had revealed. Her mother selling her jewelry during fake trips to Bath—that was likely so she could sell her jewels without being recognized. Her mother groveling at Lilias's selfish uncle's feet and it not being enough—was the marquess planning on turning them out? He knew the Mayfair home they stayed in was the smaller of the two their family owned in Town. And the Cotswold home? Did the same hold true there?

"Did your family have another country home?"

She frowned. "What?"

"Another country home. Did your family, or rather

does your uncle, currently possess two such homes?"

A distracted nod. "Yes, a much larger one in Shropshire."

"Why did you all not stay at the larger country home?"

"My father preferred the smaller."

Just then, the back door to the club opened, and a tall, wiry man stepped into the shadowy lane. "No loitering in the alley."

"We're coming in," Lilias called.

Nash scowled. She knew nothing about getting into a club such as this. "You cannot just say you're coming in. You have to be given permission."

She offered him a haughty smile, stood, and opened her cloak, letting it drop upon the bench she'd just risen from. He got a full view of the tops of her breasts again, as did the stranger whose mouth dropped open. "Send the man who tends to the carriages," she ordered, and to Nash's astonishment, the man nodded and disappeared.

Lilias grinned down at Nash. "Well," she said, her tone smug, "he did not seem to notice I have no gloves, a hole in my slippers, and a threadbare cloak. Now, if you'll excuse me..."

To his surprise, she stepped down from the gig. He had to lunge for her, and he just barely caught her by the wrist.

She glanced over her shoulder, raising her eyebrows challengingly. "You can come if you want, but don't expect me to wait for you, Nash."

He had mere seconds to find out the most important thing he wanted to know, the one fact that would determine his actions. "Did you tell Owen you love him?"

"What?" She looked utterly perplexed. "Do you... Do you mean when he asked me to wed him?"

"No. Before that. Four years ago in the Cotswolds by

the river. The one where I first met you."

He saw the moment she recalled saying it, and it felt like a blow, though it shouldn't. Everything would move forward just as it should with her and Owen.

"I did say that," she said, her voice so quiet he barely heard her. She turned fully toward him then, her head tilted back. "But I meant as a friend," she added, her voice even lower now as each word dripped misery. "He told you?"

Nash nodded, his chest tightening, the world around him spinning.

"When?"

"Four years ago," Nash replied, feeling a sort of numbness for what he was sure she would say to his next question. "Would you have wed Owen if you had not been caught on the terrace with him?"

She blanched at that, and Nash knew. Good God, he *knew*.

"I—" Her gaze dropped from his, and she shook her head. "Probably not, but who can say for certain. I—That is, my mother and my sister—"

"Need you. They need a savior, and Owen is to be it."

She nodded again, her head rising and her eyes finding his. The tears that shone there made him want to fall at her feet and offer himself if she'd have him. But maybe she wouldn't, and he could never do so anyway.

"You think me horrible?" She sounded small, broken.

"No." His body thrummed with the need to go to her, to embrace her. He had to clutch the edge of the seat he still sat upon until he was sure he could master his basest desire. "I think you are a woman trapped in a man's world."

Before anything else could be said, the back door to the club opened once more, and the tall man from before came out. But this time he was accompanied by another tall but broader, more muscled gentleman with brown hair that was tied back at the nape of his neck. He wore expensively cut clothing as a lord would, but he had the look of one who knew the streets well. It was a hard look, a wary one. He had an air of self-confidence about him that Nash recognized immediately as belonging to someone with authority. This had to be Carrington's partner in the club, Beckford.

The man looked between Nash and Lilias, and then he said, "I had to come out here myself to see what sort of lady could tempt my gatekeeper to break the rules he knows well not to break."

"What rules are those?" Lilias demanded before Nash could speak.

"I'm to meet all ladies that want entrance. I don't want any jealous husbands coming here causing me trouble. But for you—" he winked "—I could make an exception." The man stepped toward her as if to touch her, and Nash stepped in front of her to meet the man head-on.

A slow smile spread over the man's face, but it did not lighten his eyes. "It's like that, is it?" He did not have the cultured tone of one raised by tutors and nannies. He possessed a more guttural speech, as one who had been raised by their own wits on the streets.

"It is," Nash said in an unbending voice, but just in case there was any doubt, he added, "The lady is with me."

"Fine, then," the man replied. "And just who are *you*?"

"He was here last night," the sinewy man answered for him. "At the front entrance. That there is the Duke of Greybourne."

"Of course you were here last night," Lilias scoffed, cutting Nash a glare. "No doubt this is where you met the light-skirt who smeared lip paint across your face."

Nash ignored her for a moment, though he'd not

missed her jealous tone or how dangerously pleased it made him feel. Instead, he focused on the man who'd spoken. "I don't know you. We've not met. So how do you know me?"

"Carrington told me. When you got snippy with him and stormed out, I asked him if he wished me to bring you back. He didn't. He said you were a personal friend, and you were welcome here anytime. Said to give you special treatment should you require it."

"And who are you?" Nash asked of the man he suspected to be Beckford.

"That there is Beckford, the owner of the Orcus Society," the wiry man said, glaring at Nash. "You should know the owner of a club you want to get into."

"Stand down, Bear," Beckford said, then addressed Nash. "You'll have to forgive Bear. He's rather protective when he thinks I'm being disrespected."

"I meant no disrespect," Nash said easily. "I knew your name, of course, but I have never seen you. And I wasn't required to know what you looked like when I was previously given entrance."

Beckford eyed Nash and then Lilias. "You are the only one whose identity is still a mystery." The man's voice was too smooth, and his gaze lingered too long upon Lilias's chest for Nash's liking. He reached down, snatched up the cloak she'd discarded, and set it on her shoulders. She glanced at him in obvious surprise.

"She'll remain a mystery," Nash replied before Lilias could. She elbowed him for his gallant efforts, but he didn't care. She did, he noted with relief, pull the hood of her cloak up. All that concerned him was protecting her. "She's with me. That's all you need to know. Well, that and if she ever comes here without me, do not give her entrance.

That would infuriate Carrington."

A knowing look settled on Beckford's gaze, which was still upon Lilias. "Another Society lady dressed as a courtesan." He shook his head.

"What gave me away?" Lilias demanded.

"Your face is too innocent. And this one—" the man jabbed a finger in Nash's direction "—is too protective."

"Men are not protective of courtesans?" Lilias asked.

"Yes," Beckford replied, "they are, but in a different sort of way. A way that says, 'This is my paid possession.'"

Nash did not like the direction this conversation was going. "Shall we go into the club?"

"And what did Greybourne's way of being protective say to you?" Lilias asked, ignoring Nash.

"How the devil is this man supposed to know?" Nash bit out.

"Oh, I know. I've a keen eye. Your way says this woman is a part of you."

Lilias gasped, and Nash had the urge to punch Beckford in the mouth. "Your vision has turned bad."

Beckford snorted, Bear guffawed, and Lilias was utterly silent beside Nash. He purposely avoided her gaze. Nothing good could come of their eyes meeting now. "We're here in search of someone," Nash said.

Beckford nodded and motioned his hand toward Bear and then Lilias's gig. In a flash, Bear was moving toward the gig and Beckford was waving them inside the club. "You can tell me who you're in search of on the way in. I do have one question, though, and one favor."

Nash did meet Lilias's gaze then, and she looked as surprised as he was.

"What's the question?" Nash asked.

"The lady, Lady....?"

"A," Lilias said. "You can call me Lady A."

Nash raised his eyebrows and tried to convey with a look that she would need to explain this to him later.

"All right, Lady A," Beckford said agreeably, closing the door behind them, which effectively left them in a dark, narrow corridor.

Somewhere in the distance, muted conversations were happening and music was being played. The notes of both floated on the air to Nash. Scents assaulted him as before, too. Scents of burning candles and lamps. Of crackling fires and heavy perfumes. Of the tang of excitement and the sweetness of desire. He moved closer to Lilias, pressing his hand to her back, needing to have contact with her to ensure she was safe. He half expected her to pull away from him, but she leaned into his palm, the curve of her lower spine fitting perfectly there. It made him wonder how they would fit together in other instances. Without clothes.

"Damnation," he muttered, going perfectly hard.

Lilias and Beckford looked at him.

"Stubbed my toe," he lied.

Beckford looked at him skeptically but asked, "Are all rooms open to Lady A?"

As Beckford wound them down the dark, stuffy hall and passed an oil lamp that had been fashioned into the wall, the momentary pop of light highlighted Lilias's expression and showed her to be scowling at Beckford's back. Nash stifled the desire to laugh.

"Why are you asking him?" Lilias asked, sounding incensed. "I am right here, and the question is about me, so you should address it to me."

"Very well," the man said. "Do you wish to enter the pleasure rooms or avoid them?"

"She'll avoid them," Nash said quickly.

"I most certainly will not," Lilias objected. "If they are good enough for you to go into and meet your lady bird, then I'll enter as well."

"I did not meet my lady bird there," he ground out.

"So you admit you have one?"

"No," he snapped. Only Lilias had the power to confound him. "Lady A will not be entering any pleasure rooms. And if Lady A argues about it, Lady A will find herself hoisted over my shoulder, carried out of here, and taken immediately home. Does Lady A understand?"

"You're a brute," Lilias said. "But fine. I'll not enter a pleasure room unless it's necessary. Now that the matter is settled, what is your favor, Lord Beckford?"

"It's just Beckford," he said, coming to the end of the passage and opening the large double door the led into the club.

Sound and light exploded from the room. There was laughter and chatter, the notes of violins, and a pianoforte. There were glittering chandeliers and cheroot smoke swirling in the air. The rattle of dice being cast and the cheers and cries of those who'd just won fortunes and those who'd lost them. It all rushed at them at once on a roll of cool air.

Lilias shivered and pressed closer to Nash, and then she said in a voice full of awe, "This is better than any novel."

## Chapter Nine

She was certain she sounded naive, but she was also certain that she did not care. This moment, here with Nash, seeing this club that Owen would never allow her to enter, was a moment she would never forget. Nor would she forget how protective Nash was being, as if she were a part of him. Wasn't that what Beckford had said?

The words of the club owner made her remember he hadn't answered her about the favor he needed. She firmly believed in returning favors, and she suspected he'd only allowed her entrance as a favor to Carrington since Nash and Carrington were personal friends and Carrington was part owner of this club.

No one knew Carrington was an investor, of course. He was a duke, and dukes were not supposed to do things like own gaming clubs, but Guinevere's husband was his own man, born and raised in Scotland. He hadn't even known he was part of the *ton* until he was in his twenties; he had thought himself a bastard until then. He had raised himself from poverty, started a successful distillery business in Scotland, and then invested in this club. Guinevere had told her in secret, and her friend's voice had been full of pride, as well it should be. Carrington made his own choices and did not allow the *ton*, or anyone else, to dictate how he lived his life. A man like that, one who would tolerate her excursions with SLAR, would be much better suited as a husband for her than Owen. She'd always thought Nash was such a man.

She glanced at Beckford, intending to ask him what favor he needed, but the magnificence of the room captured her attention. Three glittering chandeliers cast shards of light from where they hung from an elaborate ceiling high above. The light seemed to slide into spaces in the room, which was somehow large, yet cozy. She supposed it was the thick rugs on the gleaming floors, the crackling dual fireplaces, and the plush red velvet curtains hanging from the windows that gave the room such a welcoming feeling. She wanted to go over to one of the oversized chairs by the fireplaces and order a drink. It was a scandalous and thrilling thought.

Or perhaps she would recline on one of the comfortable-looking red-and-gold settees that were positioned under the windows. Or maybe she would gamble. She could, if she knew how, which she didn't. After all, there were half a dozen large, circular gaming tables in the room with green baize tablecloths and places for ten men at each table. A man in black livery stood at the head of each table, looking very stoic. She supposed he was in charge of the cards or the dice, depending upon the game.

She scanned the room and counted six doors. She looked at Beckford. "Is this the gaming room?"

"Yes. This is the main one where most people play."

"There's another?"

"Yes. Do you see the door by the pianoforte?"

She nodded, immediately finding the door.

"There is a smaller gaming room in there that has only one table. It is a high-stakes table, and only those who can stake one hundred pounds can enter."

Her eyes widened. "One hundred pounds! That's a

fortune!"

"Yes," he said, smiling, and she noticed he had the most unusual blue eyes, the color the lightest blue she had ever seen. But no, she had seen that blue before, she thought as she stared at him. She just could not remember where, but something tugged at the back of her mind. "About my favor..."

"Yes," she said, blinking.

He withdrew a necklace from his coat and held it out to her. "This belongs to Lady Frederica. I believe she is a fellow SLAR member."

"Did Carrington tell you that?" Lilias demanded, already prepared to lecture Guinevere's husband, who seemed to be blabbing all about Town about their secret society.

"No, Lady Frederica did. But don't be vexed with her. She was quite unaware of what she was saying. It was after she'd been hit from behind and her carriage was stolen," Beckford said. "I actually carried her to the house where you picked her up. I'm the one who sent Davy to you. Freddy—I mean, Lady Frederica gave me your address. When you came for her, I was just in the other room."

Lilias smiled. "You hid in the other room to protect Frederica's reputation."

"I would not use the word *hid*," Beckford said, frowning. "I intentionally withdrew myself."

She bit her tongue on teasing him.

"Why the devil did you act like you didn't know who she was when we met you, then?" Nash demanded, his arm coming around Lilias's waist. He drew her to him and stepped a tad in front of her. Lilias's heart galloped at the protective gesture.

"I wanted to see what the two of you would say. If you'd be truthful. Just because Carrington tells me to trust someone doesn't mean I automatically do, *Greybourne*. They, woman or man, need to prove themselves worthy."

Nash grunted, but Lilias nodded her agreement to the sensible statement. "I take it you deem us honest?"

"For now," Beckford said with a smile. "But the night is young... Lady A," he went on, though she knew now he knew exactly who she was, "will you give Lady Frederica her locket for me, please?"

"I will, but if you know where Frederica lives, why do you not return it to her yourself?"

"There is your world," he said slowly, "and then there is mine. The two worlds do not normally mix except at night and on very special occasions, like when a friend from your world has a foot in both worlds, but that's rare."

"Like Carrington?" Lilias asked.

"Yes. Now, enough about me... Why are the two of you here?"

"I'm here to retrieve something from one of your members, Mr. Levine. I have it on good authority that he's here tonight."

"Whose authority?"

"That of his sister, Mrs. Porter."

"Ahh, Mrs. Porter." Beckford drew the out the words, and Lilias understood immediately that he knew Helen was a courtesan by trade. Did he know she was not even really Mrs. Helen Porter, the supposed widow, but really Miss Helen Levine, the unwed courtesan? Lilias understood why Miss Levine went by Mrs. Porter and pretended to be a widow. It was easier for widows to go about as they pleased, and people asked fewer questions of her that way than they would as the unwed Miss Levine.

"Mr. Levine is in the Gold Room. Careful with him, though. I get the sense that he can be dangerous. There is something about him. He always seems on edge, and more so lately."

Lilias frowned. "Then why do you permit him to enter?"

"My dear, if I turned away every gentleman I thought dangerous, I'd lose a fortune. The key is to watch them and swoop in if need be."

She nodded and swept her gaze around the main room, her attention coming to rest on a gold door. "The Gold Room, I presume?" she asked, pointing.

"Yes, so named because it brings me much gold. That is the *vingt-et-un* room. He's in there playing. Do either of you play? The rule is that you can only enter if playing or if you are a mistress of a man playing, as the women seem to have a calming effect on the men."

"I play," Nash said.

"Excellent," Beckford replied. "You can enter. And you"—he looked to her—"can play the part of his courtesan. I assume you wish your identity to remain secret?"

"Yes," she said, the word coming out breathless at the thought of playing Nash's mistress.

"Then play your part. The better you are at it, the less likely it will be that questions are asked."

"Who's within the room?" Nash asked. When she looked at him questioningly, he said, "I want to ensure no one you know is in there to give away who you are."

Beckford listed six men, none of whom she knew. Nash nodded, satisfied. "Keep your cloak pulled up around your face until we are in the room and the door is shut."

"If you need me," Beckford said, "ask my sister for me. She'll be the one who comes in to let the dealer know when any new players are to enter the Gold Room. That way, if someone is entering who might recognize you, you can put your cloak back on and depart immediately."

She nodded, a thrill of excitement going through her. This was the sort of adventure she loved, the sort that would be lost to her as soon as she became Owen's wife.

The Gold Room certainly lived up to its name. Everything in it glittered and was lushly opulent, from the gold velvet curtains, to the luxurious gold rug, to the gold plush chairs the players sat upon. There were six men in the room and one man who appeared to be in charge of the game, and every one of them paused to look at Nash and Lilias as they entered.

Nash grabbed her hand and pulled her close behind him, and the simple protective gesture caused a thrill that made her heart speed up and her stomach flutter. It was a reaction she could not stop.

"You'll have to wait for this hand to be over," the man who appeared in charge said, addressing Nash.

It irked her somewhat that most men rarely seemed to think a woman would be capable or interested in pursuits that men assumed required their "superior intelligence," such as cards, but she held her tongue. A mistress would never state such an opinion in public, and for now, she was Nash's mistress.

Nash helped her out of her cloak, and she felt the eyes of the men on her. Though she'd dressed the part of a paramour intentionally, the lecherous attention made her uncomfortable, so when a man dressed in gold livery approached them and asked if they'd like a drink, she said yes. She'd never imbibed before, but she'd heard talk of spirits having a calming effect.

"What will the lady have?" the footman asked Nash, which snapped her temper in two.

"The lady," she said, locking gazes with the surprised

footman, "will have—" What would she have? The only spirit she ever had was ratafia, and she highly doubted they had that here. "The lady will have her usual," she finished, her face burning. She prayed the footman had no notion if she was a regular or not.

The game of *vingt-et-un* had resumed, so thankfully, no one at the table was paying them any mind.

When the footman stood there with a confused look on his face, Nash slid his arm over the back of Lilias's chair and said, "Do not tell me you have forgotten my lady."

*His lady.* If it was possible for a heart to lurch out of one's chest, hers just did.

*This is not real. We are not a couple.*

"She is unforgettable," Nash continued, and he sounded so believable that she found warmth flowing through her, followed swiftly by a piercing ache.

"Yes, my lord," the footman rushed to say, to which Nash hitched an eyebrow. "I mean, yes, my lord," the footman hastened to correct, "she's unforgettable."

Nash nodded, playing the part of a stuffy aristocrat perfectly, especially when he said, "But you have forgotten me, apparently."

"My lord?" the poor footman squeaked. He looked to be no more than twenty years of age, and his ears had turned red.

Suddenly, a blond-haired man seated facing them said, "His Grace, you fool. You are addressing a duke. He is not 'my lord.' He is 'Your Grace.'"

The men at the table all stood, and Lilias realized the hand was over. The head man was gathering the cards, and all the players exited. The door shut, and the footman stammered, "I'm sorry, Your G-Grace."

"No harm has been done," Nash replied to the footman,

his voice taking on an understanding edge, but his gaze upon the man who'd spoken was hard. "Do we know each other?"

Bushy eyebrows arched over dark-brown eyes. "I'm surprised you don't remember me, Your Grace." But the man did not sound surprised, not truly. "My stepfather was hired by your father to teach your brother Latin when he failed to master it. I would know you anywhere, though we never formally met. When I came to your home with my stepfather, you were out each day, hunting, riding, doing all manner of physical things your frail, ailing brother could not."

Nash stiffened beside Lilias, and she squeezed his hand, offering silent support. The man smiled, but his eyes held no warmth. In fact, they chilled Lilias. He flicked his gaze to the table, then back to Nash. "You look exactly like your brother. Twins, weren't you?"

*Twins?* Nash had never said they were twins. He'd only ever called him his *younger* brother.

"We were," Nash replied, his voice devoid of emotion but his hand was now gripping hers so hard that her fingers throbbed. But looking at him and the way he was focused intently on the gentleman speaking to him, she doubted that Nash was even aware of the reaction the man was eliciting in him. "I'm sorry, but what did you say your name was?"

"Mr. Levine, but you were far more interested in my sister, Helen. She's Mrs. Helen Porter now. She's widowed."

Lilias froze in shock. Did Nash have a past with Helen Levine? Mr. Levine was smiling so knowingly at Nash that Lilias knew it had to be so.

Nash's brows dipped into a confused expression. "Does

your sister have flaming-red hair?"

The man nodded, and a slow, tauntingly smug smile tugged his lips upward. "As I said, you were more interested in her than in me the few days Helen and I came with my stepfather to your home. My stepfather was Jacob Pickering. Do you recall him?"

"Of course," Nash said stiffly. "But why do you and your sister go by different surnames than your stepfather now?"

"We always went by Levine. You just never bothered to inquire."

Lilias felt Nash flinch at the man's tone of disgust.

Mr. Levine drummed his fingers on the table as he stared at Nash. "Helen and I were from my mother's first marriage, and my stepfather did not ever deem us worthy to give us his surname."

"Oh, that's horrible!" Lilias blurted out, bringing the man's attention fully to her.

The footman still in the room discreetly turned his back, and Lilias understood the man had been trained to act as if he heard nothing and saw nothing the patrons of the club said or did. This was likely the best opportunity she would get to persuade Mr. Levine to give her Helen's manuscript. She untangled her hand from Nash's while keeping her gaze on Mr. Levine.

"I actually came here tonight to find you," she blurted, then rose from her seat next to Nash and took a seat at the table across from Mr. Levine.

By Nash's loud grunt behind her, she gathered he did not approve of the way she was choosing to handle the situation, but she pressed on. The night would not last forever, and she had to be on her way home before the sky lightened and her family woke.

Mr. Levine offered her a lascivious look as he leaned forward in his seat and traced a finger over her forearm. She forced herself not to draw away as he said, "That, my dear, is the best news I've heard all night."

She started when Nash sat beside her, not having heard him move, but she was glad. His presence was comforting, and she knew he would not let anything happen to her. And if she had questioned it at all, the intensity of his tone when he spoke next would have banished any doubt. He leaned his elbow on the table. "If you touch my lady again, I will break your hand."

Mr. Levine withdrew the offending appendage, an irritated look upon his face. "Ladies such as this one"—Mr. Levine waved a hand in her direction—"go where their desires and the coin take them. If she's looking for me…" He shrugged, letting his words trail off, but the implications were obvious enough.

"She needs something from you," Nash said, each word punctuated with his obvious distaste for the man.

Lilias didn't like Mr. Levine, either, and was particularly offended for all courtesans that they had to put up with such treatment from men. She doubted a single woman ever had dreamed of becoming a courtesan. Circumstances forced these women into their profession—no training, little choices, precious little freedom, and the desperate need to survive. And men were the main culprits of women's terrible plights, and those same men dared to look down upon women when they did what they must to survive. His own sister was a courtesan, for heaven's sake! Did he look down upon her?

Mr. Levine regarded her, and she had to bite the inside of her cheek in order not to say everything she was thinking. "What is it you wish from me, Mrs.….?"

"Artemis," she said, thinking it rather ironic, given the role she played tonight, but also appropriate to call herself by the name of the Greek goddess of the hunt. Lilias was chaste, though her thoughts were not, and she was on a hunt—for a manuscript. She didn't particularly care in this moment what Mr. Levine thought, though she highly suspected him perverse enough to like it.

Nash began to cough beside her, and Mr. Levine's eyebrows shot up in surprise and then a dark, unsettling smile settled on his face. "Interesting surname," he replied, his eyes undressing her suddenly.

She bridled, but managed to get out, "I am an interesting woman."

"I can imagine—"

"Don't," Nash interrupted, his tone ruthless. "Do not imagine. She's mine."

It shouldn't have made her heart flutter—it was an act, after all—but it did.

The man shrugged. "For now."

"Forever," Nash shot back.

"Gentlemen," Lilias interrupted, almost wishing she did not have to. It was like listening to her secret fantasy come true, except it wasn't true and never could be. She suspected what was actually occurring was what often occurred with men. They were trying to show their superiority over each other. "I'm flattered, but as His Grace has said, I'm his, and I'm quite happy with the arrangement." Saying the words made her heart suddenly hurt, and she had an overwhelming urge to flee. She no longer wanted to play this game with Nash. It had gone from fun to torturous in a breath. But she stayed in her seat, determined to help Helen and Lady Katherine.

"I'm here on behalf of your sister." She purposely left

out that she was also there on behalf of Lady Katherine. She certainly didn't need to mention that Lady Katherine had been lovers with Lord Quattelbom, who had failed to pay Helen the promised allowance that had resulted in Helen writing the manuscript in the first place. Lilias did not think any of the details would soften the man to their cause. By his demeanor thus far and his hostile interaction with Nash, Lilias actually suspected that it would only make the man more determined to publish the manuscript. He seemed to despise Nash for having been brought up in privilege, so it stood to reason that he despised all lords of privilege.

The man's brows dipped into a deep V. "My sister? What of her?"

"She sent me to implore you to return the manuscript she wrote." When irritation swept across his face and he opened his mouth to argue, she hurried to finish. "You know she has changed her mind. It is not your manuscript to see published."

"I gave her the money to stay in her home, and she gave me the manuscript as payment."

"Yes," Lilias said angrily, "and you ought to be ashamed. She's your sister. You should have helped her without requiring payment."

"And just who are you to stand as savior to *my sister*? I've never even seen you before."

"It's none of your damn business who she is," Nash bit out.

She put a staying hand on his arm, appreciating his wish to protect her, but antagonizing Mr. Levine would not help matters. And Mr. Levine and Nash obviously had a past, which she had many questions about, none of which she thought Nash would answer. He was a man of many layers, and she'd never even truly peeled back the first. She had not even known he was a twin.

"Tell me, Greybourne, why are you here accompanying your courtesan on a mission for my sister?"

"That's also none of your business," Nash growled.

"I wonder," Mr. Levine said, drumming his fingers on the table once more, "do you regret dismissing Helen from your life as if she never meant anything to you?"

Lilias's breath caught at Mr. Levine's words, which reminded her uncomfortably of what Nash had done to her.

"I regret that I allowed what happened to happen, given I did not care for your sister. If she felt mistreated, for that, I am sorry."

"I doubt it," Mr. Levine said, rising suddenly. "You're like all men of your ilk. You leave disaster in your path without a thought to who you have ruined."

"Wait, Mr. Levine!" Lilias scrambled to her feet as the man began to leave. "Many people will be gravely hurt if you see that manuscript published!"

He turned toward her, a mocking look upon his face. "You refer to people of the *ton*, I presume?"

She nodded. There was no point in lying. He'd most assuredly read the manuscript, and each chapter was about a man of the *ton* who had wronged his sister. "Those men deserve the chapters your sister gave them. I'm not denying that," Lilias said. "But some of those men are connected to women in these chapters, women who have committed no larger crime than falling in love and making a mistake. Do they deserve to have their lives ruined as your sister's was?"

He made a derisive sound. "I assure you, there are no innocents in this book."

"I'll pay you for it!" she blurted, though she had no notion where she would get the money.

His brows arched with obvious surprise. "I doubt a

woman in your position has the money to buy back this manuscript from me."

"Then I'll buy it from you," Nash said, surprising her and rising to stand beside her. Conflicting emotions washed over her. Why would he do that for her? He didn't care about her. He'd dismissed her just as he'd apparently dismissed Helen.

"It's not about the money, *Greybourne*," Mr. Levine said condescendingly. "If that's what Helen told you, she's wrong. It's about revenge. It's about striking Kilgore in his heart."

*Kilgore!* Lilias just barely contained her gasp. Of course, the manuscript would have a chapter on the most notorious rogue she had ever known, the Marquess of Kilgore! He'd been in the middle of quite a few problems the last five years.

Before she could consider the newly revealed information any more, Mr. Levine flung open the door, and just as he did, Lilias felt her cloak fall onto her shoulders. She glanced at Nash. His face was tense. "Pull up your hood," he said.

When she apparently didn't move fast enough to suit him, he started to yank the hood up for her, and his fingers grazed her cheek. Her body reacted instantly to his touch, the pull to him more than she could bear.

"Stop it," she hissed, brushing his hand away from her. "Do not touch me!" And before she said anything she would later regret, she took the lead from Mr. Levine and dashed out of the door and straight into Beckford, who'd been passing by.

"Done already?"

She nodded. "Did Mr. Levine leave?"

"I believe so. Did you not get what you wanted?"

She could feel Nash standing behind her, so close his heat warmed her back. "No," she said, swallowing. "I did not. But I'll find a way. I'd like to go home now. Would you call up my gig?"

"Of course," Beckford replied. "Do you know the way out?"

"I know it," Nash replied before she could.

With a nod, Beckford left them standing there, and Lilias had no choice but to follow Nash. He crossed the luxurious room they had come through before, which seemed less crowded, hinting that the night was winding down. But the men that were there gave her curious looks so she pulled her cloak tighter about her face. She let out a relieved breath when Nash went through a plain black door. Once they were in the passage, darkness descended except for the faint glow of the oil lanterns that stood every few feet.

Nash's heavy footsteps mingled with her lighter ones in the silence, and she was glad he was not speaking. Her thoughts and emotions were a jumble, and it was all because of Nash. She knew she should fully accept that he had never cared about her, and she could, she really thought she could. She most definitely knew she *should* and that she should forget him. She vowed to herself that she would.

Her stomach ached while she followed him through the dark shadows. She stared at his broad shoulders and slim hips as he walked with a long, sure, commanding stride. In all her interactions with him, he had always been a man whose actions supported his words—except with her in their last interaction seven years ago and now their recent ones. In particular, her mind latched on to each of his actions that contradicted his claim that he did not care for her, and she turned them over one by one, examining them.

His distraught state over her wardrobe had been surprising, and the way he'd carried on about no one keeping watch over her had astounded her, as well. Of course, he'd said he only cared that she did as she pleased for Owen's sake. Yet, the passionate way in which he seemed to care hinted otherwise. He'd acted extremely possessive in the club, too, and granted, it could simply be an act, but if it was, he could have had a career at Drury Lane.

What if he *did* care?

Her step faltered at the possibility. What if he had been running from something in his past, something he had not told her, something he was afraid to tell her? Was it something to do with his brother? Or Helen? Or both of them? Her heart began to pound harder, and when he glanced over his shoulder at her, she forced herself to keep moving. He turned around and continued, and her pulse quickened even more as she followed him, this man whom she had long loved, whom she was unsure how to quit loving, who was lost to her.

This needed to be the last time she allowed herself to be alone with him, she realized with blinding, painful clarity. Every part of her wanted him to take her in his arms and kiss her senseless, and she was afraid if he ever did such a thing, she would not be able to resist. She would betray Owen, and she could not live with that.

With each step, a war raged inside her. Should she confront Nash and ask him bluntly how he felt about her, or should she keep her silence and never know? Her emotions roiled so greatly within her that she had to take deep breaths to calm herself. By the time they reached the exit door and Nash opened it, she decided she could not bear to discover he cared. It was better to think he had not. Her nostrils flared with her resolve, and she steeled herself to simply keep her silence and let all the questions raging in her remain unanswered.

Her gig would be along any moment, and then he would drive her home and that would be the end. She could do it. She could contain herself. But then he turned to her, moonlight struck his face, and her breath hitched at the concern that was etched there.

His hands gripped her upper arms before she knew what was occurring. "Vow to me now that you'll not pursue Mr. Levine without me." It was a demand and a desperate plea at once. "I don't trust him, and I cannot abide thinking you might stride right into danger."

Each of his emotion-filled words weakened her resolve not to ask him, like stones thrown against fragile glass, and her determination shattered. Her blood roared in her ears, and she swallowed. She was facing a life of heartache with or without the truth, so she'd take the truth.

"Why?" she asked. "Why do you care so much if I'm protected?"

When he simply stared at her, she wanted to scream. "What concern am I of yours?" she tried again. Still, he stood in silence, gripping her as if he was afraid she'd disappear if he let go. It was that grip, his holding her as if his life depended on it, that made her say what she did next.

"I'll give you my vow not to pursue Mr. Levine alone *if* you tell me the truth about how you feel." She did not add *about me*. She did not feel she had to. He would know. If he cared for her as she did for him, he would know exactly what she meant.

He released her as if merely touching her scalded him, and he shoved both hands through his hair. Then he took a long, shuddering breath and let it out slowly. The breeze suddenly picked up, and in the distance, the night watchman's whistle shrieked.

"You were wearing green." Nash's voice fell low and intense. Her brow dipped into a furrow, and he offered an achingly gentle smile that made her warm despite the cool night air. "The day I met you," he said by way of explanation. "You were wearing green."

"You remember what I was wearing?" she asked, shocked.

"I remember every single thing about you. I remember details no self-respecting rogue should admit to recalling." He looked down at her worn slippers and laughed. "You were barefoot. I knew right away you were different from any girl I'd ever met. Your hair was unbound and wild, much like now." His gaze had come to her face, and it clung to her in an appreciative way that caused her toes to curl in her slippers.

She brought a self-conscious hand to her hair to try to tidy it, but he caught her fingertips and held them for just a moment, but even after he let go, the heat of his body lingered on hers.

"Don't," he said, the single word husky. "I love your hair. I love the way you wear it. I've dreamed about it, and—"

He choked off the sentence, and she wanted to fall at his feet and beg him to continue, to touch her hair, to touch her. Dear God, perhaps knowing *was* worse than not knowing. But she could not, she would not, stop him now.

His gaze softened, as if he was thinking back to something that made him happy. "You used to hum when it was silent, and I felt so terrible for you because I concluded that silence scared you. Yet, I was so in awe of your ability to face what scared you. Such a slip of a thing you are, but your force of will is greater than any man's I've ever known."

What he was revealing started a trembling in her that she could not control, so she wrapped her arms around her waist and waited.

"The way you laughed, the way you still do—so infectious. It made me once think that I might catch some of your joy just by being near you."

"And did you?" She could not keep quiet.

His mouth curved with tenderness. "God, yes. But happiness is damned slippery for someone like me."

Tears sprang to her eyes to hear him say that, and she tried to stop them but they blurred her vision and rolled down her cheeks. He reached out and brushed his fingers across her left cheek before pulling back. "I remember how warm your tears are, from when you cried that day by the river. Do you remember that? When you told me of your father?"

She nodded, then sniffed and brushed at her tears. This was her opportunity to ask him about his brother. "You told me you betrayed your brother."

"Yes." The word seemed to catch in his throat.

"Why didn't you tell me he was your twin?"

He shrugged. "It didn't seem important. I was born first—the eldest, *the heir.*" He said the last so derisively she knew instantly that he hated being the heir. He inhaled a long breath, seemed to hold it, and then released it very slowly. "Thomas, my brother, used to say that I was the heir and he was the frail, unneeded spare. My parents would scold him and act horrified in the moment, but do you know, their actions hardly ever matched what they said." She remained silent, almost certain he just needed to tell her, tell someone, and she did not want to interrupt that. "They treated him as if he could do nothing. They forced him to stay indoors almost always, as if they were afraid if he went outside he'd die, as if they were afraid that danger awaited him out in the world. I suppose, ultimately, they were correct."

Nash had threaded his fingers together, and she longed to grab his hands and take them in hers, to help him conquer his pain. But if she did that, she feared she would not be able to make herself ever let go.

"They said to him, 'You're strong, don't be ridiculous, you are not just the feeble spare,' but every action they took, every action they demanded I take to protect him, to put him first, to let him win at everything, always said to him that they believed him to be weak, that they believed him in need of their hovering, coddling, and constant protection. He hated it, I hated it, and sometimes—" his gaze became pleading, as if he was asking her to forgive him "—I hated him."

"Oh, Nash." Her throat tightened mercilessly for the pain she could see he was in. "That is normal. I cannot tell you how many times I have wished my sister, Nora, ill for threatening to tell on me, for being a pest, for blackmailing me."

Nash shook his head. "It's not the same. You've never failed to protect your sister. I got tired of letting Thomas win, so one day I simply didn't. Helen—" He swallowed, and Lilias's heart stopped. There was a connection there, after all. "Helen came to our home for a sennight with her father, like Mr. Levine said. Thomas was instantly enamored of her, but she had her sights set on me—the heir. I knew it, too, so when she kissed me on the ice, I kissed her back. Thomas saw it, charged me, and, well, you know the rest... I told you I'm not good."

She wanted to weep for the weight of the guilt he carried. "That was one moment of selfishness, Nash. That does not make you bad."

"No." The word was harsh, a total and utter denial. "I almost did it again with you, to Owen. I suspected he liked you. I tried to help him win you." He swiped his hands over his face, stayed that way for a moment, as if he could not stand to continue, and then he dropped his arms to his sides. The look of raw pain in his expression made her suck in a sharp breath. "I don't know if I was really unsure of how he felt or if I convinced myself I was unsure because I wanted you so damn much. That day, that day in the woods when I said you made me feel, what I was trying to say was that you made me feel alive. When I was with you, you made me feel again. Before that, I had barely felt anything since Thomas's death. But when I kissed you, I felt alive. I felt hopeful."

The revelation was everything she had ever longed for, dreamed of, and it hurt desperately. A sob escaped her, and as it did, Bear pulled onto the lane, driving her gig toward them. It was the worst and most perfect timing of her life. Because she knew, she absolutely knew, that if they had been alone for one more breath, she would have flung herself into his arms and kissed him. She would have betrayed Owen and her promise to him. She had one thing she needed to say, though, before Bear was upon them, before this moment was gone forever.

"I have loved you every day since the moment I met you," she said through the tears that were now streaming down her face. "And when you came back, I had hoped... Well, I went there hoping... But now—"

She didn't know what to say. She was betrothed to Owen, but she wanted to tell Nash she'd break it off. What sort of person did that make her if she did that? What sort of person was she to even think about such a horrid betrayal? And even if she did end her betrothal, would Nash court her? She feared his honor and his guilt would prevent it. She needed time to sort out her head.

"Nash, I—"

"Don't say it." He pressed one searing finger to her lips. "Whatever you were going to say, don't. I told you I wasn't good."

"Your brother's death was not your fault."

"It's not just that, Lilias. God, it's not, but that's enough. Listen to me." He pulled her close, buried his head in her neck, and inhaled long and deep. Before she could lock her hands behind his back, he pushed her away gently, and through her tears, she saw that Bear had pulled up with the gig, silent and waiting. Nash stared at her as if they were still alone. "I'm a selfish bastard, Lilias. I told you this because I have to let you go. You've haunted me like a ghost, and I need to let go. So promise me, swear to me, you won't go on any more missions alone. I thought I could accompany you until Owen returns, but I can't."

"I swear it," she choked out.

He nodded, then turned to Bear. "Can you see Lady Lilias home, please?"

She wanted to protest, to steal more time with him, but she knew this was best for both of them. So when Bear nodded, she didn't argue. Nash stepped toward her, took her right hand in his, and brought it to his lips. His gaze met hers, and the heart-rending tenderness in his eyes was everything she had dreamed of, everything she had ever wanted, but it was too late. It was too late for them. Her pulse pounded, and her heart jolted as he brushed the softest kiss to the top of her hand. His touch sent gooseflesh over her body, and when he turned her palm over and kissed the inside of her wrist, she could not stop her moan of need. Their gazes met, clinging as he released her hand. Heat smoldered in his eyes, along with need and finality. Devastation swept over her, and she began to tremble.

Bear was there suddenly, taking her by the elbow and helping her into the gig, and when she turned to look at Nash, he was gone. She had no notion if he'd returned to the club or simply disappeared into the shadows, but he was gone. Gone from sight. Gone from her life, possibly forever. But he was lodged in her heart, desperately deep and permanent. She was his in the furthest reaches. Each beat was his. Each thought was his. She did not see how she could wed Owen knowing such a thing, but she did not see how she could do anything else.

# Chapter Ten

*A* knock came at Lilias's bedchamber door, but she did not respond, nor did she move from under her covers where she had been hiding, almost exclusively, for three days. She'd only come out to see to her most urgent needs of survival; to read a note sent to her by Helen in which Helen mentioned that the publisher was, thankfully, in the country for the remainder of the month so they had some time to obtain the manuscript; and lastly, to send the news in a letter to Frederica, along with Frederica's locket and Lilias's assurances that she would call upon Frederica in the next several days so they could discuss how to retrieve the manuscript from Mr. Levine.

When another knock came, Lilias called out, "Please go away," and then she simply pulled the coverlet closer over her head, prepared to allow the same torturous thoughts about Nash that had infiltrated her mind continuously for days to do so once more. And they did—immediately. What had Nash meant when he'd said that he'd tried to help Owen win her? And when he'd said he'd almost done *it* again to Owen? Had he meant he'd almost pursued her in spite of knowing Owen liked her?

When her door banged open, she flinched and curled into a tight ball, but a throat clearing loudly and very near her compelled her to respond.

"I still have a megrim, Mama," Lilias mumbled, certain

it had to be her mother checking upon her *again*. She'd been in several times a day for three days. Lilias knew her mother was worried, but if she admitted just how much she did not want to wed Owen, her mother would be even more concerned and possibly take to her own bed.

"It is not your mama."

The coverlet was yanked from her head, and Lilias blinked, finding Guinevere standing over her, a worried look upon her face.

Behind Guinevere, Nora hovered with a rapt expression. "Nora, not now. Please," Lilias begged. For once, her sister listened and quietly left the room, shutting the door behind her.

Lilias dragged herself into a sitting position and met her friend's concerned gaze as Guinevere sat on the edge of Lilias's bed. "What are you doing here?"

"For one thing, you missed a SLAR meeting this afternoon, and you have never missed a meeting. For another," Guinevere continued, not giving Lilias time to offer an excuse, which was just as well because Lilias did not want to lie to her friend, "Greybourne came to the house today to speak with Asher, and he looked dreadful. As if he'd lost the person who meant the most to him in the world."

That got Lilias's full attention. Just the mention of Nash's name made her heart twist in her chest. She sat all the way up, her heart now pounding. "Go on," she said, knowing Guinevere well enough to understand she had a point she had just not gotten to yet.

Guinevere studied Lilias for a moment, her look going from one of concern to what Lilias considered scheming.

*She knows. Guinevere knows I'm still hopelessly in love with Nash. Please don't let her ask me. Please don't let her ask me. If she asks me, I might break down and pour my heart out.*

"He looked as if he had not slept in days. I admit to being intrigued with what would be keeping a rogue such as Greybourne awake, and do you know, I do believe he's in love!"

Lilias thought she might swoon. The room seemed to be spinning as Guinevere continued. "Isn't it funny that you both found love. You with Owen and Greybourne with some mystery woman, whom I heard him refer to as *Lady L.*" Guinevere eyed her silently, expectantly.

Lilias swallowed, but her mouth was so very dry, as were her eyes. Crying for three straight days would do that, she supposed. She wanted to tell her best friend everything, but how did one confess they were in love with one man and betrothed to another? How did one confess that their character was so weak that they'd been contemplating for three straight days just how horrid it would be to break off her engagement and had barely managed to push the selfish thought away each time? Because even if she did break off her betrothal, she could not guarantee that Nash would be as dishonorable as she was, and if he would not have her, that left her mother and sister—and her, though she hardly cared about that—near homeless and poverty stricken. Never mind that she would hurt Owen and he would hate her.

"Isn't that terribly funny?" Guinevere persisted, looking wide-eyed and innocent.

"It's hilarious," Lilias choked out.

"I also find it funny that you have not come to see me once to tell me personally of your betrothal to Owen. I had to read it in the scandal sheet."

"I…I have been busy."

Guinevere's eyebrows arched high. "Too busy to share the happy news with your best friend that you are marrying the man you now love?"

Guinevere had not said outright that Lilias was a liar, but her tone and expression implied it. And of course Guinevere knew! She was her best friend!

"I happened to overhear Greybourne tell Asher that this woman, Lady L—" Guinevere paused "—was in desperate need, and he would do anything in his power to aid her. He was there to ask Asher to help him with some task, I think in regard to her, but I could not hear what."

Lilias swallowed. Nash likely wanted Carrington to ensure she did not go on any missions alone as she had promised him. She wondered if she'd look out her window tonight to find Greybourne or someone he'd hired guarding her from below.

Guinevere looked contemplative for a moment. "Maybe he loves this Lady L and he doesn't think she'll have him."

"Did he say that?" Lilias asked miserably. "Did he say he loved me?" She no longer cared. Tears filled her eyes and slipped down her cheeks.

"Oh, dearest," Guinevere murmured, then scooted forward and pulled Lilias into a hug. "He didn't have to say the words. It's painted on his face with the dark smudges under his eyes, the dark stubble, and the mussed hair. It's in the wrinkled clothing he's wearing, as if he cannot even be bothered to change. And it's in his words, which sound filled with agony... Will you not tell me what is happening? Will you not let me try to help?"

Lilias pulled back and swiped at her tears. "You cannot help," she whispered. And then she told Guinevere of the manuscript, Mr. Levine, the trip to the Orcus Society, and of her and Nash and all they had said to each other.

Guinevere shook her head slowly, smugly. "I knew that man loved you the moment I saw him at my ball!"

Lilias smiled weakly at her friend. Guinevere did so love to be right.

"Even if it's true, it doesn't matter. I'm betrothed to Owen. I gave my word, and even if I had not, I must wed him. I cannot risk my mother's and my sister's futures to follow my heart when I do not even know if Nash would follow his."

"I surmised that, too," Guinevere pronounced, then gave Lilias a pat on the hand and a squeeze. "You are wedding because of finances, aren't you?"

Lilias nodded and then quickly told Guinevere all Lilias had learned about her mother's trips to Bath and the true state of her family's situation. "I must wed Owen," Lilias said, hating herself for even saying such a thing. "And I do not believe Nash would, in fact, make me his wife, even if I were no longer betrothed. There are things in his past that make him feel guilty, make him feel as if being with me would be a betrayal to Owen, and I don't think he could live with that."

"Tell me. Perhaps I can help?"

"You can't change his mind, Guinevere."

Guinevere smiled. "Perhaps Asher could?"

"I don't think so. It's a matter of honor, and I do believe penance. Anyway—" she plucked at a loose thread on her coverlet "—I would not want Nash to ever think I betrayed his confidence by telling you his secrets, and then you, in turn, telling your husband."

"Fine," Guinevere replied. "Let us forget Nash for a moment. Let us speak of you and Blackwood and your financial coil."

Lilias felt incredibly tired again. It was all too much to even think about. She tried to lie back once more, but Guinevere caught her by the wrist. "If you had not discovered the true severity of your family's financial problems, would you have said yes to Blackwood even after being discovered in his arms at the ball? And by the by, why did you kiss him?"

"What?" Lilias jerked all the way upright. "I did not kiss Owen. He kissed me!"

Guinevere's brow furrowed. "I vow I heard Greybourne muttering to himself as he was leaving our house, and it sounded as if he said, 'Why did she kiss Owen if she did not care for him? Why?'"

"Why would he think that?" she asked, breathing in shallow, quick breaths to calm her now roiling stomach.

"Well," Guinevere said, "my astounding powers of deduction lead me to conclude that Blackwood likely told Greybourne as much."

"No," she whispered, a fiery knot of anger pulsing to life within her. "He wouldn't."

"Darling, he has confessed to loving you forever. I think he would."

"But he knew… He knew I loved Nash."

Guinevere nodded. "Yes, and he did whatever he had to in order to ensure you were his. That is unforgivable in my humble opinion."

It was more than unforgivable. Lilias was shaking with betrayal and rage. "I cannot wed him! I cannot. But how can I not? Where will Mama, Nora, and I even live? Where—"

Guinevere took Lilias's hands. "Hush. Do you think I would let you go under? Asher and I will provide you, your mother, and sister a place to live. We will ensure the debts are paid to the ruffians who dare threaten you and your family!"

"No." Lilias shook her head. "I cannot take your charity."

"Fine. A loan, then."

"I cannot take a loan without some way to pay you back."

"Fine," Guinevere huffed. "We will find you employment and then discuss a loan."

Lilias needed to speak to her mother, but how on earth could she tell Mama that she wanted to call off her betrothal and cast them all into scandal and peril? "Guinevere, are you certain Carrington would allow us to stay at one of his homes? Just until I find employment, mind you."

"I'm certain. Does this mean you're going to break the betrothal?"

Lilias bit her lip. "I... Well, I think so, but I must talk to my mother. If she becomes too upset, if she is too fearful for me to do it, I don't know what I shall do. I don't know how I could live with myself if I cast my family into a worse position against my mother's will, and I don't know how I can hurt Nora's future so." Lilias wrung her hands. "But I cannot wed Owen. Not now." She bit her lip. "I should have never relented. I'm so, so livid with him for doing what he did!"

Guinevere hugged her. "Break the betrothal. I feel certain that your future will work itself out."

⁂

"Is it done?" Asher asked Guinevere the moment she entered their bedchamber later that night.

Guinevere had to force herself to concentrate on Asher's question. Her husband was reclining on their bed in nothing more than a pair of skintight breeches. "It is," she said, sitting on the bed, intending to talk, but Asher had her in his lap in a breath and was kissing her neck. "Darling," she said, kissing him back, "I cannot concentrate this way."

"That's the point. Focus on us. There is nothing more we can do to push them together at this time."

"Asher, she did not kiss Blackwood as that devil told Greybourne she did. You must make certain Greybourne hears this."

"I will," Asher promised, making quick work of getting her out of her gown. "We're to meet tomorrow as I am helping Greybourne with a task."

"Mmm..." she moaned as her husband nuzzled her neck. "I hope this task involves his aiding Lilias. Her family is in dire straits."

"Ye know I cannot say."

"I know." She kissed Asher's chest and then his lips. "But Lilias may well be living with us if Greybourne does not aid her."

"I can promise ye that Lady Lilias will not have any more worries soon, but I cannot promise ye anything else. Greybourne's past weighs heavily on him, and that is all I'm going to say."

"Oh, that's amazing!"

Asher looked puzzled. "How?"

She giggled. "No, not what you *said*. What you are doing with your fingers."

Her husband's response was to circle his fingers over her breast ever so gently again. After a moment, he paused and glanced at her. "Will you regret what we've done if it does not work out for them?"

Guinevere did not even hesitate. "It will work out. I am certain." She gave Asher a deep kiss, to which he responded by flipping her onto her back and coming between her thighs.

He offered a loving smile as he hovered above her. "I

love yer heart." He kissed her. "And yer breasts." He kissed each one. "And yer lips." He kissed those, as well, sending her pulse spinning. "Shall I tell ye every part of ye I love?"

She grinned wickedly. "I think in this one instance, I'd prefer you to kiss me on every part of me you love."

"Ah, my sweet, wicked wife. Ye command, and I obey."

## Chapter Eleven

A sennight after Nash had last seen Lilias at the Orcus Society, his solicitor sat in Nash's study gathering the papers Nash had just signed. "That's it, Your Grace. Lady Lilias's mother is now the proud owner of Charingworth Manor in the Cotswolds. She'll receive these papers tomorrow from the Earl of Barrowe, her late husband's brother, indicating that he has given her the house outright. That was quite a bit of luck that the house you wanted of Lord Barrowe's happened to be unentailed."

"Yes," Nash agreed, picking up his drink and taking a sip. The brandy burned a trail down his throat to his stomach. He wished it could burn away his past sins so he could have a future with the only woman he would ever love.

He finished the drink, set down the glass, and stared out the window into the meticulously designed garden of his Mayfair home. He'd trade all his property, all his money, all his worldly possessions to have had one night with Lilias to keep in his memory before he'd discovered Owen loved her, as well. Night was falling quickly, shadows overtaking the picturesque view of the garden, and with the darkness outside came the darkness within. It had been especially bad since he had said goodbye to Lilias. Every day not seeing her felt like a lifetime.

He considered once more what he'd done for her and

her family, what he'd set in motion and asked Carrington to help him do, and he decided he didn't give a damn if he'd overstepped or not. He needed to give her the freedom to have choices for her life, not to be afraid, not to be compelled to wed Owen if she truly did not wish to. Though he still did not understand why she had kissed Owen on the balcony that night if she had no feelings for him. Since they'd last parted, he had considered going to her and asking her a thousand times, but he dismissed the idea every time.

That was what a selfish person would do. He had to let things go, to let *her* go. Nash had sealed his own fate long before he'd met Lilias. He'd done what he could for her, and it would not lead back to him. He'd paid her uncle handsomely to tell Lilias and her family that the earl had decided to make the house her mother's and that Lord Barrowe had also paid his brother's, Lilias's father's, debts to the miscreants out of a suddenly discovered affection for his late brother's family. The Earl of Barrowe was to concoct an excuse that he'd almost died and had a dream in which his brother's ghost visited him and chastised him for not watching out for his nieces and sister-in-law. It was ridiculous. It was a tale worthy of a book, and that's exactly why Nash expected that his sweet dreamer Lilias would believe it. Even if she didn't, no one could prove he was the one who had taken care of the debts except his solicitor and Carrington, and neither man would betray Nash.

His solicitor, Mr. Farnsworth, cleared his throat. Nash looked up at the man and asked yet again, "You're certain we took care of all the family debts?" He wanted nothing left for Lilias or her mother to worry about. He knew Owen could have done it, but he also knew it would have shamed Lilias to ask him. This way, she did not have to ask and could choose her own fate.

"Yes, Your Grace. The man I hired is the best, and with the information you gave me that the Duke of Carrington collected on who Lady Lilias's father owed, I feel certain no one should be bothering the family anymore. And I conveyed to my man to deliver the message you requested: that you would hunt down any man who bothered them again and make his life one of misery."

"Excellent. And the other request I made of you?"

The young solicitor smiled. He had dark hair, dark eyes, and a friendly face. "That actually turned out to be much easier than I expected. My sister is a seamstress, and with a little poking around and a few passed coins, she got the measurements for all the women in the Honeyfield family. Everything you requested has been ordered, and they will think it came from Lord Barrowe."

"Very good," Nash said, grateful they could use Lilias's uncle to protect Nash's identity. "Then our business is concluded. You've done excellent work."

"It's my honor, Your Grace."

Nash rang the bell, and the butler entered the study. Unfortunately, his mother came along with him, and by the frosty look she gave him, he suspected that he'd done something else to make her unhappy.

As the solicitor followed Sterns out of the study, his mother sat across from him. "What was that about?" she asked.

"Business," he replied, then got up and poured himself another drink.

When he turned back toward her, she was frowning. "I don't suppose you were talking to your solicitor because you have plans to make an offer for a lady?"

"You are correct not to suppose that." He knocked back

his drink, welcomed the numbing burn, and set the glass on the desk.

"You are imbibing too much," his mother said, her voice cold and tone chastising.

He was tempted to pour another just to see if she would show real emotion. Become irate? Throw something at him? She so rarely displayed anything beyond the most muted responses.

"Are you playing at being my mother now?" he asked. "It's a bit late. I'm all grown up."

"It is never too late," she said, her tone full of haughty disdain, "for you to become the duke your father and I expected you to be. You owe me."

And there it was. She thought he owed her for Thomas's death. But hadn't he already given his life? His happiness? His peace? He opened his mouth to say all that, but he shut it just as quick. *Penance.* The word reverberated in his mind.

"What is it you wish me to do, Mother?"

She looked as him as if he ought to know. "Why, wed, of course."

The thought made him flinch.

"Your greatest purpose is to wed a woman who will strengthen the Greybourne bloodline and produce many healthy sons."

"Was that your greatest purpose?" he asked, her choice of the word *healthy* striking somewhere dark in him. He had never liked that they had undermined Thomas's confidence in himself simply because he was born with one leg shorter than the other and weak lungs.

"Partly, but we are not discussing me. I have a wife in mind for you. Her family line is impeccable."

"She sounds like a perfect breeding specimen." He

didn't bother to curb his cynicism.

"I've told her father you will come to supper." It was a cold, detached statement.

"When?" he said, forcing himself to accept his fate and pushing any feelings about it away.

His mother gave a rare smile, purely triumphant. "Tomorrow."

"Who is this paragon of purebred lines you'd have me wed?"

"Her name is Miss Eloise Balfour. She's the daughter of Dr. Balfour."

Nash frowned. "Our family physician?"

His mother nodded.

"I'm surprised and gladdened to discover you don't consider her beneath the family name, given she's not of the *ton.*"

"She has other things that recommend her," his mother replied in a pinched tone.

*What the devil is going on here?*

"Such as?"

"Her mother produced six sons, all healthy."

"I see." His old anger at how they viewed Thomas as a problem to be managed and fixed flared once more. "Are you concerned, Mother, about getting an unhealthy grandchild?"

"Of course, I'm concerned," she snapped. "Sins of the past always taint the future."

*His* sins. She meant his sins.

And perhaps she was right. It didn't matter that the prospect of meeting Miss Eloise Balfour did not make him feel anything. What mattered was atonement, and he was apparently far from finished atoning.

Lilias stood outside of her mother's closed bedchamber door with her fist raised to knock, but she lowered her hand, heart pounding, and stared at the dark wood. She was tortured by guilt. She could not wed Owen, but how could she willingly make her sister and mother's life more difficult? Why must things be so complicated?

"Lilias?" She jumped at the sound of her mother's voice behind her and whirled around to find Mama standing there holding a bunch of papers. "I was just coming to find you."

Lilias's stomach knotted, and her mouth went dry. "I thought you were in your bedchamber."

"Why didn't you knock?" Mama asked.

"I—Well, I, feared I might wake you," Lilias fibbed, her cheeks instantly burning with the lie. When her mother chuckled, Lilias's jaw slipped open. "Mama, you laughed!"

Mama linked her arm with Lilias's, opened her bedchamber door, and led them both inside. She closed the door behind her and motioned to the sitting area. "Your cheeks pink when you fib. They always have." She said it in a gentle tone, then motioned toward the window. "Take a seat, Daughter. I have news!"

Lilias was glad for the delay in telling her mother her own news so she immediately did as requested and sat in the burgundy chair near the window. Her mother sat on the chaise that faced the chair and set the papers she'd been holding in her lap. And then that scrutinizing look of moments before swept over her face again. Lilias assumed she'd decided to ask her why she'd been at her door again, but instead, Mama surprised her by saying, "I saw your uncle today."

"Uncle Simon was here?"

Mama nodded.

"I did not even realize…" Lilias's words drifted off at the undeniable realization of how self-absorbed she'd been.

"No," her mother said softly, leaning toward Lilias and taking her hand, "you would not have. You've been quite sad. Don't think I am totally oblivious, darling."

"Mama, I'm so sorry!"

"Don't be." Her mother patted her hand. "I suspect it has something to do with your impending marriage."

Lilias swallowed convulsively. Now was her chance. Her mother had given her the perfect opportunity to tell her, but Lilias's mouth would not form the words. She was frozen by guilt.

Mama squeezed her hand. "You do not wish to wed Blackwood." It was a statement, softly spoken. Lilias's heart pounded, and she wasn't even sure if she nodded. Her mother continued. "But you would for me and Nora."

"I intended to," Lilias sobbed, "but Mama, it's complicated."

Her mother nodded. "Life always is, dearest. Does your hesitation have to do with the Duke of Greybourne, perchance?"

"Yes." She groaned. "But we can never be together. That is not the only reason I do not wish to wed Blackwood, though."

"Why could you not be together? Does he think himself too good for you?"

Lilias smiled at her mother's protective tone. She had not heard it in so many years.

"No, it's not that." She took a deep breath and told her mother what she knew of Nash and how he blamed himself for both his brother's death and Owen's accident, and that he would never allow himself a future with her because of

Owen. Then she explained how Owen had lied and told Nash she had kissed him.

"Oh, dear, that is an unfortunate turn of events. And what of you? If you didn't have to wed Blackwood, would you fight for a future with the Duke of Greybourne, even though he might reject you?"

"Yes," she whispered without hesitation. "I would fight for him until I had no fight left."

Mama grinned. "Then it's a very good thing you don't have to wed Blackwood."

Confusion and hope filled Lilias. "How can you say that?"

Her mother held up the papers. "Your uncle came here to tell me he's seen the error of his ways."

"Uncle Simon?" Lilias could hardly imagine.

"I was surprised, as well, but he has given me Charingworth Manor, and he has paid all your father's debts. You are free!" Her mother frowned. "Well, the *ton* will consider you ruined, but I don't care and neither should you. I'm tired of caring what people of the *ton* think. It has nearly killed me. Don't let the man you love simply walk away from you. Though, I daresay you have some explaining to do as to how you came to love a man I do not even know." Her mother eyed her sternly.

Lilias took a deep breath once again and shared her adventures years before in the Cotswolds with her mother. Once she was done talking, silence fell.

Her mother looked contemplative for a moment. "I fear I did you an injustice not to stand firmer with your father on the companion and not keeping my own eye upon you." Worry and guilt etched her mother's face.

Lilias took her hand and squeezed it. "No, Mama. I had a wonderful childhood. Truly." She realized in that moment how true it was. No, she had not felt protected as many girls did, but that had made her into the woman she was now. A strong one. One who would bear the *ton's* scorn and fight for the man she loved. One who would carve her own path as her father had wished her to do.

Her mother pursed her lips and then said, "Be that as it may, first thing tomorrow, I'm going to secure you and Nora a companion. Your father had such a force of will, and I, well, I was no match for him. And then I was just trying to survive the financial problems and my sadness. Your father made you strong. I see that. Let me do my part to protect you."

It seemed easier not to argue against the companion, and if she knew Mama, who had always had a horrible time making decisions, it would be a while before a companion would be secured. That was time enough to plot with Guinevere about Nash and address the problem of securing Helen's manuscript.

"Oh!" Mama said, sifting through the papers she was holding and plucking a sealed letter out. She extended it to Lilias. "This came from Blackwood."

Lilias quickly tore it open and read.

*Dearest Lilias,*

*I've returned to Town, and I shall call on you this afternoon. I cannot wait to see you.*

*Yours,*
*Owen*

Anger with Owen flared as Lilias folded the note and looked at her mother. "Blackwood is to call upon me this afternoon, and—"

A scratch at the bedchamber door interrupted Lilias.

"My lady," the butler called out, "Lord Blackwood is here to call upon Lady Lilias. Shall I see him to the drawing room?"

"Yes, do," her mother replied. She stood and motioned for Lilias to do the same. "Go on, darling. Time to take your future into your own hands. You cannot win the man who has your heart until you break this betrothal."

She wasn't at all certain she could win Nash even after the betrothal was broken, but she was going to try. This was likely her last chance. He loved her. He'd practically said so. If only he'd accept that their love had the power to heal the scars on his heart, as it had done with hers.

## Chapter Twelve

Truth was the only way forward. No matter how painful, it had to be truth. As she opened the parlor door, Lilias realized that as angry as she was with Owen, now that her ire was cooling a bit, she felt sorry for him. He didn't really love her. Love was not selfish and possessive to the point of lying to keep someone with you. Owen feared being left again by someone close to him. So as she shut the door and he turned away from the window to face her and a smile lit his face, she restrained the simmering fury she felt.

"You lied to Nash," she said softly.

His whole demeanor changed. The smile faded, his eyes grew hard, and his shoulders stiffened. She had hoped he would be remorseful, that they could somehow salvage their friendship, but he was clearly far from ready for that. It left her with the need to put distance between them, and it filled her with aching sadness.

"I have devoted my life to you," he said. The words held an edge that she didn't like. She took a step back. "I would do anything for you. Yes, I lied. But that's because I love you. He'll do nothing but hurt you."

"You cannot keep someone with lies, Owen. You knew I loved him." She had thought about it a lot over the last day since Guinevere's revelation about Owen's lie. "You knew I loved him, and you did all in your power to ensure he and I never had a chance. That is not love."

"Isn't it?" he snarled. "Tell me what love is, then. I don't know." He shook his head. "Everyone I love leaves. You. My mother."

He'd never wanted to speak of his mother before. Lilias had tried, but he'd always refused. Tears sprang to her eyes now at the hurt inside him. "I won't abandon you, Owen, not if you don't force me to, but the way I love you is in friendship. It's always been friendship."

"Why?" he demanded, his voice like thunder in the silence. "I'm better for you."

"No." She shook her head, her heart so heavy. "I would make you crazed with my love for adventure, my need for freedom."

"You need a protector, Lilias! Someone to guide you and keep you from harm. I'm that man! I'll keep you from doing foolish things."

"I don't want or need that sort of protector," she said through the tears that were now falling. Her father had given her that gift, as had her mother, even if she hadn't wanted it at the time. All those years Lilias had longed to feel protected, and she had unknowingly learned to protect herself.

Owen advanced so quickly she did not have time to react. He grabbed her by the arms as his expression twisted in agony and fear. "He is not who you believe he is! You don't know Nash, not really. You never did."

"Release me, Owen," she demanded. "You're hurting me."

He stared at her for a moment, as if he might not do as she asked, but he finally released her. He turned and kicked out at the side table. It toppled over, the vase upon it shattering and water spilling across the floor.

Right away, a scratch came at the door. "My lady?" the

butler called. "Do you need assistance?"

Owen shook his head and raked his hands through his hair, visibly trembling. "I'm sorry," he said, sounding frustrated. "I won't lose control again. That was not acceptable."

"I'm fine," she called to the butler as she touched Owen's arm lightly. "It's understandable, Owen. I've hurt you."

"I'll take the hurt, if you will only but see. I am best for you. He will not even have you. I vow it. You'd not want him, either. He'd hurt you as he hurts everyone. He killed his brother."

Her heart dropped at his continued lies. "That's not true."

"It is! My father told me years ago that Nash stole the girl his brother loved from him, and the brother charged him on the ice, the ice broke, and when he fell through, Nash stood there and watched him drown. My father heard the truth in Town."

She could hardly believe how Owen was turning on Nash. "Your father heard gossip," she said, fiercely angry. "Nash told me what happened."

"And you think he'd tell you the truth?" Owen demanded harshly.

"Yes," she said, "he would. I know him."

"Do you?" he sneered. "Did you know that the day I challenged him to a race in front of you, he had told me the night before that he'd let me win. He knew he was better. He told me that to shame me, to best me just as he had his brother. And I almost died—just like his brother."

"No!" she vehemently denied. "He would never want to hurt you. He's denied himself to protect you!"

Nash's words from the night they stood outside the Orcus Society rang in her head then. *It's not just that, Lilias.*

*God, it's not, but that's enough.* Had he been referring to Owen? She had suspected all along that Nash blamed himself for Owen's fall, but if they'd had this conversation and Nash had said he'd let Owen win, she understood why he might blame himself. But she knew Nash. He would have never hurt Owen purposely, and the fact that Owen would try to make her think so infuriated her.

"He would never have intentionally hurt you like your mother did when she left you and your father," she said.

"Maybe not," he said, "but he can't help himself. He'll hurt you next."

"Get out," she said in a firm but quiet voice. She had not wanted it to be like this, but this was how it had to be.

"Don't do this, Lilias," Owen said, his voice suddenly pleading, his face softening. "I love you. I'm the best man for you. I have always been there for you. He left you. He left you, and he will never wed you. Then where will you be?"

"Alone," she said. "But I'd rather be alone than wed to a man I don't love. Goodbye, Owen." She turned before he could say more, marched to the door, and opened it.

"When he abandons you, Lilias, I'll be here," Owen said, now facing her. "That's what love is. You'll come back and I'll be here waiting for you. You'll see."

Lilias wanted to reach out and hug him for the pain his mother's leaving him long ago had put deep inside him, but that would only give him false hope with her. Instead, she shook her head and said, "One day, when *you* are ready, *I* will be here, Owen, waiting as your friend. Nothing more. And I feel certain Nash will be there as your friend, as well."

"He's no friend of mine!" Owen bit out and brushed past her. He stormed past the gawking butler, her wide-eyed mother, and Nora, and a moment later, the front door slammed so loudly that Lilias swore she felt it in her bones.

The butler quietly disappeared, and her mother said, "Well, that did not appear to go well."

"No," Lilias said on a long sigh. "I wonder if I should warn Greybourne."

Her mother smiled. "That would give you an excellent reason to see him, but not," she admonished, "until tomorrow, and not if Guinevere cannot accompany you, dearest. It's time you start behaving like a proper lady. If Greybourne doesn't come to heel, then—"

"Mama!" Lilias moaned. "I thought you understood. I cannot wed another man. I love Greybourne. I will not stop loving him simply because he may not want me. It is a love so deep I ache with it."

Nora sighed, and a dreamy smile tugged her lips upward. Mama slid an arm around Lilias's shoulder. "I do understand," she soothed. "I was going to say that if Greybourne does not come to heel, then perhaps you can become a companion or some such thing, but you will need to start acting within the expected boundaries immediately."

"That sounds dreadful!" Nora announced, to which Lilias could not agree more.

The minute Guinevere pulled up in her gig late the next afternoon, Lilias flew out the door, barely giving the footman time to open it. She'd been waiting all day for the appointed hour Guinevere said she could accompany Lilias to call upon Nash, as Lilias's mother's had demanded, and Guinevere had been engaged all day until now. Lilias bounded down the steps and into the gig, and Guinevere laughed at her.

"My, you're eager," she said, her voice holding a knowing note. She'd told Guinevere in her note earlier that morning that she'd broken her betrothal to Owen. As Guinevere maneuvered the horse onto the lane to go to Nash's, Lilias quickly told her of what her Uncle Simon had done. When she was finished, Guinevere gave a snort that sounded strangely derisive. Lilias frowned but continued. "I intend to call upon my uncle and thank him."

"Ha!" Guinevere said.

"What do you mean, 'ha'?" Lilias asked, confused.

"Oh, did I say 'ha'? I was—Well, I was thinking about something Asher said earlier."

"You're acting very odd," Lilias said, though she did know from being in love herself how easy it was to let the object of one's affections consume one's thoughts, even when they were not present.

"Sorry, dearest. How did Blackwood take your breaking the betrothal?"

"Not well at all." As Guinevere drove them along, Lilias told her of Owen's reaction, his accusation that Nash had killed his own brother, and his claiming that Nash meant to shame Owen in front of Lilias by luring him into a race he had never intended to allow Owen to win.

"From what I have observed of Greybourne personally since his return, I sincerely doubt that," Guinevere said. "His actions have been very honorable."

"What actions?" Lilias asked, intrigued.

"This and that," Guinevere replied in an evasive manner. Lilias was about to ask for specifics, but then Guinevere went on, "So you are calling upon him simply to warn him that Blackwood may now wish him ill?"

Lilias blushed, and her stomach roiled with anxiousness.

"Well, I suppose I was hoping that if Greybourne heard the news of my broken betrothal to Owen, it might possibly come to him that we could have a future together."

"And if it does not?" Guinevere asked, looking from the lane to Lilias.

"I'll fight for him," she said, conviction coursing through her. "I'll try to break through the guilt I think is consuming him. I can't let go, Guin. Not yet. Not until there's no hope. Do you think me a fool?"

Guinevere grinned at her. "No, dearest. I think you are marvelous, and strong, and determined. And I think Greybourne is lucky you love him."

Not long later, they pulled up to Nash's home in Mayfair. They handed the gig off to a servant who had appeared and made their way up the steps.

Guinevere eyed her. "Is that a new cloak, and slippers, and gloves?"

Lilias ran a finger over her new fur-lined cloak as they ascended the last few stairs and she knocked on the door. She turned to Guinevere, her pulse racing with expectation, and she tried to calm herself by continuing the conversation. "Uncle Simon sent it all this morning. Can you believe it?"

"No, as a matter of fact, I cannot. Listen, Lilias. I should not say anything, but—"

Just then, the door to Nash's home opened, and Guinevere winked at Lilias, took out her calling card, and quickly explained that she was there to see Nash's sister and that Lilias had business with the duke.

They followed the butler as he explained that Nash was with his mother in his study and Lady Adaline was in the garden, which was on the way to the study, so they stopped at the garden first. Guinevere grasped Lilias's hand and, squeezing it, whispered, "Good luck," before she disappeared behind the servant and out into the garden.

Lilias waited in the passage, her nerves mounting, but the butler returned before she could work herself up into too great a state. They continued to the study, which was, thankfully, not far from the garden entrance.

The butler knocked on the shut door, then stepped in, pulling the door almost closed behind him. Lilias heard a woman's voice. It must have been Nash's mother. Lilias swallowed, suddenly even more nervous. The study door opened, and the butler came out and instructed her to enter. When she did, she was surprised to see that Nash was nowhere to be found. There was only a woman—Nash's mother, she assumed—sitting on a blue velvet settee. The woman was beautiful in a cool and aloof way. She had dark hair, much like Nash's, but where Nash had light-gray eyes, this woman's eyes were so dark they were almost black.

"How can I help ye? Lady Lilias, is it?"

Lilias nodded, feeling acutely self-conscious that Nash was not there and that she had no good reason to give this woman for why she was calling. She noted Nash's mother did not ask her to sit down, and neither her tone nor her expression were welcoming. "Yes, Your Grace. I have business to discuss with your son."

The duchess's mouth pulled into a pucker of obvious annoyance. "What business is that?" Lilias's mind went blank and her mouth went dry, and the duchess's eyes narrowed, then widened. "Ye're the girl from the Cotswolds!" It was said as an accusation.

"Yes," Lilias replied. "I knew your son from the Cotswolds. He, the Earl of Blackwood, and I were friends."

"Ye," she said, pointing at Lilias, "must be what lured him from the house at unspeakable hours of the night."

Lilias winced. "Is your son home?" she asked, feeling as if the situation with his mother was fast disintegrating. It was obvious the woman did not like her.

"He is not. He is at supper with his betrothed."

She recoiled as if the duchess had slapped her. No. No. That could not be. Her heart refused to believe what his mother had just said. Lilias swallowed, anxiety tightening her throat. "Did you... Did you say your son was betrothed?"

"Aye," the woman replied, the word clipped. "So whatever business ye think ye have with my son, I daresay ye do not."

A tide of hopelessness washed over Lilias, threatening to pull her under. *Betrothed.* Had he done it simply to move on with his life? He'd said he wanted to let her go, that he had to. Heaven above, was this his way of doing so? Her legs felt suddenly too weak to keep her standing.

"Thank you," she mumbled and blindly pushed her way out of the room.

The butler was there, hovering just outside the door. No doubt Nash's mother had instructed him that Lilias would not be staying long. It took all her reserve to hold back her tears as the butler led her out and assured her he would inform Guinevere that she was ready to depart.

Once outside, Lilias started walking. She didn't even know where she was going, but she knew she could not stand in front of Nash's house where his mother could look out a window and see Lilias sobbing. Nor did she want to be lurking there if he happened to come home early. She had no notion what to say, what to do. She wanted to fight for him, for them, but if Nash had taken this step, she feared the guilt he already carried would not allow him to break his promise to the woman he was to wed. Lilias's step faltered as she realized she didn't even know to whom he was betrothed.

"Lilias!"

She turned at the sound of Guinevere's voice and her gig upon the street. Her friend was upon her in moments. "What on earth, Lilias? Where are you going? Why—" Guinevere's mouth slipped open, and she scrambled down from the gig, grabbing Lilias by the arms. "Why are you crying? What did *that man* say to you?"

Despite the sorrow drowning her, Lilias smiled at her sweet friend and how incensed she sounded on Lilias's behalf. "That man," she said, swiping at the tears that would not stop, "was not even home. His mother told me he was having supper at his betrothed's home."

"What?" Guinevere gasped. "No! No, that cannot be. I don't believe it."

Lilias frowned. There was that bit of oddness from earlier in her friend's voice again. "Why do you not believe it? I told you of the guilt I believe he lives with, and he told me he wanted to let me go. I suppose this is his way of doing it," she said, sobbing again.

"How would he even have time to become betrothed?" Guinevere muttered, pinching the bridge of her nose. "Asher would have said something, I'm certain of it. Though, I suppose there is the slightest chance he might not have. He's been very mum about what they discuss because he owes Greybourne some sort of life debt, and apparently the man demanded payment in the form of Asher not speaking to me about the duke. It's all been so tedious. I've had to work very hard to learn anything about Greybourne, and—"

"Guinevere!" Lilias interrupted. "What are you talking about? What have you learned?"

"Well, for starters, your uncle did not give your mother the Cotswold home. Greybourne purchased it from him for an exorbitant sum so you and your family would not have to leave!"

She stared at Guinevere for a moment, speechless, and her heart exploded. "Nash purchased the home?"

Guinevere nodded, grinning. "And he paid all your father's debts. I heard Asher and Nash discussing the particulars of how Nash could do it and ensure he remained anonymous. I vow I think my husband wanted me to hear. He knows my habit of eavesdropping at doors, and he took no obvious precautions such as having the conversation outside or when I was not at home. Greybourne loves you. He must if he's done these things for you."

Lilias could hardly believe it. She was alternately joyous and terrified. She believed he loved her, though he'd never said those three words. Yet, what he'd told her outside the club that night seemed to indicate it. His actions then, and his actions in regard to her uncle, her home, and her father's debt, certainly indicated love, so how could he get betrothed?

*You did.*

She groaned, her jaw clenching, and her hands curling into fists.

"Let's go to my home and talk to Asher," Guinevere said. "He will know if Greybourne is betrothed, and perhaps he can help you get through to the man."

Lilias shook her head. "I don't want you to put Carrington in that position. If he promised Nash he'd not talk to you about this matter, then he should keep his promise. I don't want to be the cause of Nash losing another friend." She had already cost Nash his friendship with Owen.

"Then what are you going to do?" Guinevere demanded.

"I don't know," Lilias said helplessly. "I need time to contemplate it all." Her head pounded, and her heart ached. "I think I'll walk home."

"Lilias, no. Let me drive you."

Lilias shook her head. "It's not far. I've done it before." Of course, Nash had been following her then. He'd followed her to ensure she was safe, supposedly for Owen's sake, but she knew now it had been because he'd wanted to ensure she was safe for her own sake. Tears threatened, but she blinked them away, seeing another gig headed down the lane toward them.

"Lilias Honeyfield, I refuse to allow you to walk home alone. I—"

"On second thought," Lilias said as the driver of the oncoming gig came into perfect view and she realized it was the Marquess of Kilgore, "I don't think I'll be going home just yet."

With that, she held up her hand to wave Kilgore to a stop. As the rogue slowed his gig to a halt in front of her and Guinevere, Guinevere's eyes narrowed upon Lilias. "What is this about? Are you going to try to make Greybourne come to his senses by using Kilgore?"

"That's quite the intriguing proposition without even a hello," Kilgore said, a suggestive grin coming to his handsome face.

"I have no intention of using you to make Greybourne jealous," she said, her mind turning. She didn't know where Nash was, and her heart and head were a mess. She needed something else to concentrate on at the moment, and her unfinished mission to secure the manuscript from Mr. Levine was the perfect thing. A chapter of that manuscript *had* to be about Kilgore if Mr. Levine intended to see it published to gain revenge on the marquess, so Kilgore should be motivated to help her retrieve it. Besides, she highly suspected Kilgore was a man well acquainted with guilt. Perhaps some time alone with him and some conversation would give her some thoughts on how to reach Nash before he was lost to her forever.

"Well, that's rather disappointing," he said, his voice like silk. "I rather enjoyed the idea of being used by you."

She studied him for a long moment. The way his mouth curved in a bored half smile. The seemingly carefree way he lounged on his seat. But he was not carefree. He was tense. His left hand clutched his thigh, and his right foot tapped. Kilgore was a man who wanted her and everyone else to think he was no good. She'd play along—for now.

"Don't fret," she said. "I *do* intend to use you."

"Lilias!" Guinevere gasped.

Lilias smiled reassuringly at her friend. "Don't worry, dearest. I intend to use Kilgore to help me solve a problem he has somewhat helped create." With that, she launched into a quick explanation of the manuscript by Helen Levine and her brother's refusal to return it. She also mentioned what he had said at the Orcus Society: it wasn't about money but about striking Kilgore in the heart.

When she finished, she studied him. "Do you know to what he was referring?"

"Yes," Kilgore said, his face as tight as the one word. "I—" He glanced at them both almost apologetically. "It's not fit for a lady's ears."

"I'm not much of a 'lady' in the prim-and-proper sense so do go on. That is—" Lilias cast a look at Guinevere, whose face was alight with eagerness, "if Guinevere will not be shocked," she finished, feeling sure Guinevere would not care, but Lilias was compelled to allow her friend to decide for herself.

"Ha!" Guinevere pronounced. "You know better! Both of you do. Do tell us, Kilgore."

A breeze blew and ruffled Kilgore's dark hair off his forehead to reveal a white scar down the right side. It appeared to start at his hairline and stop midway to his eyebrow. He touched his forefinger to the scar and appeared lost in the past for a moment. Then he took a deep breath and spoke. "I take it you have not read Helen's manuscript?"

Lilias and Guinevere both shook their heads, to which Kilgore nodded. "As I have not, either, so some of this is speculation, but it is grounded, I believe, in facts. "I have never touched Helen in my life, but I have an enemy who was her client, and I have no doubt he did not pay her what he promised. He very likely has a scathing chapter in her book."

"And this would be…?" Lilias asked.

Kilgore's gaze locked on Guinevere, and he raised his eyebrows. "You know," he said quietly.

"Oh!" Guinevere exclaimed, and when Lilias looked at her, she was goggling at Kilgore. "Are you referring to Asher's brother?"

"Indeed," Kilgore answered. "Talbot met with Helen a great deal, and I would not be surprised if he spoke too freely in the throes of passion, and after, about his many schemes and goings on. As you likely know, one of which involved me and a certain wager on the books at White's."

"Oh goodness," Lilias said as her mind pulled the threads together. She knew the wager on White's books of which Kilgore spoke had involved Lady Constantine. "You think there is a chapter in the book that must give details of you and Lady Constantine."

Kilgore's jaw was like flint, and the flicker of fury in his eyes was so intense in the moment before his lashes fell that gooseflesh rose on her arms. "I do," he ground out. "But you must believe me that Lady Constantine is a woman above reproach. She would not allow the likes of me to touch her with even the longest pole I could find."

The statement was emphatic, and Lilias did not know what was true, nor was it truly her concern. The matter was private and should stay that way. "Why would Helen write a chapter that would hurt you?"

"I do not think it would have been intended to hurt me. I think she intended to hurt Talbot. He pursued Lady Constantine, and she turned him down, and he undoubtedly said something to the effect that she was not so pure, that she and I—" He stopped and sucked in a ragged breath. "I could swear it to be lies, but no one would care. And it is already whispered about, bandied around in Society."

"This book would make it seem as fact," Guinevere said. "And Lady Constantine's ruin would be official."

A strangled sound of pain came from Kilgore. "Yes."

"So now we understand how Mr. Levine intends to strike at you," Lilias said.

The three of them stood there for a moment, the unspoken truth that hurting Lady Constantine would be a death blow to Kilgore hanging between them.

"But why?" Lilias asked.

A dark smile tilted up the corner of Kilgore's lips ever so slightly. "I recently gave him a thrashing he richly deserved and likely will never forget, and then I helped a woman he claimed to love flee him and disappear. He thought to show his love for her with his fists, and I thought to give him justice. In his twisted mind, he thinks I seduced her away from him. So I suppose now he is coming for me."

"Kilgore!" Lilias exclaimed. "You are rather like a hero."

"No," he said flatly, "I am not. Pray, don't ever forget it."

She didn't know why he hated himself so much, but it was quite obvious he did. Now was not the time to unravel that coil, however. "Do you know where Mr. Levine lives?"

"Why?" Guinevere demanded.

Lilias ignored her friend, as did Kilgore, his gaze boring into Lilias. "Yes. He lives in St. Giles."

Lilias was somehow not surprised to hear that Mr. Levine lived in the most notorious rookery in London. Many families there were hardworking, but there were also pickpockets and criminals aplenty crammed into slum-like housing where the poorest, most unfortunate souls often turned to crime in desperation.

Kilgore arched his dark eyebrows. "Shall we go there now and see if we can retrieve the manuscript? I happen to know a bit about Mr. Levine's nighty routine."

Lilias didn't doubt it. Kilgore was quite clearly a man of many layers, and it seemed one of them might by spying.

"No!" Guinevere exclaimed, but Lilias nodded at Kilgore. Guinevere grabbed Lilias's hand and jerked her around so they were face-to-face. "Dearest, no! I'm for going, as well, but not without Asher. He would be livid if I went into St. Giles without him. I shudder to think on it."

"*You* should not go," Lilias said. "I quite agree that Carrington would be beyond reason, but I do not have a husband." And she no longer had a man to whom she was betrothed, either. She had only herself, and she had no doubt that Kilgore could protect her.

## Chapter Thirteen

"I've been looking for ye," Carrington said, pulling out the chair beside Nash in the Gold Room of the Orcus Society. The game of *vingt-et-un* had just ended and another was not set to start for a few minutes.

"Well, you've found me," Nash replied, shoving his cards toward the dealer, who quickly took them.

"Dennington," Carrington said to the dealer, "give me a few minutes alone with Greybourne."

The man immediately nodded, set down the cards he'd been about to shuffle, and exited the room, shutting the door behind him.

Wariness settled heavy on Nash. "If this is about Lady Lilias…" Carrington had been very vocal about how he thought Nash was making a mistake. Nash didn't have the patience for it tonight. It had been a devil of a long one already.

He'd gone to Dr. Balfour's house to appease his mother, but he'd known the moment he met Eloise Balfour that he could never wed her or any woman. He could not pledge to hold another woman in his heart besides Lilias, especially not before God. It would not be true.

"It is about Lady Lilias but not as ye think. She sent a missive to Guinevere this morning, and Guinevere told me Lady Lilias has broken her betrothal to Blackwood. And Greybourne, Blackwood lied to ye. Lady Lilias did not kiss him on the balcony that night at the ball. *He* kissed *her.* She told Guinevere so."

A queer buzzing filled Nash's ears for a moment, then darkness started at the edges of his vision, blotting out everything but a pinpoint of light. In that light was an image of Owen. His supposed friend had purposely lied to him. Nash would find him and kill him. No, no. Murdering a peer would keep Nash separated from Lilias, and nothing, *nothing,* could keep him from her now. Not after learning of this betrayal. Before he even knew what he was doing, he was rising and shoving his chair back to go to her. She needed him, and he needed her. And in this moment, everything else paled in comparison to the news Carrington had relayed. Owen was a liar. Owen was not Thomas, not anything like Thomas, who had been good and honest. What else had Owen lied about? Rage seared Nash's veins. He'd been so consumed by guilt, so determined to live a life of penance that he had hurt Lilias, almost forced her to wed someone she didn't love.

He was at the door when a thought struck, and he stilled. "She may not have me," he said, more to himself than Carrington.

His friend answered, anyway. "I would wager my entire fortune that she will have ye."

Nash tugged a hand through his hair, doubt rising. "She doesn't know everything." He told Carrington then about the horse race with Owen and then about his brother and the ice. Shame curled within him.

"Good God, Greybourne. Those things were not yer fault. Letting Lady Lilias slip through yer fingers *will* be yer fault, but yer brother charging ye on the ice was not. Ye tried to save him, didn't ye?"

"God, yes." Nash stared down at his hands, a memory

tickling the back of his mind, but before he could delve into it, the door to the Gold Room burst open and Owen stalked in, his uneven gait more pronounced at his clipped pace.

"You," he snarled, pointing his cane at Nash. "You took her from me!" He started toward Nash, but Carrington stepped in front of him to block his path.

"Let him pass," Nash said to Carrington as Nash concentrated on the man he wanted to throttle.

Carrington immediately moved, and Owen shoved a chair out of his way, knocking it over in his haste to stand in front of Nash. "You vowed not to pursue her," Owen spat, his face turning red and his expression twisting.

"I kept my vow," Nash said, his own fury climbing.

"She's mine!" Owen roared, pushing Nash in the chest. "And if I cannot have her, I'll ensure you don't, either."

The threat snapped the last thread of control Nash possessed. He reared back and hit Owen in the jaw, shutting him up and sending the man staggering backward and falling onto his arse. Nash's pulse thumped in his ears as he came to stand over Owen, who was struggling to get back up. Nash raised his foot and pressed the man down to his back. "Make no mistake, Owen. I'll kill you if you so much as touch a hair on Lilias's head or dare to ever kiss her again. You lied about her kissing you on the balcony. You manipulated me, and now I know it."

His nostrils flared as he stared down at the man he'd almost helped wed the woman Nash loved. "Do not go near her," he managed through clenched teeth. "She's broken her betrothal to you, and made her wishes known, and if you cause her one more second of pain, I'll cause you a lifetime of it."

"Get off me!" Owen demanded, trying to knock Nash's foot away but not succeeding. "She can't love someone like you! I did everything right. I was there for her! I stayed by her side for seven years listening to her carry on about you, pine over—"

"What?" Nash interrupted, realization hitting him full force. He leaned down, grabbed a fistful of Owen's overcoat and yanked him up. "You told me she never asked about me." His head pounded with the understanding of just how much Owen had manipulated him through the years. A fury, like he'd never felt, pulsed through him. He'd practically carved out his heart to step aside for Owen to win Lilias. He reared his fist back to punch Owen again, but a woman's voice rang out, freezing him mid-motion.

"You!" Asher's wife bellowed, coming into the room in a swirl of silk. She pointed a finger at Nash. "How dare you betroth yourself to another woman and break my friend's heart all over again! Your actions will be her undoing! She's gone and run off with Kilgore!"

<hr />

Lilias sat on the seat of Kilgore's gig, shivering as he drove them deeper into St. Giles. As the gig bumped over the dirt road turned to slush by the earlier heavy rain and the fog grew thicker, the night took on an ominous air and she began to doubt her decision. But she could not turn back now. Kilgore was here, and she did not see how she could manage this confrontation in the daylight. Someone might see her.

Though the hour was late, people loitered on the street, and as Lilias and Kilgore passed them in the gig, she studied them. The women were selling their wares, and many of the people sitting against ramshackle buildings with blankets pulled up around them likely did not have homes.

But it wasn't all gloomy. Several corners blazed with light, and when they passed a building where music flowed out into the cool night air, Kilgore told her it was a gaming hell.

The houses grew closer to one another and smaller as they moved into the underbelly of St. Giles, and the stench of garbage made Lilias cover her mouth with her hand.

Kilgore handed her a handkerchief as he drove the gig. "For the smell."

She nodded gratefully and took it from him, and then said, her voice muffled from the cloth, "Shall we go over the plan again?"

"Yes. Levine should not be home. He always gambles at the Cross and Crown on Saturday night until nearly dawn. But regardless, I have my pistol with me." Kilgore lifted his right leg, and she gazed down with a mixture of relief and concern. She'd never gone on a mission as dangerous as this one was working out to be, but she would not turn back now.

"How will you get in if the door is locked?" She only now thought to ask.

Kilgore laughed, but it was a mirthless sound. "Let's just say I learned long ago how to get out of rooms in which I had been locked."

She nodded, repressing the urge to ask him about it. The mysteries of Kilgore would have to wait until this mission was complete.

"You will keep watch on the corner by Clyde's Pub, which is a stone's throw from Levine's house, while I try to find the manuscript inside his home, assuming it is even there," Kilgore continued. "There is always a line of vendor carts there, and you will hide behind those. If you should see Levine coming, give the bird call so I'm prepared for him but he's not alerted to my presence. If I have not found the manuscript, I'll confront him about it with my pistol in hand."

She nodded, feeling fairly secure in their plan. Kilgore had told her he made it his business to know what his enemies were up to so that was why he knew Mr. Levine's routine. And thank goodness he did!

"Let me hear the bird call again," he demanded.

She gave it, pleased with how loud it was.

"You're as good at it as any man I've ever worked with."

"Do you care to expand?" she asked, rubbing her arms to ward off the chill that was settling into her bones.

"No," he replied. "Some stories are best left buried."

"What if the manuscript is not there and we cannot persuade Mr. Levine to give it to us?" Lilias asked, nibbling on her lip and staring down at the pretty new gloves that Nash had bought for her. Nash, who might be betrothed to someone else.

A dark chuckle came from Kilgore. "Lady Lilias, there are always ways to persuade men to part with things they don't wish to. But don't fret about that now. We're here."

She followed his pointed finger and felt her mouth slip open at the dark, tiny, dilapidated house that was Mr. Levine's residence. And she had thought her life was hard! Shame rolled over her. She knew nothing of true poverty, but tomorrow, she was going to do something about that. Somehow, she was going to help those less fortunate. Mr. Levine had not started out wicked. He had come into the world pure, as all babies do, and the circumstances of his life had molded him. That was no excuse for the things he had done, of course, but it did make her wonder how the Mr. Levines of the world could turn out if they had more of a chance.

Kilgore pulled the gig up to the pub. Though the door was closed, laughter and bawdy songs flowed from the tiny establishment. Light illuminated it, and Lilias could see men in dirty work clothes and women dressed to catch the men's attention all packed inside, tankards raised and smiles on their faces. It was not all sadness here, and that lifted Lilias's gloom just a bit.

After Kilgore secured the gig, he helped her down. Her slippers sank into a layer of slosh that made disgust roil in her stomach as he led her to the vendor carts. Just as he'd said, there were five of them lined up on the street.

"What are these for exactly?" she asked.

"Oh, most of the people who live here don't know how to cook, nor do they have the means to do so in their homes, so the vendors sell food."

"For a peer, you know a great deal about life in St. Giles."

"As I said, I make it my business to know my enemies."

Somehow she thought it was more than that, but again, questions would have to wait.

Kilgore's hand came to her shoulder. "I'll open the window as soon as I get in the house so I will be sure to hear your bird call."

She nodded, her heartbeat increasing now that their plan was about to come to fruition.

"I'll be back before you know I'm gone," he said, winking at her. And then he withdrew his pistol, straightened, and made his way to the front door of Mr. Levine's home.

It was thirty steps from where she was, exactly as he had said it would be. He knocked with his pistol raised, and when the door remained closed, she exhaled with relief. She gasped in admiration as Kilgore made quick work of getting past whatever lock Mr. Levine surely had in place. The door opened and closed behind Kilgore, and she was left to wait.

Anxiousness turned in her stomach, and her palms grew damp as she stared at the dark house, willing him to hurry. Something rustled by her feet, startling her, then that same something scampered across her foot. Shock made a scream rise swiftly, but she clamped her teeth down and kicked her feet to rid herself of what had to be a rat. To her horror, however, instead of kicking the rat away, the creature seemed to multiply in the dim light, and squeaking sounds rose from the ground. As the rustling increased, she could just make out a stream of rats flooding out of one of the carts. She did scream then, slapping a palm over her mouth and scampering back, away from the cart and straight into something solid.

Her pulse exploded as steely arms encircled her, and a deep, rough voice said, "Hello, Mrs. Artemis."

Just as she opened her mouth to scream yet again, Mr. Levine's door banged open across the street and Kilgore charged from the home roaring, pistol raised.

Mr. Levine jerked her roughly against him, one arm releasing her and the other locking her in place. A blade suddenly shimmered in the moonlight, and then the sharp point of it came to her throat, and she cried out in fear.

"I'll slit her throat if you don't lower your pistol," Mr. Levine called out, and when Kilgore took another step toward them, to her relief, Mr. Levine jerked the blade away from her throat. But it was short lived as the dagger glinted above her for a moment before the heavy handle met her skull and darkness descended.

※

Nash drove the gig hell-bent on reaching Lilias. Beside him,

Carrington held on, which was wise. Nash took the turns to St. Giles at a pace that caused alarm to slither through him, but he did not slow down. As the roads grew narrower and the stench increased, so did his fear. It had seeped into every part of him as Carrington's wife had told him of Lilias's latest mission with Kilgore. If anything happened to Lilias, Nash didn't know what he would do, who he would hate the most—himself for denying them for so long, his mother for lying to Lilias and telling her he was betrothed to Miss Balfour, or Kilgore for agreeing to accompany Lilias into the rookery at night to steal from a man Nash sensed was unstable.

The fog was pervasive tonight, making seeing conditions deplorable, and as he rounded the dark corner where Clyde's Pub was, a man appeared from the thick, white mist and staggered toward them. Nash had to pull back sharply on the horse's reins in order to avoid running the man down. "Get the hell out of the way!" he yelled at the drunk, his blood pumping through him so fast all his senses were on fire.

"Greybourne!" Carrington bit out. "That's Kilgore!"

Nash frowned, black fright sweeping over him because he did not see Lilias. Kilgore fell to one knee.

"He's injured," Carrington said, but Nash was already out of the gig and closed the distance between him and Kilgore in a heartbeat. He reached for the marquess just as the man glanced up, and Nash froze. The left side of Kilgore's face appeared wet in the moonlight, and the metallic smell of blood hit Nash's nostrils. Kilgore had been cut, and a quick perusal also showed that he appeared to have been stabbed in his right leg.

"Kilgore," he said, gripping the man by the forearms. "It's Greybourne."

"And Carrington," the duke said, now standing by Nash.

"I bloody well see you," Kilgore panted, revealing the pain he was in when his whole body shuddered.

"Who did this?" Nash asked, the light bright enough for a moment that he could see a long gash down the left side of Kilgore's face.

"Levine." The one word came out as a curse. "He stabbed me in my leg, cut me across the face, and knocked me out. I awoke in his home with this on my chest."

Kilgore shoved a crumpled missive at Nash, but in the moonlight, Nash could not see what it said. "Tell me," he ordered, fear rampant within him.

"It says he's going to use my woman for what I did."

Rage made Nash shake. "Lilias?" Kilgore nodded. "Why does Levine think Lilias is your woman? He just met her with me not long ago."

"She saved me," Kilgore said, coughing. "He'd knocked her out and forced me into his home with her. He was going to kill me, but when she awoke, she pleaded for my life. She made up the most unbelievable tale right on the spot, and Levine believed her. She told him that she loved me and I loved her, and it would be much worse on me, much better vengeance, if Levine took her from me and left me alive."

Fury nearly stole his ability to speak. "Where did he take her?"

"To my house," he replied. "He thinks—" Kilgore swayed, and Nash gripped him more tightly. "He thinks that's where I seduced the woman he claims to have loved." Kilgore shook violently and coughed before he continued. "But all I did was shelter her there while making plans for her escape. That's it." He sucked in a ragged breath and swayed once more.

"What of your servants? Won't they stop—"

"Don't have any," Kilgore choked out while shaking his head. "Levine knows." He grabbed Nash's overcoat, and Kilgore's gaze clung to him. "He must have been studying me even as I watched him. I'm sorry," Kilgore said, misery in his voice. "I thought myself so damn clever."

"Jesus," Nash said, glancing to Carrington and then back at Kilgore. Worry clawed at him now, causing him to tremble as badly as Kilgore. "No one is there? No one is at your home to help Lilias?"

"No," Kilgore rasped. "My aunt is away at Bath."

The thoughts going through Nash's head would drive him mad. He thrust Kilgore at Carrington. "Take Kilgore and get him help."

On a nod from Carrington, Nash left them both standing there and ascended the gig, praying he would get to Lilias before it was too late.

## Chapter Fourteen

This was not how her story was supposed to end. Lilias jerked on her wrists once more, which were tied painfully tight to the bedposts of Kilgore's bed. Her gaze darted across the candlelit room to the closed bedchamber door, and she yanked against her bindings repeatedly, the rope cutting into her skin, burning and causing her to whimper. But white-hot fear drove her to continue trying until warm blood trickled from her wrists. She was trapped.

Her throat tightened with the need to scream her fear and rage, but she refused to give Levine the satisfaction of believing he'd broken her. She was a fool to have gone to his home, to have made up that ridiculous lie, but she'd been desperate to save Kilgore.

*Heaven above, Kilgore!*

Her stomach roiled recalling all the blood on his face and leg, and then her stomach heaved recalling how Levine had told her he intended to use her so Kilgore would have to spend the rest of his life tormented by images of Levine touching her. The man was insane!

Heavy footsteps suddenly thudded on the stairs, and her pulse spiked as she began to yank again, wincing against the pain. Even if she didn't care about Levine thinking he'd broken her spirit, it would do no good to yell. The house was utterly empty of servants. And by its exquisite furnishings, she didn't think that had to do with a lack of funds, which meant Kilgore had sent everyone away to isolate himself.

"Mrs. Artemis," Levine called as the bedchamber door creaked open and he appeared in the threshold. "I'm here for you. Are you ready for me?"

"You make me sick," she cried out, frantic now and yanking on her wrists so hard that tears sprang to her eyes.

Levine moved into the room, stripping off his clothing as he went. He threw his overcoat to the floor and yanked off his neckcloth. Lilias's stomach clenched. She was going to be sick, but by heaven, if it was the last thing she did, she'd keep the contents of her stomach down until she could lose them all over Levine.

He tugged off his boots, loosened his breeches, and offered her a sick, twisted grin. "You are far too overdressed, my dear. Let me help you."

The bed dipped with his weight, and she screamed with all her fear and frustration, kicking out at him. He let out a strange laugh, catching her ankles deftly and yanking her legs apart. As she squeezed her eyes shut for the worst, a near inhuman roar filled the bedchamber. Her eyes flew open just in time to see Nash striding through the room like an angry god bent on destruction. He was upon Levine before the man could react, and he went flying backward—Nash having thrown him—and crashed into a set of chairs by the window. Then Nash turned, his massive shoulders heaving, and swallowed the distance between him and his prey.

Lilias could not see to the other side of the room, but she heard the *thunk* of Nash's fist against the man's body, bone crunching, and moans of pain. "Nash!" she screamed. "Nash! Stop it. Stop it! He's not worth the guilt if you kill him! I'm here. I need you!"

Silence fell, then a moment of shuffling, followed by more groans from Levine. Heavy footsteps came toward her, and Nash appeared, agony twisting his face. He towered over her for a moment, then a string of curse words she'd never heard flowed from his mouth as he made quick work undoing her binds.

"Lilias," he said, his voice a cry of regret and need. He gathered her into his protective arms, bringing her to his chest and cradling her. "Lilias, my Lilias," he said, then kissed her nose, her chin, her cheeks. He cupped her face and looked at her, his visage a mix of undeniable love and pain. Lilias's heart pounded as he stared at her. "Did he—"

"No!" she said, her voice breaking on a sob. "Is he dead? Did you—"

"No. He's tied up."

"Go on and kill me!" Levine bellowed.

Instead of answering, Nash scooped her off the bed and carried her away from Levine and into the hall. He set her on her feet, his gaze holding hers. "We'll deal with him soon enough."

She could not stop the smile from creeping onto her face and the hope filling her heart as he pressed her against his full, solid length. "We?"

"Lilias." His deep voice broke on her name. "God, I want to kiss you."

She wanted that so bad she could have wept with the desire. "What of your betrothal?" she asked, her body still trembling with what had happened, and her head aching from the hit Levine had given her.

"There is no betrothal," Nash replied, running the pad of his thumb over her lips as if he were memorizing the shape of them. "My mother lied to you. I'll deal with her later, too. Right now you come first. *We* come first. Are you all right?"

She nodded. "We?" she asked again, clinging to him for support.

"We," he repeated, his voice a slide of velvet over her. "It has always been you and me. You are the only one for me, though I do not deserve you. You don't even know all my sins. I—"

"Shh," she whispered, rising on her tiptoes, her body sliding along his—hard flesh to her softness. She found her intended mark and brushed her lips to his. "I know them. I know of you not pulling back in the race with Owen, and you already told me of your brother and Helen. I know your heart, too. You never set out to intentionally hurt either of them, Nash." She met his eyes. "I know your sins, and I command you to forgive yourself—for you and me."

He cupped her face, his large hand splaying hotly against her skin. "I love you, Lilias. I have loved you since the day I first saw you crossing that log barefoot."

"And I love you," she said, melting into him as he brushed his lips to hers now. "I have loved you since the day you jumped into the river to save me, then dragged me out and chastised me like the moody, imperfect hero you are."

Nash arched his eyebrows. "There's such a thing as an imperfect hero?"

"Oh yes," she said, sighing into his mouth as it covered her in a greedy kiss. His lips were warm and persuasive, and the series of slow, deep kisses he gave her made her knees weak. When he pulled back, she said, "The most glorious heroes are imperfect ones, Nash, because they, more than any others, need their heroines."

"Ah," he replied, tracing a line of feathery kisses up to her mouth once more. "That sounds just like me, because I need you with me from this moment until forever. Marry me, Lilias," he said, sliding his hands from her face to her back to hold her tight. "Marry me and let me spend my life loving you."

"I thought you would never ask," she said, circling her arms around his neck, and meeting his hungry kiss with one of her own.

---

The next day, Lilias stood hand in hand with Nash as he confronted his mother. Lilias wasn't the least bit worried when the dowager duchess shot her a withering glare. Lilias had seen what Nash was capable of last night, the lengths he would go to in order to keep her safe. Not only had he stopped Levine from hurting her but Nash had deftly dealt with the authorities in getting Levine carted off. She suspected, Levine would end up in Bedlam with his actions and the way he'd raved as they'd taken him away.

Nash had seen her safely home after that and had placated her mother, who was awake and frantic, and then charmingly and politely asked her mother for permission to marry Lilias. Of course, Mama had promptly granted it. And then this morning, he'd shown up as soon as the calling hour had rolled around, Helen Levine's manuscript in hand. After assuring her mother he'd have her home at an appropriate hour, he'd taken her to Lady Katherine's and sat in his carriage as Lilias assured the woman that the manuscript would be properly destroyed.

And now they were here so Nash could confront the past that had haunted him most of his adult life. He had not spoken much of it, but his mood had grown increasingly quiet as they approached his home and his face had become set in hard lines. But still, she wasn't worried. They had each other, and whatever secrets might be revealed, if they faced them together, she felt sure they would only grow stronger in their love.

"Why is she here?" his mother demanded, her glare turning glacial. "I demand she leave," the duchess said before Nash could respond to her.

"Lilias is not leaving, Mother, or not permanently anyway. You are."

"What do ye mean?" his mother asked coolly, and she quickly followed the question with, "Do not be ridiculous. This... This—" his mother waved a hand at Lilias "—*person* needs to go. She's not yer family. I am. Yer sister is."

Nash's fingers tightened around Lilias's, and his shoulders subtly stiffened. She squeezed to remind him she was there for him. She caught his side glance and grateful smile, and then the fierce scowl he directed at his mother. "Lilias has agreed to become my wife, so very soon she will be staying forever, and there is no room in this house for the darkness you bring it. You can move to any house of mine you wish, except the Cotswold home or this one."

"Ye cannot wed this woman. Ye must wed Miss Balfour. I've...I've promised Dr. Balfour."

Annoyance settled on his face. "Why would you do that, Mother?"

Lilias found herself almost leaning toward the woman to see what she would say, but she said nothing. Instead, the woman pressed her lips together.

Nash shifted and then spoke again. "I've been recalling things, Mother. Things about the day Thomas died. Things I suppose I buried because they were too painful."

Lilias felt his hurt in her own chest. She moved closer to him, and he slid his arm around her waist as if he needed her strength as much as she needed his. "My hands were cut so badly from clawing at the ice to get to Thomas that Dr. Balfour said I might not get complete use of my forefinger and thumb back on my left hand. I'd forgotten that." Lilias looked at his hand, imagining the torment it must have been for him to try and fail to save his twin brother. "I also recalled just this morning how I very nearly drowned, as well. How Father and the stable master had to pull me out because I would not come out of the frigid water, I would not quit diving under searching for Thomas."

"Greybourne, do not do this," his mother said, suddenly looking frightened and sounding small.

He didn't acknowledge her, and Lilias realized he was lost in memories he'd repressed for so long. "Dr. Balfour said I was lucky I had not died from the cold and the blood loss from the cuts. But you... Do you remember what you said to me when I awoke?"

"Greybourne." She moaned in such an animalistic way that Lilias's breath caught in her throat.

"I am your *son*," he said, "and you have never called me by my given name. So formal. So distant. So damn cruel."

Tears filled Lilias's eyes at the pain Nash had been living with caused by his own mother. "There were no kind words from you when I awoke, nor from Father. But *you*, you said that I *let* Thomas drown. You demanded to know what I had done to make him charge me on the ice. Never once did you offer comfort. You offered condemnation, guilt, and silence. Bloody deafening silence."

Lilias swiped at the warm tears now gliding down her cheeks and squeezed Nash's waist. When he squeezed her back, she exhaled with relief. This moment with his mother was painful but necessary if he was ever to heal and if the life they wanted together was to have a real chance.

"I couldn't," Nash's mother said on a sob. "I couldn't give ye those things. Not because I blamed ye but because I blamed myself. And yer father blamed himself, too."

"Explain," Nash said, the word cold, but Lilias understood why. She understood his need to protect himself now.

Nash's mother's gaze darted to Lilias for a moment, then fell on Nash once more. "Ye were not the firstborn," she whispered, sounding utterly broken now. "Thomas was. Ye were not the heir." A bitter laugh escaped her.

"What?" Nash said, sounding shocked. Lilias herself could not have even formed that one word in this moment.

"Ye were born second, a breath after Thomas, but ye came out perfect. Strong. Healthy. But Thomas—" The duchess shook her head violently. "He was blue and so quiet, and he had that twisted leg. Yer father and I both knew before Dr. Balfour even told us that Thomas would never be strong enough to carry on the family name."

"Dear God," Nash muttered, and Lilias found herself nodding in mute agreement.

"Ye do not understand!" his mother sobbed. "Thomas could not have handled the weight of being the heir. Dr. Balfour said his lungs, like his leg, were not properly formed, and he would always be weak. That's why—That's why we did what we did to protect him. Ye were to be his protector with us, and in the end, ye failed him and we failed ye both. And…and to make matters dreadfully worse, Dr. Balfour has been blackmailing yer father and me for years! He threatened to expose what we had done unless we paid him and unless ye one day wed his daughter. I wanted to tell ye, I did, but how do ye tell someone how miserably ye have failed them? How do ye tell someone the terrible choices ye've made?" She buried her face in her hands and cried.

Partly in shock and partly relieved it all seemed to be out in the open now, Lilias looked at Nash, and she could see the indecision on his face as to whether to go to his mother or not. Lilias knew he could likely not totally forgive the horrible things she'd done, and it would take a lot of time to even accept what had happened, but she knew he'd feel guilty if he didn't go to her now.

Lilias set her hand on Nash's back and gave him a little push, which did not move him at all, but he knew what she meant. He smiled lovingly at her, and then he took the first step toward his mother and toward the possibility of healing. And when he put his arms around his mother and said, "I love you," Lilias knew, without a doubt, that she had found her perfect love, her perfect hero.

# Epilogue

"Come here, my duchess," Nash said two weeks later, his seductive voice shooting thrills through Lilias that she was positive would never lessen.

She walked toward Nash, who was sitting bare chested on the edge of their bed in nothing but a kilt, and as she drew near, he gave her a smile that promised another night of bliss in his arms.

"Is it true," she said, placing her hands on his thighs and nudging them apart while holding his gaze, "that Scots do not wear anything under their kilts?"

He smirked up at her, grabbed her by the waist, and lifted her as he stood, swinging her gently around to playfully toss her on their bed. She squealed with delight, and then laughter bubbled forth, followed by a rush of excitement as her husband came to kneel over her, caging her in with his powerful arms planted by each of hers and his strong thighs touching each of her hips. "I don't know whether it's true or not," he said in a husky voice, kissing the skin of her chest that her gown revealed, "but I do know that this half Scot wears nothing under his kilt."

"Oh, how deliciously scandalous." She slid her hands between his thighs to their juncture. She smiled slowly as she felt the truth of his words. "I must say I'm glad," she whispered wickedly. "It will make trysts in the gardens so much easier. If only I didn't have to wear so many layers…"

"Ah, ye of little faith," he said, placing dizzying kisses up one side of her neck and then down the other. "Let me show you how easy it is to deal with your layers." His mouth descended to hers, sucking, pulling, nipping. By the time he was done with his kiss and he pulled back, she realized, bemused, that he'd shoved up her gown and had rid her of any underlayers that would hinder his loving her thoroughly.

"I think I'm too proper a lady for this wicked behavior," she teased.

He chuckled as his hands slid under her buttocks to hoist her up to meet him and he slid slowly and deliciously into her. "Thank God you are not, nor have you ever been. I like that most about you."

It was hard to concentrate enough to form a coherent reply because the way he moved in and out of her was building a fire that was burning her all over. With every stroke of his body, he was hitting the spot she had discovered with him, the one that made her splinter in his arms. But somehow she found the thread of her reply as her hands splayed over her husband's own perfectly formed buttocks. "That's what you like most about me?" she panted.

Another chuckle came from Nash, this time darkly rich. "In this moment," he said, his voice ragged as his pace increased, making the blood in her veins rush faster and roar in her ears, along with the loud beat of her heart, "I most like that you are so warm, so inviting, so very wanton with me. I like—" he managed to lower himself, capture her right nipple in his mouth, and suck it in a way that made her arch on a moan toward him "—this breast," he finished with a release of her now-puckered nipple.

"But that is so unfair to the left breast," he said, sounding every bit like the devil she loved. "It—" he swirled his tongue around her left nipple "—is just as lovely and gives me just as much delight."

"Prove it," she choked out, both her breasts now heavy and tight.

And he did. He used his mouth to torment her nipple with sweet strokes, even as his body moved in and out of hers, pushing her toward that peak she'd discovered in his arms, the glorious one where all thought fled and all that remained was pure bliss. And just when she thought she would splinter, he released her breast and caught her by the underside of her thighs. He spread her legs farther apart and then set one of them over his back and brought his hand to the juncture of her thighs.

"Here," he said, separating her to find the spot that pulsed only for him, "is another part of you I love, because when I touch it, I know it brings you exquisite enjoyment, and that brings me so much happiness that I ache with it. Shall I remind you?"

"Yes, please," she begged, lost in him now.

His thumb pressed gently to the swollen secret spot, and he moved it in small circles. As he increased his speed with his thumb, he increased the speed of his strokes in and out of her, and she could see the top where he would take her, and she would fly. "What of you?" she gasped. "What shall I do for you?"

"This," he said, moving faster. "Exactly this. Give yourself to me entirely always and that's all I need."

On that statement, she reached the top, and heat washed over her, her body tensing and then constricting around Nash over and over again. She let out a scream of satisfaction as he released his own rough moan to grip her thighs and find his own fulfillment.

They fell together to the bed, breathless in the candlelight until their chests slowly rose and fell evenly. Then Nash rolled off her, went to the washbasin, cleansed himself, then returned and lovingly tended to her. When he was done, he held out his hand to her, and they stood. He stripped himself of his kilt fairly quickly and climbed onto their bed once more, and then he watched her as she removed the clothing she still had on. She loved the intensity of his gaze, the hunger she saw there, and the love. When she was finished, she cocked her head at him, and he offered a slow, roguish smile.

"Come here." He opened his powerful arms wide for her. "It's been quite the sennight."

She crawled between his hard thighs and lay across his chest, resting her chin there so she could look in his beautiful eyes. He smelled divinely of fresh soap, and she inhaled his scent, savoring it. "I'd say it's been quite the frantic fortnight, but the sennights were hectic in very different ways." Today, Miss Balfour had called upon them to say thank you for stopping her father's plans. It had been quite unexpected.

He nodded and smiled lovingly down at her as he stroked a hand over her head and along her back, causing gooseflesh to race across her skin.

"I always imagined our life together would be exciting," Lilias said, "but I daresay, not even I could have imagined we would stop a man like Levine and take care of a blackmailer like Dr. Balfour only to have his daughter call upon us to thank us for letting her know what her father was up to."

"I would not have known exactly how to take care of him if it were not for your marvelous suggestion," Nash replied.

Lilias grinned up at Nash. "Well, when you told me

how you suspected someone else held Miss Balfour's affections entirely and that she, too, had been forced to appear for supper the night you joined them, I simply knew we had an ally in her."

"Yes, you did, my dear, and you handled it brilliantly."

"*We* did," Lilias replied, thinking of how Miss Balfour truly had been the one to stop her father's blackmail. She'd threatened to cut the man from her life, and it seemed everything he had done had been an attempt to ensure his daughter had the best life possible. When he'd realized what he was doing would cause him to lose his daughter, he ceased immediately. "I wish, though, that we had not lost Owen as a friend and that Kilgore had not been so horribly injured."

"I do, too, darling," Nash replied, running his hands over her bottom and cupping her buttocks.

When he squeezed her, her entire core tightened. One of the astonishing advantages of being wed was the marriage bed. She had never read about *those* pleasures in any of her Gothic romances.

"I cannot say what the future holds for either of those men," he said, "except if my own life is any guide, I know it cannot hold true happiness until they face the pain and secrets keeping them in the darkness. For Owen, I do believe it all starts with his mother's leaving him, and though I don't like it because you are mine, he did truly think himself in love with you."

She nodded, swallowing. "If I had known, I would have dissuaded him much sooner. I was yours from the moment I saw you standing there in that kilt."

"And to think I took to wearing it in an effort to get my mother to show some emotion," Nash said with a chuckle.

She pressed a kiss to her husband's muscled chest. "I'm

very glad you are such a devil."

"And I'm very glad that you have such a love for Gothic romances," he replied, claiming her mouth. "Otherwise, you might not have had the notion that I was your hero and waited for me."

"I would have waited," she assured him. "It was always you for me, Gothic romances or not."

"And it was always you for me," he agreed, hugging her tightly and pressing a tender kiss to the top of her head. "You are mine to cherish, mine to love, mine to protect. You are my free-spirited duchess."

Thank you for reading. I hope you enjoyed Nash and Lilias's story. The next book in this series is the story of Lady Constantine and Lord Kilgore—*Lady Constantine and the Sins of Lord Kilgore*. If you have read the series from the beginning, you know that these two have a very complicated past, and that Lord Kilgore has many secrets that need to be unraveled. You'll be surprised to discover that Lady Constantine has some secrets of her own!

Pre-order of **LADY CONSTANTINE AND THE SINS OF LORD KILGORE** is coming soon!

If you are a fan of Scottish romances set in the medieval period, I think you will love my *Highlander Vows: Entangled Hearts* series. You can read a bit about book 1 below.

*Not even her careful preparations could prepare her for the barbarian who rescues her.* Don't miss the USA Today bestselling *Highlander Vows: Entangled Hearts* series, starting with the critically acclaimed When a Laird Loves a Lady. Faking her death would be simple, it was escaping her home that would be difficult.

I appreciate your help in spreading the word about my books, including letting your friends know. Reviews help other readers find my books. Please leave one on your favorite site!

# Keep In Touch

**Get Julie Johnstone's Newsletter**
https://juliejohnstoneauthor.com

**Join her Reading Group**
facebook.com/groups/1500294650186536

**Like her Facebook Page**
facebook.com/authorjuliejohnstone

**Stalk her Instagram**
instagram.com/authorjuliejohnstone

**Hang out with her on Goodreads**
goodreads.com/author/show/2354638.Julie_Johnstone

**Hear about her sales via Bookbub**
bookbub.com/authors/julie-johnstone

**Follow her Amazon Page**
amazon.com/Julie-Johnstone/e/B0062AW98S

Excerpt of When a Laird Loves a Lady

## One

**England, 1357**

Faking her death would be simple. It was escaping her home that would be difficult. Marion de Lacy stared hard into the slowly darkening sky, thinking about the plan she intended to put into action tomorrow—if all went well—but growing uneasiness tightened her belly. From where she stood in the bailey, she counted the guards up in the tower. It was not her imagination: Father had tripled the knights keeping guard at all times, as if he was expecting trouble.

Taking a deep breath of the damp air, she pulled her mother's cloak tighter around her to ward off the twilight chill. A lump lodged in her throat as the wool scratched her neck. In the many years since her mother had been gone, Marion had both hated and loved this cloak for the death and life it represented. Her mother's freesia scent had long since faded from the garment, yet simply calling up a memory of her mother wearing it gave Marion comfort.

She rubbed her fingers against the rough material. When she fled, she couldn't chance taking anything with her but the clothes on her body and this cloak. Her death had to appear accidental, and the cloak that everyone knew she prized would ensure her freedom. Finding it tangled in the branches at the edge of the sea cliff ought to be just the thing to convince her father and William Froste that she'd drowned. After all, neither man thought she could swim. They didn't truly care about her anyway. Her marriage to the blackhearted knight was only about what her hand could give the two men. Her father, Baron de Lacy, wanted more power, and Froste wanted her family's prized land. A match made in Heaven, if only the match didn't involve her...but it did.

Father would set the hounds of Hell themselves to track her down if he had the slightest suspicion that she was still alive. She was an inestimable possession to be given to secure Froste's unwavering allegiance and, therefore, that of the renowned ferocious knights who served him. Whatever small sliver of hope she had that her father would grant her mercy and not marry her to Froste had been destroyed by the lashing she'd received when she'd pleaded for him to do so.

The moon crested above the watchtower, reminding her why she was out here so close to mealtime: to meet Angus. The Scotsman may have been her father's stable master, but he was *her* ally, and when he'd proposed she flee England for Scotland, she'd readily consented.

Marion looked to the west, the direction from which Angus would return from Newcastle. He should be back any minute now from meeting his cousin and clansman Neil, who was to escort her to Scotland. She prayed all was set and that Angus's kin was ready to depart. With her wedding to Froste to take place in six days, she wanted to be far away before there was even the slightest chance he'd be making his way here. And since he was set to arrive the night before the wedding, leaving tomorrow promised she'd not encounter him.

A sense of urgency enveloped her, and Marion forced

herself to stroll across the bailey toward the gatehouse that led to the tunnel preceding the drawbridge. She couldn't risk raising suspicion from the tower guards. At the gatehouse, she nodded to Albert, one of the knights who operated the drawbridge mechanism. He was young and rarely questioned her excursions to pick flowers or find herbs.

"Off to get some medicine?" he inquired.

"Yes," she lied with a smile and a little pang of guilt. But this was survival, she reminded herself as she entered the tunnel. When she exited the heavy wooden door that led to freedom, she wasn't surprised to find Peter and Andrew not yet up in the twin towers that flanked the entrance to the drawbridge. It was, after all, time for the changing of the guard.

They smiled at her as they put on their helmets and demi-gauntlets. They were an imposing presence to any who crossed the drawbridge and dared to approach the castle gate. Both men were tall and looked particularly daunting in their full armor, which Father insisted upon at all times. The men were certainly a fortress in their own right.

She nodded to them. "I'll not be long. I want to gather some more flowers for the supper table." Her voice didn't even wobble with the lie.

Peter grinned at her, his kind brown eyes crinkling at the edges. "Will you pick me one of those pale winter flowers for my wife again, Marion?"

She returned his smile. "It took away her anger as I said it would, didn't it?"

"It did," he replied. "You always know just how to help with her."

"I'll get a pink one if I can find it. The colors are becoming scarcer as the weather cools."

Andrew, the younger of the two knights, smiled, displaying a set of straight teeth. He held up his covered arm. "My cut is almost healed."

Marion nodded. "I told you! Now maybe you'll listen to me sooner next time you're wounded in training."

He gave a soft laugh. "I will. Should I put more of your paste on tonight?"

"Yes, keep using it. I'll have to gather some more yarrow, if I can find any, and mix up another batch of the medicine for you." And she'd have to do it before she escaped. "I better get going if I'm going to find those things." She knew she should not have agreed to search for the flowers and offered to find the yarrow when she still had to speak to Angus and return to the castle in time for supper, but both men had been kind to her when many had not. It was her way of thanking them.

After Peter lowered the bridge and opened the door, she departed the castle grounds, considering her plan once more. Had she forgotten anything? She didn't think so. She was simply going to walk straight out of her father's castle and never come back. Tomorrow, she'd announce she was going out to collect more winter blooms, and then, instead, she would go down to the edge of the cliff overlooking the sea. She would slip off her cloak and leave it for a search party to find. Her breath caught deep in her chest at the simple yet dangerous plot. The last detail to see to was Angus.

She stared down the long dirt path that led to the sea and stilled, listening for hoofbeats. A slight vibration of the ground tingled her feet, and her heart sped in hopeful anticipation that it was Angus coming down the dirt road on his horse. When the crafty stable master appeared with a grin spread across his face, the worry that was squeezing her heart loosened. For the first time since he had ridden out that morning, she took a proper breath. He stopped his stallion alongside her and dismounted.

She tilted her head back to look up at him as he towered over her. An errant thought struck. "Angus, are all Scots as tall as you?"

"Nay, but ye ken Scots are bigger than all the wee Englishmen." Suppressed laughter filled his deep voice. "So even the ones nae as tall as me are giants compared te the scrawny men here."

"You're teasing me," she replied, even as she arched her eyebrows in uncertainty.

"A wee bit," he agreed and tousled her hair. The laughter vanished from his eyes as he rubbed a hand over his square jaw and then stared down his bumpy nose at her, fixing what he called his "lecturing look" on her. "We've nae much time. Neil is in Newcastle just as he's supposed te be, but there's been a slight change."

She frowned. "For the last month, every time I wanted to simply make haste and flee, you refused my suggestion, and now you say there's a slight change?"

His ruddy complexion darkened. She'd pricked that MacLeod temper her mother had always said Angus's clan was known for throughout the Isle of Skye, where they lived in the farthest reaches of Scotland. Marion could remember her mother chuckling and teasing Angus about how no one knew the MacLeod temperament better than their neighboring clan, the MacDonalds of Sleat, to which her mother had been born. The two clans had a history of feuding.

Angus cleared his throat and recaptured Marion's attention. Without warning, his hand closed over her shoulder, and he squeezed gently. "I'm sorry te say it so plain, but ye must die at once."

Her eyes widened as dread settled in the pit of her stomach. "What? Why?" The sudden fear she felt was unreasonable. She knew he didn't mean she was really going to die, but her palms were sweating and her lungs had tightened all the same. She sucked in air and wiped her damp hands down the length of her cotton skirts. Suddenly, the idea of going to a foreign land and living with her mother's clan, people she'd never met, made her apprehensive.

She didn't even know if the MacDonalds—her uncle, in particular, who was now the laird—would accept her or not. She was half-English, after all, and Angus had told her that when a Scot considered her English bloodline and the fact that she'd been raised there, they would most likely brand her fully English, which was not a good thing in a Scottish mind. And if her uncle was anything like her grandfather had been, the man was not going to be very reasonable. But she didn't have any other family to turn to who would dare defy her father, and Angus hadn't offered for her to go to his clan, so she'd not asked. He likely didn't want to bring trouble to his clan's doorstep, and she didn't blame him.

Panic bubbled inside her. She needed more time, even if it was only the day she'd thought she had, to gather her courage.

"Why must I flee tonight? I was to teach Eustice how to dress a wound. She might serve as a maid, but then she will be able to help the knights when I'm gone. And her little brother, Bernard, needs a few more lessons before he's mastered writing his name and reading. And Eustice's youngest sister has begged me to speak to Father about allowing her to visit her mother next week."

"Ye kinnae watch out for everyone here anymore, Marion."

She placed her hand over his on her shoulder. "Neither can you."

Their gazes locked in understanding and disagreement.

He slipped his hand from her shoulder, and then crossed his arms over his chest in a gesture that screamed stubborn, unyielding protector. "If I leave at the same time ye feign yer death," he said, changing the subject, "it could stir yer father's suspicion and make him ask questions when none need te be asked. I'll be going home te Scotland soon after ye." Angus reached into a satchel attached to his horse and pulled out a dagger, which he slipped to her. "I had this made for ye."

Marion took the weapon and turned it over, her heart pounding. "It's beautiful." She held it by its black handle while withdrawing it from the sheath and examining it. "It's much sharper than the one I have."

"Aye," he said grimly. "It is. Dunnae forget that just because I taught ye te wield a dagger does nae mean ye can defend yerself from *all* harm. Listen te my cousin and do as he says. Follow his lead."

She gave a tight nod. "I will. But why must I leave now and not tomorrow?"

Concern filled Angus's eyes. "Because I ran into Froste's brother in town and he told me that Froste sent word that he would be arriving in two days."

Marion gasped. "That's earlier than expected."

"Aye," Angus said and took her arm with gentle authority. "So ye must go now. I'd rather be trying te trick only yer father than yer father, Froste, and his savage knights. I want ye long gone and yer death accepted when Froste arrives."

She shivered as her mind began to race with all that could go wrong.

"I see the worry darkening yer green eyes," Angus said, interrupting her thoughts. He whipped off his hat and his hair, still shockingly red in spite of his years, fell down around his shoulders. He only ever wore it that way when he was riding. He said the wind in his hair reminded him of riding his own horse when he was in Scotland. "I was going to talk to ye tonight, but now that I kinnae..." He shifted from foot to foot, as if uncomfortable. "I want te offer ye something. I'd have proposed it sooner, but I did nae want ye te feel ye had te take my offer so as nae te hurt me, but I kinnae hold my tongue, even so."

She furrowed her brow. "What is it?"

"I'd be proud if ye wanted te stay with the MacLeod clan instead of going te the MacDonalds. Then ye'd nae have te leave everyone ye ken behind. Ye'd have me."

A surge of relief filled her. She threw her arms around Angus, and he returned her hug quick and hard before setting her away. Her eyes misted at once. "I had hoped you would ask me," she admitted.

For a moment, he looked astonished, but then he spoke. "Yer mother risked her life te come into MacLeod territory at a time when we were fighting terrible with the MacDonalds, as ye well ken."

Marion nodded. She knew the story of how Angus had ended up here. He'd told her many times. Her mother had been somewhat of a renowned healer from a young age, and when Angus's wife had a hard birthing, her mother had gone to help. The knowledge that his wife and child had died anyway still made Marion want to cry.

"I pledged my life te keep yer mother safe for the kindness she'd done me, which brought me here, but, lass, long ago ye became like a daughter te me, and I pledge the rest of my miserable life te defending ye."

She gripped Angus's hand. "I wish you were my father."

He gave her a proud yet smug look, one she was used to seeing. She chortled to herself. The man did have a terrible streak of pride. She'd have to give Father John another coin for penance for Angus, since the Scot refused to take up the custom himself.

Angus hooked his thumb in his gray tunic. "Ye'll make a fine MacLeod because ye already ken we're the best clan in Scotland."

Mentally, she added another coin to her dues. "Do you think they'll let me become a MacLeod, though, since my mother was the daughter of the previous MacDonald laird and I've an English father?"

"They will," he answered without hesitation, but she heard the slight catch in his voice.

"Angus." She narrowed her eyes. "You said you would never lie to me."

His brows dipped together, and he gave her a long, disgruntled look. "They may be a bit wary," he finally admitted. "But I'll nae let them turn ye away. Dunnae worry," he finished, his Scottish brogue becoming thick with emotion.

She bit her lip. "Yes, but you won't be with me when I first get there. What should I do to make certain that they will let me stay?"

He quirked his mouth as he considered her question. "Ye must first get the laird te like ye. Tell Neil te take ye directly te the MacLeod te get his consent for ye te live there. I kinnae vouch for the man myself as I've never met him, but Neil says he's verra honorable, fierce in battle, patient, and reasonable." Angus cocked his head as if in thought. "Now that I think about it, I'm sure the MacLeod can get ye a husband, and then the clan will more readily accept ye. Aye." He nodded. "Get in the laird's good graces as soon as ye meet him and ask him te find ye a husband." A scowl twisted his lips. "Preferably one who will accept yer acting like a man sometimes."

She frowned at him. "*You* are the one who taught me how to ride bareback, wield a dagger, and shoot an arrow true."

"Aye." He nodded. "I did. But when I started teaching ye, I thought yer mama would be around te add her woman's touch. I did nae ken at the time that she'd pass when ye'd only seen eight summers in yer life."

"You're lying again," Marion said. "You continued those lessons long after Mama's death. You weren't a bit worried how I'd turn out."

"I sure was!" he objected, even as a guilty look crossed his face. "But what could I do? Ye insisted on hunting for the widows so they'd have food in the winter, and ye insisted on going out in the dark te help injured knights when I could nae go with ye. I had te teach ye te hunt and defend yerself. Plus, you were a sad, lonely thing, and I could nae verra well overlook ye when ye came te the stables and asked me te teach ye things."

"Oh, you could have," she replied. "Father overlooked me all the time, but your heart is too big to treat someone like that." She patted him on the chest. "I think you taught me the best things in the world, and it seems to me any man would want his woman to be able to defend herself."

"Shows how much ye ken about men," Angus muttered with a shake of his head. "Men like te think a woman needs *them*."

"I dunnae need a man," she said in her best Scottish accent.

He threw up his hands. "Ye do. Ye're just afeared."

The fear was true enough. Part of her longed for love, to feel as if she belonged to a family. For so long she'd wanted those things from her father, but she had never gotten them, no matter what she did. It was difficult to believe it would be any different in the future. She'd rather not be disappointed.

Angus tilted his head, looking at her uncertainly. "Ye want a wee bairn some day, dunnae ye?"

"Well, yes," she admitted and peered down at the ground, feeling foolish.

"Then ye need a man," he crowed.

She drew her gaze up to his. "Not just any man. I want a man who will truly love me."

He waved a hand dismissively. Marriages of convenience were a part of life, she knew, but she would not marry unless she was in love and her potential husband loved her in return. She would support herself if she needed to.

"The other big problem with a husband for ye," he continued, purposely avoiding, she suspected, her mention of the word *love*, "as I see it, is yer tender heart."

"What's wrong with a tender heart?" She raised her brow in question.

"'Tis more likely te get broken, aye?" His response was matter-of-fact.

"Nay. 'Tis more likely to have compassion," she replied with a grin.

"We're both right," he announced. "Yer mama had a tender heart like ye. 'Tis why yer father's black heart hurt her so. I dunnae care te watch the light dim in ye as it did yer mother."

"I don't wish for that fate, either," she replied, trying hard not to think about how sad and distant her mother had often seemed. "Which is why I will only marry for love. And why I need to get out of England."

"I ken that, lass, truly I do, but ye kinnae go through life alone."

"I don't wish to," she defended. "But if I have to, I have you, so I'll not be alone." With a shudder, her heart denied the possibility that she may never find love, but she squared her shoulders.

"'Tis nae the same as a husband," he said. "I'm old. Ye need a younger man who has the power te defend ye. And if Sir Frosty Pants ever comes after ye, you're going te need a strong man te go against him."

Marion snorted to cover the worry that was creeping in.

Angus moved his mouth to speak, but his reply was drowned by the sound of the supper horn blowing. "God's bones!" Angus muttered when the sound died. "I've flapped my jaw too long. Ye must go now. I'll head te the stables and start the fire as we intended. It'll draw Andrew and Peter away if they are watching ye too closely."

Marion looked over her shoulder at the knights, her stomach turning. She had known the plan since the day they had formed it, but now the reality of it scared her into a cold sweat. She turned back to Angus and gripped her dagger hard. "I'm afraid."

Determination filled his expression, as if his will for her to stay out of harm would make it so. "Ye will stay safe," he commanded. "Make yer way through the path in the woods that I showed ye, straight te Newcastle. I left ye a bag of coins under the first tree ye come te, the one with the rope tied te it. Neil will be waiting for ye by Pilgrim Gate on Pilgrim Street. The two of ye will depart from there."

She worried her lip but nodded all the same.

"Neil has become friends with a friar who can get the two of ye out," Angus went on. "Dunnae talk te anyone, especially any men. Ye should go unnoticed, as ye've never been there and won't likely see anyone ye've ever come in contact with here."

Fear tightened her lungs, but she swallowed. "I didn't even bid anyone farewell." Not that she really could have, nor did she think anyone would miss her other than Angus, and she would be seeing him again. Peter and Andrew *had* been kind to her, but they were her father's men, and she knew it well. She had been taken to the dungeon by the knights several times for punishment for transgressions that ranged from her tone not pleasing her father to his thinking she gave him a disrespectful look. Other times, they'd carried out the duty of tying her to the post for a thrashing when she'd angered her father. They had begged her forgiveness profusely but done their duties all the same. They would likely be somewhat glad they did not have to contend with such things anymore.

Eustice was both kind *and* thankful for Marion teaching her brother how to read, but Eustice lost all color any time someone mentioned the maid going with Marion to Froste's home after Marion was married. She suspected the woman was afraid to go to the home of the infamous "Merciless Knight." Eustice would likely be relieved when Marion disappeared. Not that Marion blamed her.

A small lump lodged in her throat. Would her father even mourn her loss? It wasn't likely, and her stomach knotted at the thought.

"You'll come as soon as you can?" she asked Angus.

"Aye. Dunnae fash yerself."

She forced a smile. "You are already sounding like

you're back in Scotland. Don't forget to curb that when speaking with Father."

"I'll remember. Now, make haste te the cliff te leave yer cloak, then head straight for Newcastle."

"I don't want to leave you," she said, ashamed at the sudden rise of cowardliness in her chest and at the way her eyes stung with unshed tears.

"Gather yer courage, lass. I'll be seeing ye soon, and Neil will keep ye safe."

She sniffed. "I'll do the same for Neil."

"I've nay doubt ye'll try," Angus said, sounding proud and wary at the same time.

"I'm not afraid for myself," she told him in a shaky voice. "You're taking a great risk for me. How will I ever make it up to you?"

"Ye already have," Angus said hastily, glancing around and directing a worried look toward the drawbridge. "Ye want te live with my clan, which means I can go te my dying day treating ye as my daughter. Now, dunnae cry when I walk away. I ken how sorely ye'll miss me," he boasted with a wink. "I'll miss ye just as much."

With that, he swung up onto his mount. He had just given the signal for his beast to go when Marion realized she didn't know what Neil looked like.

"Angus!"

He pulled back on the reins and turned toward her. "Aye?"

"I need Neil's description."

Angus's eyes widened. "I'm getting old," he grumbled. "I dunnae believe I forgot such a detail. He's got hair redder than mine, and wears it tied back always. Oh, and he's missing his right ear, thanks te Froste. Took it when Neil came through these parts te see me last year."

"What?" She gaped at him. "You never told me that!"

"I did nae because I knew ye would try te go after Neil and patch him up, and that surely would have cost ye another beating if ye were caught." His gaze bore into her. "Ye're verra courageous. I reckon I had a hand in that 'cause I knew ye needed te be strong te withstand yer father. But dunnae be mindless. Courageous men and women who are mindless get killed. Ye ken?"

She nodded.

"Tread carefully," he warned.

"You too." She said the words to his back, for he was already turned and headed toward the drawbridge.

She made her way slowly to the edge of the steep embankment as tears filled her eyes. She wasn't upset because she was leaving her father—she'd certainly need to say a prayer of forgiveness for that sin tonight—but she couldn't shake the feeling that she'd never see Angus again. It was silly; everything would go as they had planned. Before she could fret further, the blast of the fire horn jerked her into motion. There was no time for any thoughts but those of escape.

# About the Author

Julie Johnstone is a *USA Today* and #1 Amazon bestselling author. Scottish historical romance, Regency historical romance, and historical time travel romance featuring highlanders, aristocrats, and modern-day bad billionaire bad boys are her love, and she enjoys creating both with a hefty dose of twists, plenty of heartstring tugs, and a guaranteed happily ever after.

Her books have been dubbed "fabulously entertaining and engaging," making readers cry, laugh, and swoon. Johnstone lives in Alabama with her very own lowlander husband, her two children – the heir and the spare, her snobby cat, and her perpetually happy dog.

In her spare time she enjoys way too much coffee balanced by hot yoga, reading, and traveling.

Made in the USA
Middletown, DE
30 October 2020